ISLAND
of
SILVER

Book One

BONNIE HENDERSON

Publish Authority

Editor: Janet Silburn
Interior Design: Teresa Evans

ISBN 978-1-967213-10-8 (Paperback)
ISBN 978-1-967213-11-5 (eBook)

Published 2026 by Publish Authority,
300 Colonial Center Parkway, Suite 100
Roswell, GA, USA
PublishAuthority.com

Printed in the United States of America

To my husband, Joseph,
and
Marc, Jeff and Cassandra

To see a world in a grain of sand
And a heaven in a wild flower,
Hold infinity in the palm of your hand
And eternity in an hour.

William Blake

contents

foreword

In writing about the beautiful island of Guernsey, I aspired to be as true to its history as possible. In terms of geography, however, I allowed my imagination some creative licence. All of the key settings, such as St. Saviour's Parish, St. Peter Port, Bluebell Woods, Rocquaine Bay, and the Creux Mahie, exist, but for the story to be told as it needed to be, I moved some of these places to different locations. As well, I had to change a shingle beach to one that had golden sand. And although the woods in Guernsey are truly beautiful, my imagination spread the trees in even greater loveliness over the island.

chapter
one

I DID NOT GO to church on the day I met the heavenly silver witch.

I had every intention of going to St. Saviour's – because every Sunday, for as long as I could remember, I attended with my Papa and my Mamma and my four brothers. Even though I was only five years old, I had an awful lot of Sundays inside me already, hours and hours of sitting in the Vidamour pew, where my grandparents and great-grandparents and great-great-grandparents, had always sat. Papa told me that every pew in St. Saviour's Church had a family of ancestors attached to it from hundreds and hundreds of years ago, further back than I could really imagine – ancestors gleaming in the great distance like the pale turquoise horizon that shimmered around our island of Guernsey.

And every Sunday, I imagined the ancestors sharing the pew with us. They would descend from their spots in heaven to crowd onto the seat with Papa and Mamma, and Reginald,

Herbert, Lloyd, Randolph, and me, their bodies gliding gently into the narrow spaces between us.

Their clothes sparkled from being in heaven for so long, and I could easily see what they were wearing – sometimes it was their church clothes, just like in the photographs that Mamma displayed in the front parlour, and sometimes they wore long gowns as filmy as butterfly wings, the kind of clothing I thought people would wear living on the clouds of heaven.

I had a harder time with their faces, though. In the few photographs we had of them, arranged neatly on the mahogany table, it was difficult to see what they looked like. Partly it was because the sun shone so brightly through the wide casement window in the front parlour, the picture frames radiant in the light, a glimmering silver that made the sepia photographs even paler, the faces soft smudges. But even in late afternoon, when the light faded, still they were misty, blurry faces floating in the silver frames, as if wisps of pale brown smoke had spread under the glass.

But I hoped that if I kept trying to imagine their faces, they would eventually be revealed to me, appearing suddenly as I sat very quietly in the pew. And so, my eyes were always ready for a glimpse of their heavenly faces.

I didn't spend all that time, though, imagining my ancestors. The service was very long, and there was lots of time to dream of a great many beautiful things, dream in colours as brilliant as the stained-glass windows.

And thankfully, when I let my thoughts flow around me, I was able to sit as still as one of my dolls. With the bow on top of my head, a great swirl of ribbon that Mamma carefully arranged there, and the black patent leather shoes on my feet that Papa polished for me the night before, I could remain motionless, the light dancing inside me, with my eyes fixed on Rev. Pelletier. Far ahead at the altar, he would wave his long arms over his head, warming up more and more during the sermon, teaching us about hell, working hard praying at us, his face almost as hazy as my ancestors – all while I sat, unmoving, staring as if I had my doll's unblinking marble eyes.

Mamma called it daydreaming, or sometimes, she called it my imagination running away from me. It worried her.

I didn't know why – because I loved letting it go – but I didn't feel like it was running. It felt like flying – like a bird must surely feel when its wings, in one great lovely swoosh, lift into the sky.

And often, I found myself imagining the ancestors.

But just as much, it seemed, sitting on the hard wooden pew in St. Saviour's Church, I dreamt of the magnificent Guernsey cliffs – dreamt of them so vividly that I truly felt as if I were perched on the edge of one of the steep cliff faces.

Where I gazed at the turquoise sea that spread like a halo around our small island of Guernsey, our magical island that floated in the jewel bright waters.

The cliffs rose high into the sky, looming over the water, granite cliffs that glistened in the crashing, sunburst waves. At the bottom, the rocks jutted out of the depths like the great horny claws of an enormous sea monster lurking in its deep lair, one that could rise any day with the mighty cliffs on its back.

I never minded dreaming about a sea monster living underneath Guernsey, a sea monster that I wasn't sure was imaginary at all. Because I never believed it could ever hurt us.

For when I thought of the white mist shimmering over the water, it seemed as if surely angels had just been there, leaving the mist in their wake as they flew back to heaven on silent wings.

Angels that would keep us safe in Guernsey from a sea monster, angels in a heaven that did not seem too far away.

Even when the clouds came, and the light vanished for a while, Guernsey still seemed magical and holy, a place where I still felt protected from any sea monster gnashing its teeth underneath our island.

Because when the grey skies came, it seemed then that God, with his long wispy hair and great grey beard, was leaning over our little island in the vast sea.

And sometimes, the ancestors would be there too, high in the sky, as hazy as God's beard, as hazy as they were in the photographs.

I would become so lost in all my imaginings in church that I could barely hear Rev. Pelletier's voice at the altar – and the longer I dreamt the more his voice faded away.

Heavenly silver moments spent in church. When time stopped.

But I missed it all that day. Because of the witch, the heavenly silver witch. When time stopped again.

On that Sunday morning, I awakened to the sound of the screen door slapping quietly shut. I leapt out of my bed and rushed into the spare room across the hall. Looking through the wide window, I saw my brothers running from our back porch into the vineyard. Reginald, with his long legs, led the way, closely followed by Herbert, and then Lloyd and Randolph, who ran side by side. Even though Lloyd was two years older than Randolph, and tall for his age, all legs, as Mamma would say, putting her arms around him when she said it and smiling into his quiet brown eyes, Lloyd always liked to run right alongside Randolph. But then Randolph was awfully quick, and surely did not seem to be slowing Lloyd down very much, his legs moving like the lion-hearted boy he was.

All my brothers had lion hearts, for they were very brave and strong – in my eyes, they could do anything. Lloyd's heart was a little different, though, because Mamma said he wore his on his sleeve, which confused me, because it seemed to me that Lloyd wore his huge heart in his light brown eyes.

I told myself that when I was older, it would all make more sense. What I knew for sure, though, was that their lion hearts seemed to make my own heart grow much bigger inside me.

And that morning, watching my brothers running through our vineyard, all that I longed to do was to follow them, through the vineyard and to the cliffs of Rocquaine Bay.

I knew that was where they were going.

I even knew that Randolph let the screen door shut with a little slap because he wanted to let me know. He couldn't wake me up and tell me – Reginald wouldn't let him – for Mamma said I was too young to go the cliffs.

But I followed them whenever I could. And because it was Sunday morning, the only day of the week that Papa did not rise before dawn to work in the vineyard, the only day he and

Mamma stayed in their bed until after the sun rose, it was the very best day for running after my brothers to the cliffs.

I put on a sweater that would keep out the damp morning air, and a matching skirt and long stockings that Mamma had knitted for me. Usually, Mamma attached a ribbon in my hair as pink as the roses that grew in our garden. It made me feel a little silly, as if one of the flowers had sprouted on my head, but Mamma would gaze at me with a smile, telling me it was perfect.

I didn't bother with the hair ribbon that morning, although for Mamma, I tried to wear it most days. But at the cliffs, it would blow away in the wind like a baby bird torn out of its nest – so I tied my long hair back with a piece of white wool instead. Then I crept through the kitchen as soundlessly as I could, past the enormous stove, the stove that was as black as the devil, Randolph said once, even though Mamma told him to hush. But after that, I couldn't look at that stove without thinking that I could see the devil's dark, sinister face peering at me, its red tongue licking in the bright flames when Mamma lifted a burner. Now, as I slipped out of the house, I tried to be especially quiet, telling myself to think of a field of Guernsey lilies, their crimson petals waving in perfect silence in the wind. I did my best not to look at the stove, but I could still see it out of the corner of my eye, just a glimpse, and in that brief moment I was sure I saw a devil's leering face, his dull black eyes filled with malice. I ran out through the screen door, letting it slam just a little, and then froze, whispering a prayer, hoping that Mamma and Papa, if they heard anything, would think it was the boys going to the cliffs, and go back to their Sunday morning rest. But as I stood there, I heard nothing, the house as quiet as its stone walls.

I stepped off the porch and sped as fast as I could towards the cliffs. My brothers were long out of sight, probably already on the shore of Rocquaine Bay. And so I ran towards the cliffs. In the early light that shone on the wild daisies, and the deep pink lilies, and the bright green grass, I felt myself flowing into a swift, joyful dance.

Towards the cliffs, where Guernsey was especially magical.

Abram heard Lorley leave the house.

He wondered if she was wearing the hair ribbon that Marie tended so carefully. Probably not. When Lorley tried to fix the bow in place herself, it took her such a long time; she would be too eager to follow her brothers to the cliffs to bother with all that.

He looked at his wife, still sleeping deeply. Thank God she hadn't heard the boys or Lorley – not that it had ever bothered her to let her sons explore the cliffs and the caves. Boys in Guernsey, easily starting as young as Randolph, grew up doing that; it was really only Lorley that she worried about so much.

But Lorley, who looked like his beautiful Marie, with her soft fair hair and eyes the colour of the sea, wasn't content just doing chores at her Mamma's side. She loved to explore, like her brothers; they would know that she would be following them and would watch out for her.

If Abram hadn't been so afraid of waking her, he would have stroked his wife's hair that fell in long, silky strands over her pillow, and caressed her forehead, to somehow ease all the worries in her mind. Lately, she had been hovering over the children, watching them too closely – but he knew that it was really not about them at all, but about the trouble in Europe. That was what had kept them up so late last night. And there was cause for concern – there was no doubt about that – but he had tried to assure her that all would be well.

But he couldn't promise her, as she had begged, that he wouldn't fight for his country if it came to that.

He got out of the bed, careful not to wake her, but moving quickly. He could never understand how people could lie in bed after they awakened. Once the sunlight shone through the window, he would wake up immediately. This morning he had lingered a bit, but only because it had been so hard to take his eyes off Marie.

After five children in their sixteen years of marriage, she was as beautiful to him as on the day of their wedding at St. Saviour's Church. He hated to see her so unhappy now. But knowing that he had to fight in France was devastating to her. When he voluntarily joined the Militia three years ago, in 1914, he told her then that if Guernseymen were sent to war, he would have no choice but to go with the Regiment. And now that the Royal Guernsey Light Infantry had been formed from the Militia, it was certain that the men from Guernsey would be serving their King overseas. Last night she had cried, sitting in the wicker chair by the stone hearth in the kitchen. They were quiet tears, not enough to wake the children. But her long hair had come undone, covering most of her face.

He had stood there, unable to do anything other than watch her cry.

He hoped she wouldn't be so worried today, that they

would have a calm Sunday. He threw on his clothes, the rough trousers and sweater of a farmer. He had to get some fresh air. Leaving the house quietly, he stood on the back porch, looking at the fields. The grapevines were brilliant in the morning sunlight; the mist that hung over the cliffs never lingered on the fields. Last night Marie had said how proud she was of their farm, and how grateful she was that they would have something important to one day leave to their sons. And then she had asked him what would happen to the land if he went away to war.

Marie opened her eyes as soon as Abram left the room. Despite the fears that had kept her awake most of the night, she had to smile a little. He thought he was being so quiet, believing that she was in some deep dream. Even if she had been asleep, she surely would have awakened when he stared at her with his large, dark eyes. He might as well have been moving his hands over her body.

She covered her eyes then, as the morning light streamed through the casement window, making the lead around the glass gleam a dull gold. Before Abram had awakened, she had been staring at him. And she knew for certain that he had been sleeping, because she had touched his arm, gently, the way she always did when she wanted him. That was all it took, usually, just a single caress, and he would wake up, and they would make love. At first, not long after they were married, when she had reached out to him like that, she had been ashamed. A woman wasn't supposed to care about such things or wake her husband in that way. But Abram loved it.

Even after five children, he desired her, loved her as if she were still twenty years old. And she felt the same, even though she knew that a woman should not even think about such things.

But she couldn't help it with Abram.

Now he was talking about going away to war. She couldn't bear it.

Without Abram, she imagined their large farmhouse, which had been in his family for over three hundred years, made from Guernsey granite, large stone blocks that shone caramel and deep brown in the morning light, falling apart, crumbling as if it were made of chalk.

Look at what was already happening, she thought.

Her little Lorley was out there running towards the cliffs after her brothers; of course she heard her slip out of the house. It wasn't the first time she had done this – and even though Marie knew that the boys would be bringing her back soon enough, she didn't like it at all. If she hadn't been so desperately worried about Abram going off to war, she would have been out of her bed and in the kitchen like a proper Guernsey mother and kept her little girl safe by her side. What was she doing, lying in bed, remembering Abram's lovemaking when Lorley was running like a lost lamb by the cliffs? And when Abram was determined to join the Guernseymen if they went off to war?

She got out of bed then, quickly.

And she began to dress hurriedly, looking at herself in the oval mirror hanging over the dresser. Her hair was too long, falling to her waist, but she didn't cut it because Abram liked it that way. When she was working in the house, he would tell her not to pin it into a chignon, but to let it fall over her shoulders and down her back, soft and shining, the colour of a pale golden fawn, he said. She would only do that when they went to bed, even though she knew that the proper way to sleep was to keep your hair in a braid. But during the day, she had to at least tie it back; otherwise, she would never be able to get her housework done.

She grabbed a ribbon out of the little drawer in her dressing table and began fastening it in her hair. It was a pink one, cut from the same spool that she used for her daughter's hair. She was about to take it out, to save it for Lorley, but she was in too much of a rush now, so she left it in her hair and, without giving it any thought, slipped into the first dress in the wardrobe, the lavender one, tying the strings at the back as tightly as she could, so that it cinched the way it was supposed to around her waist. It was still a little loose. She had lost more weight.

When she walked into the kitchen, she saw Abram on the back porch. He had his back to her, gazing at their vineyard.

He turned as she joined him on the porch.

"Abram, I'm sure that Lorley has gone with the boys to the cliffs again. You better go after her before she gets too far."

"Don't worry now. The boys know when she tags along. I've told Reginald many times that he and his brothers must always be watching for her when they go to the cliffs."

She felt a little better then, thinking about her eldest son, her Reginald, fourteen years old and almost as tall as Abram. The last time Lorley followed her brothers, less than a month ago, they returned with her sitting on Reginald's broad shoulders, looking as majestic as the Queen of England riding her horse.

She looked past Abram to the fields now, gleaming bright

green in the morning sun, the purple myrtle blooming, the hedgerows dividing their land from their neighbours, the thick leaves as soft as velvet.

She felt his arm tighten around her shoulders. "Marie, try not to worry about anything – about the children or the war." He paused, knowing it was really the war that was pressing on her mind. "When I joined the Militia, we both knew that this could happen. Now that the Royal Guernsey Light Infantry has been formed, I have to go when they sail overseas."

"The British generals won't hesitate to put Colonials like the men from Guernsey in great danger, Abram, you must know that," she said, turning to look at him, the words coming too quickly out of her mouth.

He shook his head, saying, "Marie, our island has been part of Great Britain for almost nine hundred years. We have always served the Sovereign."

Marie stared at her husband in silence. He spoke the way too many in Guernsey were speaking now – this island of brave men, descendants of Huguenots who centuries ago fled France to escape religious persecution, and settled on this small island, still speaking the French of their Norman ancestors, but fiercely loyal to the British Crown. At least Abram could speak English as fluently as he spoke their dialect, Guernésiais – as could their children, but that was her influence really, for English was her first language, being from one of the families on the island of British descent.

Now, she spoke Guernésiais more than she spoke English, and the children could slip easily from one language to the other – although at home they most often spoke in the Guernsey dialect. But many on the island could not speak

English. Those Guernseymen in the Militia would have a hard time with the British generals, she knew.

And despite what Abram said, she feared that those in the British Command would not do as much to keep the Guernsey Colonials out of harm's way; they would protect their own from England first.

But she could never make Abram understand that.

So she said nothing as she returned her gaze to their land. He said, "We'll get through it somehow, Marie, I promise you. Reginald is fourteen now, such a strong boy, and a good farmer. And you know that Herbert sticks as closely to Reginald as moss on an oak tree; he works his heart out with his older brother in the fields. Even Lloyd and Randolph do pretty well in the vines."

"Abram, they are still such young boys; Randolph is only seven years old and Lloyd, nine. You know as well as I do that all they do is chase after each other, hiding behind the vines, and then they run off to the cliffs the first chance that they get."

"But Marie, they can –"

She ran her fingers through her hair then, some of the long strands falling out of the loose ribbon. "I can't talk about this anymore. I don't know what I'm going to do without you."

"It will be all right. You'll see," he said, putting his arm around her slight shoulders. His voice was as soft as lamb's wool; when she looked up at him, he was smiling. He held her even closer to him then, saying, "This will be all over soon enough. Let's just enjoy our Sunday with the children, please, Marie."

She looked into his large, dark eyes, and saw, despite his

brave words and smiling face, how much he needed her to be happy.

I wasn't worried that I hadn't found my brothers yet.

They always went to Rocquaine Bay. The sand on the beach there was as silky smooth as the ribbons Mamma tied in my hair, the water as bright as crystal. As soon as they climbed down the cliff, my brothers would roll up their pant legs and wade in the shallow water along the shore, looking for Chancre crabs, and the sparkling fish that swam in on the tide, the secretive, exotic blennies, the spiny dogfish, and the conger eels. But before too long, they would explore a cave, with Reginald always leading the way.

I finally made it to the top of the cliff and stood there, looking down over the bay. I could see my brothers splashing in the smooth water. The climb down on this part of the slope was a bit steep, but it was filled with lichens and brambles, and lots of bracken ferns to hold onto if my foot slipped. So beautiful to gaze upon, the flora grew as if painted on the granite rock in brilliant green and yellow brushstrokes. And especially lush and green were the bracken ferns, their fronds reaching into the sky, spread wide, as if in silent prayer.

I knew how much Mamma didn't want me to go to the cliffs, but I had been doing it now for almost a year, just like all of my brothers had when they were little. And I was very careful; I never climbed the really steep slopes, not like Lloyd and Randolph, who especially loved the cliffs farther down the bay, where the granite was as dark and jagged as a snaggle-toothed beast.

I began making my way slowly down to the beach, thankful that my brothers hadn't yet gone into one of the caves. When that happened, I had to wait for them, walking up and down the beach as I stared at the cliffs, wondering which cave they had gone into that day. Once, too weary of waiting for them, and convinced I knew which one they were exploring, I ventured into the cave, the grey rocks jutting around the narrow opening like the jaws of a sea monster, glistening darkly from the spume of the waves lashing against them. I saw footprints in the sand by the entrance, so I walked, very slowly, into the cave, calling out my brothers' names. I didn't go very far; the beach was still shining through the opening, but in front of me there was thick darkness. I stared hard at the rough walls, peering into the still, midnight air. And then a devil's face began glimmering before me, as jagged and black as the wet granite, with awful eyes that smouldered like coals, and I ran out of the cave. No longer mindful of the slippery dark sand, almost falling as I rushed to get out of there, too frightened to look back at the rock walls of the cave, I lurched towards the light, scrambling over the rocks as quickly as though Satan himself was snapping at my heels.

On the beach waiting for me were my brothers, all four of them, looming very large, dark silhouettes against the light blue water and sky.

Reginald was bigger than ever that day, a giant. I had never seen him so angry.

I could do nothing but stand silently on the sand.

I had done what Reginald and all of my brothers had told me never to do.

Reginald's face was as dark as thunder, and the others

looked just as grim, even Lloyd and Randolph, although I could see in their eyes how badly they felt for me. And on Randolph's face, I saw the flicker of the slightest wink.

I felt a burst of love for him then, and I wanted to tell him not to worry. I was so happy to have escaped the devil lurking in the deep crevices of the rock walls, that to be safe on the beach was heaven, regardless of whatever fierce words Reginald spoke.

"If you ever go into a cave again, Lorley, we will never let you come with us. Do you understand?"

I nodded. I could have shouted loudly into the brilliant blue sky that I never wanted to go into another cave for the rest of my life anyway. I was so happy to have my feet firmly planted in the sand, to feel the spray of the waves as they lapped over my ankles, to be in what felt like another world compared to that cave.

But I said nothing, because if I had told my brothers that I believed I had looked into the eyes of Satan himself in that black cave, I would be banned from the cliffs for life. Reginald would decide, sounding like Mamma, that my imagination was out of control.

Whenever I heard those words, I ended up losing my freedom, usually being kept in the kitchen with Mamma making fruit bread and potage for a few days. And so I tried to keep my imagination tucked firmly inside of me. Sometimes, there were so many whirling thoughts that I grew a little lightheaded trying to sort them out; it was like being in a meadow, gazing at too many wildflowers all at once. But sometimes, still, thoughts crept out of my mind, and I paid the price. I had learned never to tell anyone, again, that I was sure I could see, staring from my bedroom window after everyone had gone to bed, the witches from the South Shore flying on their broomsticks over our woods. I had mentioned it once to the entire family when we were sitting at the long, wooden table in our kitchen. As Mamma used her ladle to pour the vegetable potage into our thick soup bowls, I told them. And because there were so many stories about the witches who lurked on the South Shore, I thought everyone would be amazed by what I saw – proof that the witches in the stories were real.

It didn't turn out that way.

I was in the kitchen for almost a week after that, and I even slept in a little trundle bed for a few days at the foot of the great mahogany one that Mamma and Papa shared, an ignominy that I endured.

So as I stood on Rocquaine Bay that day, I knew there was absolutely no way that I could tell my brothers about the devil who lurked in those granite walls. I looked at them all, saying, being more truthful than I perhaps had been in all my life, "I will never go into that cave again." And then I had to add, because I loved my brothers, "None of you should either."

Reginald said, his eyes boring into me, "Why Lorley?"

But I wasn't going to fall into that trap and end up chopping carrots and potatoes and fruit forever. "It's just not a nice cave," I said, as I shrugged and shook my head.

Herbert, standing close to Reginald, piped up then, not looking at me but at my brothers. "That cave has a lot of strange rocks, remember? It probably scared her to death."

I inadvertently nodded, but no one noticed, and that was all for the best. I didn't want Reginald to start questioning me and make me unravel all that had happened in that cave. Then he would have to report to Mamma and Papa, and I would be seen, once more, as the child with too much imagination, one who had to be kept hidden away in the kitchen making fruit bread.

But that awful day was long behind me now, almost six months past, and I never ventured into another cave, but waited for my brothers on the beach, regardless of how long it took them to do their exploring.

Now, as I crept down the cliff amidst the bracken ferns and lichens and brambles, I watched my brothers running quickly along the shore, their cries as cheerful as if they were flying with the seabirds that swept over the bright water. I was anxious to join them, but I forced myself to go slowly, not moving forward until I was sure each footstep was secure. And I had to be even more careful once I was closer to the bottom, because there the rocks were bare, dark granite jutting over the beach like the stones of an ancient castle that had fallen into the sea.

I wasn't even halfway down when I saw Lloyd and Randolph run towards a cave at the very end of the beach, a cave known as the Creux Mahie. It was one of their favourites, with a roof as high as St. Saviour's Church, they said. Reginald and Herbert ran off with them, quickly overtaking them. Reginald was soon leading the way, holding a furze branch high in the air, the torch he would light when he entered the cave.

They were about to walk into the cave, when Lloyd looked back at the cliffs. He began waving his long arm at me, and then the others turned their heads. Reginald called to me in his booming voice, "Wait for us, Lorley, by the shore. We won't be long." And then they all waved and moved swiftly into the cave.

My heart sank. They would be there for at least an hour.

I stood still, listening to the water lapping on the smooth, pale brown sand of Rocquaine Bay. And I heard the larger waves, unfurled like great white sails, crashing against the heavy, jagged rocks. Without even trying, I began to feel like an ancient queen, standing high on the cliffs of my kingdom, staring into the bright horizon with fearless eyes, waiting for my country's ship to return from some exotic land.

I was especially happy that I hadn't worn my ribbon. The wind, although still fairly mild, was strong enough to have sent it twirling away, a crazed, pink thing flying with the seabirds. Reaching behind my head, I pulled out the piece of wool that I had used to tie it back, and set my hair free. Like Mamma's, it fell to my waist, and with the wind on the cliff, it blew around me, making me feel more like an ancient queen than ever.

I began climbing up the cliff again to survey my kingdom all around me. For some reason I always found it easier climbing up, looking into the wide cerulean sky, than down towards the water and the rocks. My hair streamed behind me, and I had to be careful to make sure that it didn't get caught on any of the thorny bushes. My Mamma would not be pleased, at all, to see my hair whirling around me, the fine strands getting knotted and tangled. I would have to comb through it with my fingers before I went home. But when I wanted to imagine being an ancient Guernsey Queen from Castle Cornet, I had to let my hair fall down to my waist.

Soon, I was at the top of the cliff once more. My brothers disappeared into the cave, and I stood, alone, looking at the great expanse of water below, blending seamlessly into the enormous, shining sky, I, an ancient queen in her high castle, looking over her magical lands.

I began walking along the top of the cliffs. I tried not to think about my brothers in the cave. With Reginald leading the way, holding his torch in front of him, they would explore the dark abyss, huddled together to share the dim amber light. I shuddered, thinking about it. I could see their faces, brave, fearless – Lloyd and Randolph would be behind Reginald, with Herbert last, edging past the rock walls and the deep black crevices.

Breathing deeply, I looked up at the sky, saying a prayer to the Blessed Virgin Mary to keep them safe – although when I thought of my brothers and their bright, courageous eyes whenever they tried anything dangerous, I wasn't sure that they needed much help from heaven.

But I prayed anyway, because I loved to think of her living in heaven in her flowing gown and fluttery veil the colour of bluebells. In the holy picture that I saw once, she had fair hair as long as mine and Mamma's, but it was brighter, as yellow as daffodils, shining in an aura around her beautiful face, like a golden queen of heaven.

My worship of the Blessed Virgin Mary was a secret, though, I had to keep safely tucked inside of me, because praying to her was what Catholics, not Anglicans like my family, were supposed to do. I had first heard about her when my Mamma's church group from St. Saviour's met to talk in our front parlour. Mamma had not said much in the conversation, but then she had been busy serving the tea and cakes and fruit bread. I had managed one tray myself, doing quite well I thought, until I nearly tripped, being so taken with the enormous hat worn by Mme. Laporte. After that,

Mamma told me to just sit quietly and listen, and that was when Mme. Laporte held up a picture, saying this was what the Catholics prayed to instead of God. I couldn't take my eyes off the beautiful image. In Mme. Laporte's fleshy palm, it didn't seem very large, but it sparkled as if she were cradling a jewel, or a handful of gold. I stretched my neck as long as I could to get a good look at the picture, at the glittering gold border, as shiny as the woman's beautiful yellow hair. And her blue eyes were so bright it seemed as if there were sprinkles of gold on her long eyelashes.

Mme. Laporte then held the picture even higher, to make sure that everyone could see it, saying, "The Catholics call this a holy picture. They keep all sorts of them in their prayer books." She shook her head, and her enormous hat jiggled quite a bit, like a ship in rough waters, but I didn't pay much attention to that because the holy picture was so incredibly beautiful, looking as if it were about to float to heaven in a swirl of blue and gold. After a long pause, she said, "And they call her the Blessed Virgin Mary, mind you." Then, for some strange reason that I did not understand, all the ladies shook their heads also and pursed their lips. Mamma did not, being so busy with the tea and cakes and fruit bread that she did not seem to be listening. I let the words Blessed Virgin Mary fall over my ears, and I thought how beautiful her name was.

I asked Mamma about it afterwards, when we were washing the bone china that she used for the ladies' visit. She was very carefully cleaning each piece of Limoges separately, rinsing it in another tub of warm water before handing it to me. I longed to do the washing, dipping my hands in the sudsy water, as foamy as the sea in a storm, cleaning each beautiful piece of china, but Mamma said firmly that I was not ready for that task yet.

That day, I couldn't keep the holy picture out of my mind. As I slowly dried a dessert plate, holding it as if it were the chalice from the altar at St. Saviour's, I said, trying to choose my words carefully, "Don't you think that holy picture of the Blessed Virgin Mary is beautiful?"

Mamma looked at me, frowning, and said, "We don't pray to her. You know that, Lorley."

"But why not?"

Mamma, keeping her gaze fixed on the Limoges china, sighed a little, and said, "People who go to our church don't do that. We pray to Jesus and God."

I stopped talking about it then. I didn't want to risk Mamma thinking I was getting too many dangerous ideas in my head and worry her. I felt the same when I overheard Lloyd and Randolph telling each other stories about the old women who practised witchcraft, stories about these strange hags who lived in thatched cottages on the far South Shore of Guernsey; I knew that I could not share any of what I learned with Mamma.

Their stories about the Guernsey witches – about those who once haunted the island with their black sorcery and potions, the hundreds who long ago were tortured and burnt on stakes in St. Peter Port and even Le Catioroc in St. Saviour's, and the old, cunning women who still lurked in isolated cottages in the South, casting their spells like spiders weaving glistening, gossamer webs – frightened me an awful lot. But I never told Mamma about what I heard; never did I want her to worry about me knowing so much about witchcraft.

And so after I saw the holy picture of the beautiful blue Blessed Virgin Mary and began praying to her, to avoid worrying my Mamma, I kept it a secret.

I prayed to her often. I would imagine her floating above a forest not far from where I now walked along the cliffs, called Bluebell Woods, where the ground was covered with wild bluebells. They grew beneath tall ash trees with quiet grey bark, their high branches crisscrossing the sky in a green haze. The light that shone through them illuminated the bluebells, seeming to cast a spell on them, a spell that made them glow with a blue so intense, it was as though the Blessed Virgin Mary herself was resting there in her lovely gown, her eyes wide open and full of heaven.

I looked down at the deserted beach, my brothers now gone, and stared at the lonely waves lapping on the shore. Suddenly, it felt as if they had never been there, that no one that morning had been running in the silky sand, that no one had been scrambling over the grey rocks in the spray of the frothy water. Their footprints had now washed away. Standing there, listening to the seabirds' importunate cries, shrill in the enormous, blue sky, and the loud crashing of the waves, Rocquaine Bay now felt too empty without my brothers.

It was then I decided to go to Bluebell Woods. It wasn't a very long hike from the cliffs, and I could go there and be back on the beach before my brothers emerged from the cave. Often when I had been thinking about the Blessed Virgin Mary, I felt like going to Bluebell Woods; it was only natural; the closest thing to all her beautiful blueness was in the flowers that grew in wild profusion there.

I ran towards the woods. It was so much easier than climbing on the cliffs. The ground was uneven but covered in such soft grasses and ferns that it never hurt if I fell. Once I came to the woods, I slowed my pace – it felt too much like a church to move very quickly – a sacred place where the hours melted away as if time had never been there at all. I let myself drop down into the blue flowers, a blue so intense that when the light shone, the flowers were almost purple, as luminous as the stained glass in St. Saviour's Church.

I was not tired from climbing the cliff and then running to the woods. I just wanted to feel the soft flowers against my face and my hair – and wonder, as I always did, if some of the blue could ever rub off on me, my cheeks no longer pink but a beautiful, brilliant blue. It never happened, but I never stopped hoping that it would.

I stared into the sky through the light, green veil of the tall, overhanging branches, a sky as bright as if the bluebells were growing in wild abundance there also.

And then I fell into a deep, blue sleep.

I don't know how long I slept, lying there in my soft bed of flowers, the long, thin branches swaying overhead, the breeze stirring the narrow leaves.

When I awakened, I could hear in the distance the cry of the seabirds from Rocquaine Bay, and the sound of the sea, the large waves crashing as they washed onshore. Closer, the dry clicking of the insects' wings was all around me and the lovely, light sway of the branches filled the gentle air. At that moment, I would have loved to lie like that forever, to become one of the bluebells.

Then I heard something moving ever so slowly in the woods.

chapter
two

MY FIRST THOUGHT was that perhaps it was one of the red deer that had been brought to the island by a man from England. The deer had been spotted all over; I knew that Lloyd and Randolph had seen a few of them just recently on one of their hikes. I lay very still, not wanting to disturb it – the longer I listened, the more I was certain that the almost imperceptible rustling through the ferns and the wildflowers and the dry, feathery grasses of Bluebell Woods had to be a deer. I opened my eyes, and sat up very slowly, lifting my body out of the bluebells as quietly as if I were a flower opening my petals.

The woman was standing on the edge of the woods, turned away from me, her long hair falling past her waist. In the light shining through the trees and the iridescent glow from the wildflowers, her hair looked like the lovely blue veil of the Blessed Virgin Mary.

She was cutting strips of bark from a willow tree, using a small sharp knife, and then tucking the shavings into the wicker basket that was slung over her shoulder. It looked quite full – I could see green leaves, and brown stems with the roots still attached, and wildflowers, their petals still vibrant with colour – though there did not appear to be any bluebells, and I was relieved at that. Even though they grew so thickly in these woods, I hated to see a single one being picked. It seemed so unfair to take it away from its family – but that was another thought I could not share with anyone, other than, perhaps, Lloyd and Randolph, who never felt the need to report anything to Mamma and Papa – nor did they laugh. They smiled a little sometimes, their eyes always kind.

I tried to breathe as quietly as I could. I thought about slipping away, dancing as lightly as I could over the bluebells, back to the cliffs before she ever turned around.

But I couldn't.

Because I couldn't take my eyes off her. The long hair that at first seemed like the blue veil of the Blessed Virgin Mary herself, I now saw was really silver, seeming to shine softly blue, a mirror reflecting the bluebells growing around her ankles.

It was then that I realized that she wasn't wearing any boots, but walked lightly through the bluebells in bare feet as she cut away the long strips of bark. Even though I hadn't yet seen her face, I knew that I had never seen her before. None of the mothers or grandmothers in Guernsey would ever leave their homes with their hair falling down their backs like that – even I, at five years old, was being reckless and wild, letting my hair fly freely all around me the way I did when I went to the cliffs. Mamma sometimes did it in our home, but I knew that was unusual – other mothers did not do that, and when anyone came to the farm, Mamma would pin her hair into a chignon before she ever went outside.

I was sitting as still as the bluebells when the woman said, very softly, without turning around, "Can you hear the bluebells singing?"

Then she turned her head, looking over her narrow shoulder at me. Her silver hair was parted in the middle, falling in a soft sheen that framed her thin face. Her eyes were large – grey eyes that were so light that the colour seemed barely there at all, and they glittered like clear gemstones, the colour of the sea sometimes, when the water appeared crystalline from the sun shining so brightly.

Sitting as still as the bluebells all around me, I stared at her, and I kept thinking of the Blessed Virgin Mary, although her face wasn't like Mary's at all. In the holy picture, Mary had such brilliant blue eyes, brighter even than the wildflowers in Bluebell Woods, and she had creamy pink cheeks and yellow hair that grew in long, fluffy waves, like an exquisite doll.

The woman who was now staring at me, with a sharp knife in her hand, had no creamy pink in her face – her cheeks and her lips were almost colourless but, like her eyes, had a peculiar brightness, like a beautiful mirror that shines deeply. Perhaps, I told myself, it was her unearthly beauty that made me keep thinking of the Blessed Virgin Mary as I gazed at her.

She spoke again, smiling softly, saying, "Can you hear the bluebells singing?" Her voice was low and very quiet, each word enunciated with great care. The woods, strangely, seemed to have fallen completely silent now.

I only heard the woman's voice, asking me if I could hear the bluebells singing, her voice falling over me, a voice filled with a silvery blue light.

And then I gazed at the radiant blue flowers in the sunlight, and I heard the singing.

Coming from the wide-open petals, a song that made me suddenly feel as though I was floating in a bright blue heaven, with voices full of joy, shining inside me and all around me.

I nodded my head slowly.

She raised one of her long, thin arms high above her, and drew in the air with graceful, sweeping strokes.

And then she slipped away, without making a sound, into the long grey tree trunks behind her. For a few moments, I could see her, but if I hadn't known that she was there, I don't think I would have seen her grey hair and skin blending into the bark, like watercolours in a grey palette.

I stared hard at the grove of ash and willow trees, but then it seemed as if she just vanished, in a sudden flicker of silver light.

And the song of the bluebells vanished with her. Then my ears started hearing other sounds, a cacophony of sounds bursting through, and in that sudden rush of noise I heard my brothers loudly calling out my name, and I knew that they had to be on top of the cliffs, and very near.

I rose out of the bluebells, about to run towards the sound of their voices – but then I looked at the grey trees where the woman had been standing, and at the bluebells growing like a lush blue endless dream, and I hated to leave this enchanted place.

Where I had heard the song of the bluebells. Where it felt as if heaven had been singing to me.

Why, I thought suddenly, hadn't I tried to talk to her?

Perhaps, I told myself, it was because she had cast a spell over me, so that I could hear the bluebells singing.

And then the thought blossomed like a beautiful bluebell in my mind that perhaps this woman who shone like fine sterling was really the Blessed Virgin Mary, but grown a little older. I knew that you weren't supposed to age once you were in heaven, but maybe, if you had to come down to earth once in a while, you aged a bit, like antique silver.

It all seemed to make so much sense.

And I had to tell my brothers what happened.

I ran away from Bluebell Woods then, looking back once at the place where, possibly, a miracle had occurred. Even though my brothers' cries were very loud now, I wondered, for a moment, if I should go back to the woods, to lean down over the bluebells, to listen, to try to hear their song one more time. But I knew that the miracle had vanished, a single silvery moment in time that was gone.

I wasn't far from Bluebell Woods when Lloyd and Randolph found me.

"Why weren't you waiting for us by the cave?" Randolph said. He had been running hard, his breathing heavy. Then he turned towards the cliffs, calling, "Reginald! Herbert! We found her!"

Before I had a chance to say anything, Lloyd broke in, his voice very quiet, one that truly belonged in Bluebell Woods, "Are you all right?"

I nodded, feeling as if I were going to burst with all that I had to tell. I hardly knew where to begin.

Then Reginald and Herbert came running over the hill, racing in long strides towards me.

"Lorley!" Reginald cried out, before he even got to me. "Where were you? We've been looking all over for you. You know that you were supposed to wait for us by the cave."

"I just went to Bluebell Woods. I didn't realize how long I was gone." And then my words came out in a rush – lying down in the flowers, as if they were a magic carpet, a deep blue magical carpet from the Arabian Nights – and then the beautiful, silver woman appearing.

But before I had a chance to tell them about the bluebells singing, and about the woman who seemed to have floated right down from heaven to shine like starlight in Bluebell Woods, Reginald interrupted me, holding up his hand, suddenly acting as old as if he were Papa himself.

"What woman appeared?"

I looked at Reginald, and then at each of my brothers, who were all staring at me, their eyes intense, and suddenly, in that moment, the sun seemed to be beating down very hard, too round and too yellow.

I rubbed my eyes. Before Reginald interrupted me, my words were dancing out of me, as if they were being carried along in a swirl of magic. Perhaps, I thought, it had been the last sparkles from the beautiful woman still working on me, and now that they were gone – floating back into the trees with her and up to heaven, I imagined. Now, I was not sure how to tell them.

Then I heard Herbert say quietly to Reginald, "I think maybe she bumped her head."

And as Reginald silently nodded, muttering something that sounded like 'probably,' I found the words, once more, I wanted to say: "I didn't hurt my head." And as I spoke, I thought how impossible it would be to ever bump your head on that deep soft bed of bluebells. Even the trees in those woods, with their pale grey trunks, looked as gentle as Mamma's angora wool. "And I saw the most beautiful woman with hair that floated down her back like a silver blue veil –"

"What was she doing?" Reginald said, and I was relieved that at least he seemed willing to believe that I had really seen someone.

"She was cutting strips of bark from a willow tree, and she was carrying a wide basket filled with all sorts of plants. She just seemed to float among the bluebells, and then she asked me –"

This time it was Randolph who interrupted me, smiling as he said, "I think you saw one of the witches from the South Shore."

Before I had a chance to tell them she wasn't a witch, that the beautiful woman could never have been a witch but could be the Blessed Virgin Mary herself, Lloyd said, his eyes very big and kind, "I've heard that they have hair like that."

Randolph, nodding his head, asked me, "Did she wave her arms into the air, standing there in her bare feet?"

"Yes," I said very quietly, forcing the word out of my mouth.

"It looks like Lorley saw a witch, all right," Randolph said, looking at my brothers, and I shook my head, not believing that the woman I saw was a witch. No witch could shine like starlight. And surely, I thought, waving her arms and being in her bare feet didn't mean she was a witch. I imagined that everyone in heaven must wave their arms a lot with all the praying they had to do, and no one would bother with shoes when they lived among the clouds.

"But she wasn't like a witch at all," I said. "She was beautiful, with eyes that seemed very kind." I wanted to say there were sparkles of goodness pouring out of the grey light of her eyes, goodness like starlight in the night sky, goodness that seemed to come straight from heaven, but I stopped myself from saying too much all at once – for none of them yet really seemed to understand what I was talking about.

"Witches can make themselves appear in all sorts of disguises, they say," Randolph said, looking first at me and then at Reginald, who was shaking his head darkly.

Then Reginald said, looking in the direction of Bluebell Woods, "I don't believe they have magical powers. The old women who live on the South Shore call themselves white witches, and they believe they are healers, making these strange concoctions from plants and sea creatures. It's just a bunch of hocus-pocus."

Randolph, standing very closely beside Lloyd, said quickly, "Jack Quenneville said he saw a witch once when he was hiking with his brother on the cliffs on the South Shore. She jumped right out of the trees in front of them and raised her arms, these long, skeletal things, and tried to cast a spell on them. He said they ran away so fast they almost fell down the cliffs."

"I think the old hag women are just crazy now, living all alone the way they do on the South Shore," Herbert said.

"Crazy, and evil," Reginald said.

I could not bear to hear any more words like that about the beautiful woman I saw. So I said, in a clear voice, and I thought that perhaps I could hear a faint chorus of bluebell voices in the background, giving me strength, "She was not some weird old witch woman – that's not who I saw."

"She must have come from deep in the woods on the South Shore," Herbert said.

Then I burst out, "This lady came from a beautiful place." And I wanted to say I thought she came from heaven.

And I wanted to say that I even thought she could be the Blessed Virgin Mary herself, and that she used her special magic to let me hear the bluebells sing, when Reginald said, "She didn't touch you with her arms, did she?"

I shook my head, looking down at my shoes, wishing suddenly that my feet were bare. And thinking how much I wished she had touched me.

Because the woman I saw was not strange, nor evil – and she had eyes that I had definitely seen before –

In a holy picture. Her gaze seeing heaven everywhere.

Reginald and Herbert ran like soldiers with long, stiff strides, but at a slower pace than usual. If Lloyd and Randolph hadn't been with me, though, grabbing my hands to keep me moving fast enough, even then I could not have kept up with them. But they pulled me along – so smoothly and effortlessly, it seemed, that my feet were barely touching the ground, as though a magic carpet was fluttering under my feet and whisking me home.

I had not meant to cause any trouble – although the more I thought about their faces when I described the beautiful silver lady in Bluebell Woods, I realized it was really only Reginald who seemed upset. Nothing ever bothered Herbert very much – he seemed to think I had hit my head and dreamt everything – which was what he seemed to think about me quite a bit. And Lloyd and Randolph weren't angry, either – I even thought that they both wished they had been there with me.

When we finally made it to the edge of our vineyard, I could see our house. Mamma and Papa must have seen us at the same time because the screen door opened and they rushed onto the porch. Even though Mamma was already in her fine silk dress for church, and Papa had changed into his stiff collar and suit jacket, they ran to meet us. Mamma was a little behind Papa, because of her fancy shoes, but then I saw Papa stop and hold out his hand to her.

"What happened?" Mamma called, when she and Papa were still several steps away from us.

I kept my head down, because I did not want Mamma and Papa to see my eyes yet. The beautiful lady from Bluebell Woods was still shining inside me, the magic tingling all over me, and I was not sure how to explain it to them. If I could look in the mirror at that moment, I believed that I must surely have soft blue edges, as though the bluebells were still glowing all around me, as though the silver blue lady was with me at that moment.

Suddenly, I wanted it all to come pouring out of me, and I opened my mouth to speak, to somehow describe the magic in Bluebell Woods, but Reginald, his eyes fixed on me, spoke before I had a chance to say a single word.

"We were exploring a cave on Rocquaine Bay, and Lorley, instead of waiting for us by the Giant's Toe, ran off to Bluebell Woods. It took us quite a while to find her."

I looked up at Reginald and realized suddenly how much trouble I had caused him – the spell of Bluebell Woods must have stopped me from really seeing how hard I had made things for him. I said, the words rushing out of my mouth,

"I'm sorry. I shouldn't have run off." My eyes were on Reginald's face as I spoke, and then I looked at Mamma, and Papa, and all of my brothers.

No one said anything for a few long moments, but finally Mamma said, "Well, thankfully everyone is fine. And Lorley, you know that I don't like you going to the cliffs. You worried Papa and me half to death."

I nodded my head, and I knew she was right, but I could still feel the magic from Bluebell Woods, as if little blue sparks were all over me, and I still could not feel as badly as I should have for disobeying everyone, even though I was trying my hardest.

Papa spoke then, his voice sounding calm and reassuring in my ears. "Let's just put it all behind us. But I'm afraid it's too late for church now. I want you to get cleaned up, though. Most likely we'll have Sunday visitors."

I glanced at Reginald and then at all of my brothers, waiting for someone to tell Mamma and Papa the rest of the story, the really important part of the Bluebell Woods story.

Papa began walking towards the house, holding out his hand to me, and Mamma reached out her arms to the boys, moving with Reginald and Herbert on one side of her and Lloyd and Randolph on the other. I looked at Reginald, wondering if he was going to say anything.

He didn't look as if he wanted to, but then, seeing my face, he suddenly said, "I think Lorley saw one of the witches from the South Shore in Bluebell Woods."

"What?" Mamma said, and I heard Randolph murmur something, his eyes cast down.

In the silence that followed, Herbert said, "She might have bumped her head and just dreamt the whole thing up." But as he spoke, he looked at Reginald, and his voice trailed off like a wisp of smoke.

"Maybe she did bump her head – but I think she really saw someone, and I'm pretty sure it was one of the witches from the South Shore," Reginald said.

As I looked at Mamma's face, I wished at that moment that I had just imagined everything in a bluebell daze or hit my head a bit against a tree root and didn't know what I was saying – because I did not want to cause Mamma any more worries.

I also wanted to tell her not to be frightened – that the woman I saw could not have been a witch and may even have been the Blessed Virgin Mary. But Reginald gave me the look that told me to let him speak, that froze me as if he himself had cast a spell on me, and he told Mamma and Papa the story of what he thought happened in Bluebell Woods that day.

Mamma's face grew more and more worried as Reginald spoke.

Strangely though, as I stood beside Papa holding his hand, I thought that his face looked as calm as if Reginald were describing me doing nothing more than lying on a bed of bluebells, my eyes seeing only the sky overhead, a pure, simple sky without even a flutter of an angel wing high above.

As Reginald finished with his description of the woman waving ugly arms at me and muttering gibberish, a story so wrong, really, that it hurt my heart to hear it, Mamma said, "Thank goodness you did not come to any harm, Lorley."

I looked at her, relieved that I finally had a chance to say, "No one shining the way she did would ever hurt me,

Mamma." And my heart became full again thinking about the silver woman.

Mamma stared at me, shaking her head a little, but I continued, saying, "Her arms weren't ugly, nothing was ugly about her – she was beautiful. Her hair was like a mirror, with long silver ripples that fell past her waist."

Reginald opened his mouth to speak, but Papa stopped him, and said, looking at Mamma, "I think I know who Lorley saw."

I looked up at Papa, and for a moment I thought he was about to say what I was bursting to tell them all – that the beautiful silvery lady was no witch, but perhaps the Blessed Virgin Mary herself.

But then I told myself that was surely impossible. I doubted that Papa had ever seen her holy picture.

"The woman is known as Mme. de la Rue."

None of my brothers said a word, and I couldn't find any words either. The fact that Papa knew her name, knew who the beautiful woman in Bluebell Woods was, made me feel as if there really were angel wings high above and that a few soft feathers had just fallen on my head – a little dazzled, but dazzled in a wondrous way.

"Is she one of the old healers who still lives on the South Shore?" Mamma said.

Papa nodded his head. "It has to be her – with that long grey hair. I wasn't sure if she was still alive."

"Is she a witch, Papa?" Randolph burst out.

Papa shrugged his shoulders, shaking his head a little. "Some still call the old women who live high on the cliffs on the South Shore that – but they are really just healers who make their remedies from plants in the woods and the sea. I don't think there are many of them left. But this Mme. de la Rue was talked about a lot when I was young. There was a bad bout of flu on the island, and many who were sick made the trek to her house, deep in the woods on the South Shore, for her remedies, which were said to be the best cures." Papa smiled then and said, "But it was probably just a walk in the fresh sea breeze that healed people more than anything."

"Did you ever see her Papa?" I asked, my voice a little breathless.

Papa, still smiling, shook his head again. "No, I never have, but ever since I was a young boy, I've heard about Mme. de la Rue with her long grey hair." As Papa spoke, his voice sounded calm and quiet, without a ripple of worry anywhere.

But Mamma said anxiously, "Mme. Laporte has told the ladies in my church group awful stories about those old women making strange potions and trying to cast spells," Mamma said, and I could see the concern bright in her eyes.

"That's all hogwash, Dear. I have told you before not to listen to any of it. Mme. Laporte loves the sound of her own voice more than anyone I know – anything she can trumpet about comes out of her mouth," Papa said, and his words did not sound unkind at all. She did trumpet a lot, her voice bellowing as if a long trunk hung out of her face. And then I thought of her enormous hats, nearly as big as elephant ears, really. I had never touched her, but I could easily imagine her skin feeling as tough as a hide.

Mamma looked at me and said, in her gentle voice, so different from Mme. Laporte's, which was still blaring in my head a little from thinking about her elephant trunk, "Well thank goodness no harm came to anyone."

I stood there, and I wanted to tell them everything that had happened.

That the woman's hair was not grey – but a radiant silver blue, a beautiful veil of hair, that the woman's eyes shone as brightly as if they were full of heaven, that none of them realized how wondrous the woman was – that if she was this Mme. de la Rue, and not the Blessed Virgin Mary herself, she was a kind of sister to Mary, living on this earth, and was surely as magical – that she had made the bluebells sing for me.

But I did not speak. And as I looked at everyone standing there, at Papa and Mamma and my brothers, everything seemed to stop for a moment, as still and quiet as if a magical spell had been cast over us all. Even the leaves on the vines were motionless, part of the spell, too – and I felt as if we were all in a painting hanging in the sunlight.

In that moment, I knew that it was best that I did not say anything.

By the afternoon of that day, everything changed, changed so much that I could imagine Bluebell Woods going far away, the gentle grey trees and the deep blue flowers pulling up their roots and following the beautiful silver lady to the South Shore.

Papa was standing on the back porch gazing at our vineyard, and I was still sitting at my place at the table. Mamma was combing through my hair that had become so tangled in the woods – as if the bluebells had been dancing all over my head while I was lying on the forest floor. I wished that some had even become stuck in my long strands of hair. If I had been that lucky, I would have begged Mamma to leave them, for they were far prettier than any ribbon could possibly be.

But it was while Papa stood on the porch, and Mamma combed through my hair with her gentle hands, that M. Laporte came riding into our yard – and everything changed.

At first, I did not know who it was because there was no loud "Hello" called out in greeting, the way neighbours in Guernsey always did when they came for a visit. All I could hear were the heavy wheels of a wagon crunching on the dry gravel of our lane.

Then Papa moved from the porch, walking slowly, very slowly for my Papa, his shoulders straight, and I heard him say, "Any news?"

I looked at Mamma, who had stopped combing my hair and was staring into the yard, watching Papa. "Can you see who it is?" I asked.

"I can't," she said, her eyes still fixed on Papa walking so slowly away from us. Then she put down the comb and went to the wide casement window. "It's M. Laporte," she said, and I could not understand why her voice sounded fearful.

Because M. Laporte visited us all the time, and he was such a jolly man. For some reason, just looking at him made me smile because his big round face was always creased in a great shining grin that spread like a sun all around him.

A grin that never even went away when he was with Mme. Laporte, who could scare the smiles off the faces of most people. He would walk happily at her side, his short legs moving quickly beside her heavy torso, like a merry tugboat beside a great, billowing barge – her huge hats making her appear even larger.

But that day, as Mamma took my hand without saying a word, and walked with me onto the back porch, M. Laporte didn't look small.

And, for the first time I could ever remember, there was no smile on his face. The words he spoke were so quiet that I could not hear what he was saying. My brothers, who had been in the vineyard, crowded around him closely.

I could see Papa's face clearly as he listened to M. Laporte, a strangely still face, a face that I wasn't used to seeing on my Papa.

Then Mamma and I left the porch, our footsteps loud on the dusty gravel, much louder than the hushed voice of M. Laporte, a sad, dry sound, as if we walked on crushed grey bone.

As soon as we reached them, Papa held out his arm, gently pulling Mamma close to his side, and, looking into her eyes, said, "The Regiment leaves within a week."

Mamma nodded, a nod as light as a breath, and, gazing into his face, she seemed to be speaking to him without saying a single word.

I did not understand what Papa was talking about when he said the Regiment was leaving – although when I looked at my brothers' faces, I could tell they knew what he meant. Their eyes were shining, looking as excited as if they had just discovered a cave – a cave even greater than the Creux Mahie – and were about to explore it, to plunge into its black depths.

Everyone was silent now, Papa's words, "The Regiment leaves within a week," hanging over our little group, the air so silent I wished for any sound to break the heavy stillness, even the sad crunch of the gravel.

Finally, into that silence, I said, "But where is the Regiment going?"

I was used to the Regiment marching up and down the streets of St. Peter Port in their uniforms, as stiff and straight as the toy soldiers that Lloyd and Randolph liked to play with so much.

And I was always proud that Papa marched with them, with all the other Papas that I knew.

Papa had carefully explained to me that the Regiment was there to protect Guernsey if the War ever came to our island. But Papa had also told me over and over that would never happen.

So I had always thought that when the faraway War in France was finally over, the soldiers in the Regiment would be no more – but would disappear from sight quickly – as if they were tin soldiers scattered over the floor in Lloyd and Randolph's room, and packed away in the toy chest forever.

Papa said, his eyes and his voice gentle, as gentle as Mme. de la Rue asking me if I could hear the bluebells singing, "The Regiment must go to the War in France."

But with those words, the song of the bluebells went away, very, very far away, impossibly far away.

"Do you have to go, Papa?" I asked.

"Yes, Honey. I must go – but I will return soon. Everyone in the Regiment believes that – the War cannot last much longer."

I looked down at the dusty gravel then, and as I moved my feet, the sad swish of the stones sounded like long sighs.

And at that moment, my throat was as dry as the gravel at

my feet, and I could not say anything to my Papa. All that I could do was stare down at the grey ground.

"Lorley," Papa said. "Look at me, Honey."

I raised my head and stared into his eyes, eyes that were still so gentle, but now I saw a great sadness there also.

A sadness coming from deep inside him, as if the gravel had somehow scraped his heart, and it was weeping great drops of blood.

Then I thought suddenly of another holy picture, one that people who went to St. Saviour's were allowed to worship, for it hung in the vestibule of the church, in full display for everyone to see.

It was a painting of Jesus, with eyes as gentle as Papa's now were as he gazed down at me. Jesus, with his long flowing chestnut brown hair and his robe draped over his shoulders, Jesus with his heart exposed, pierced with thorns and dripping blood.

I had never really understood the picture before, never understood how the eyes of Jesus could be loving and gentle and calm as his heart cried great drops of blood.

But now I did.

Looking at my Papa.

And even though I thought that surely it must be a sin, probably a bad one, to think that my Papa seemed just like Jesus in the holy picture, I could not stop myself.

Then, as I looked at my Papa, staring at his face hard so that I would never forget what he looked like, he said, "You must promise not to be sad, Lorley. Everything will turn out – you'll see, Honey."

I nodded my head, saying, "Yes, Papa," hoping that I could keep my promise, but not at all sure that I ever could.

I even managed to smile, and Papa smiled at me, and at all of us, then, and he repeated, "No one must be sad."

And more than anything, I knew that Papa wanted the sadness to be in his heart alone.

When M. Laporte said that he had to leave, to tell other men in the Regiment, Abram walked down the lane with him. M. Laporte trudged slowly by his side, leading his horse, the empty wagon rumbling over the gravel.

"That was very hard, Roger. So hard to tell my family that I must leave them."

M. Laporte nodded his head, the wrinkles in his face that were usually lifted in a wide smile now hung in heavy creases. "Your children are still so young. Too much for Lloyd and Randolph and especially little Lorley to understand, I know Abram."

Abram said nothing, but sighed as he looked at the vines that grew to the edges of the lane. He loved this land, the land that his father and grandfather and great-grandfather had farmed before him. Now the vines were lush and fecund, and the hedgerows lining his fields were in bloom, the purple myrtle bright in the dark green leaves. The vines were beautiful to him, always so beautiful to him, even when winter came, when the bare branches were gnarled and brown – like old women bent over as if leaning on rickety canes, barely able to rise out of the soft earth.

Today though, the vines gleamed emerald, the sky above as clear as the waves he could hear in the distance, filling the air as he listened.

He wanted all this to remain in his heart, so that he could take it with him to the War.

Shining around the beautiful faces of his Marie and his children.

Abram glanced then at M. Laporte, who, he saw, was staring at him, his eyes heavy with the sadness in his own heart. Sad for both of them.

Then Abram said, "How did Mme. Laporte take the news?"

He looked down for a moment, and when he turned his face to Abram again, a smile had returned to his lips. Not like the wide smile that usually lit up his whole face, but a smile, one that Abram was grateful for on that day.

"She took it in stride, my wife did, Abram," he said, and his smile deepened, and his eyes danced with some of their old twinkle. "If the generals would let her, she'd go with me. And the War would be over even faster."

Abram smiled now, too. Mme. Laporte wouldn't hesitate to tell those generals what she thought they should do. And God help the enemy with her in the trenches. Armed with a bayonet and one of her hats.

Then he thought about the Laporte boys. One was the same age as Reginald, and the other one was about a year older. "How are your sons taking this, Roger?"

M. Laporte shook his head, and his face fell back into thick creases again. Sighing heavily, he said, "They are so eager to fight, Abram. They want to go with me as much as their Mamma."

"I know, I know, Roger, believe me. Reginald and Herbert are desperate to fight, too – Reginald is fourteen years old and Herbert just turned thirteen last month. I tell you, Roger, I thank God every day that Guernsey is such a small island where everybody knows each other pretty much. If not for that, I know Reginald would lie about his age and try to enlist, and Herbert would be right behind him."

"So would my sons, Abram. So would mine," he repeated as he stared down at the ground.

"But they will not be able to do that Roger. Remember that."

"I keep telling myself that." There was a pause, and then he said in a voice much quieter than Abram had ever heard him use, "I pray that this War will be over long before our boys are able to join."

"I do too, Roger, believe me. We all do." And then he smiled again at his friend, and said in a much lighter voice, "Besides, Roger, your wife would never let your boys join any Regiment. God help them if they tried –"

Abram was relieved to hear M. Laporte chuckle a little at that, and when he finally waved goodbye to him at the end of the long lane, he knew that his friend's heart was a little easier.

As he walked back to the house, though, his own heart was not easy. He could jest about Mme. Laporte – but he knew that she was a very strong woman. He wished Marie had some of her toughness, because he feared for his Marie, feared how hard this was going to be for her.

He began walking quickly, eager to get back to his family. He could see them all, still standing by the back porch, his children in a circle around their Mamma.

Then he was with them again.

And gazing long into Marie's face, he felt all the love and

light in her heart. And in that precious moment he felt a rush
of gratitude much stronger than his fear.

I watched Papa stare into Mamma's face, as though there was
a halo all around her.

And I told myself to stop thinking about the picture of
Jesus with his bleeding heart, which made me feel too sad for
my Papa.

It was not what Papa wanted.

When I looked at my brothers, there was no sadness –
except in Lloyd's face, quiet bits of sadness in his eyes, but
then I told myself that was how his soft brown eyes always
were, really. Even when Mamma would tell him to put his
mind at ease, when she saw that his worries were wringing
away at his insides, and she would hold him close, placing her
hand gently on his forehead, the worry deep in his eyes never
seemed to leave him.

But I could see that his eyes shone also. At first, I thought
it was just the light in Randolph's face spilling over onto him,
but I could tell that it was coming from Lloyd's own heart, a
light woven with the sadness.

In Randolph, and Herbert, and Reginald, there was not
even a tincture of sadness, but a shining in their eyes that, at
first, I could not understand. The only sense I could make of
it was that they were just trying to be brave for Papa, their
faces as bright as the wrapping paper Mamma used at
Christmastime. But as soon as that thought came into my
mind, I knew that it was wrong.

They were shining with pride for Papa because he was going far away to France to win the War.

Their hearts were not dripping great drops of blood, but were full, beating like the drums that march soldiers into battle.

"Do you go to France right away, Papa?" Reginald said. I looked at him quickly. Reginald's eyes were shining more brightly than any of my brothers, a great longing in his eyes, and in his voice.

Papa shook his head, his eyes fixed on Reginald for what seemed like an awfully long time before he said, "No. We sail to England for training – and then to France." Then he paused, tearing his eyes away from Reginald, smiling again at all of us before he said, in a softer voice, "The War may well be over before the Guernsey Regiment ever gets to France."

My brothers' faces didn't shine as much when Papa said that, especially Reginald's, but I told myself that was because they wanted to march like toy soldiers so badly, that they wanted the War to last long enough for them to sail bravely to France and help Papa win the War.

They did not want to be hurled back into the toy chest before they had a chance to become real soldiers.

But when I looked at my Mamma, her face was shining more brightly than ever, loving Papa and seeming to hang on his every word. She said, "Papa is right. This War cannot last much longer. He will return to us very soon."

After Mamma spoke, I felt as if the light that was shimmering around her, that lovely halo of light, had spread to me.

And I suddenly found myself saying a prayer, with all the

love in my heart for Papa, that this was true, this was exactly what would happen.

I asked the Blessed Virgin Mary, with her blue beauty filling the sky, becoming one with the sky, to shine over France and make everyone stop fighting and send Papa home to us quickly.

And although I could still hear Mamma and Papa talking in smooth, quiet voices, I did not stop praying to listen to what they were saying – and I did not even have to shut my eyes to pray.

But suddenly, Mary, in all her lovely blueness, vanished before my eyes.

And the woman Papa said was Mme. de la Rue appeared before me.

In an even greater rush of wonder and hope, I prayed that Papa would return to us very soon.

And that the bluebells would sing to me again.

chapter
three

MARIE REMEMBERED the stars in her sons' eyes after seeing the Regiment, the Royal Guernsey Light Infantry, which even Randolph, as young as he was, could say proudly, gather in St. Peter Port before leaving the island.

The boys, so proud of their Papa, watched the soldiers in their uniforms marching in the square by Castle Cornet, looking, amazingly, as if they had been fighting men together for years. It was difficult, at first, to find Abram in that great green sea – a sea, though, that was unlike any of those on Guernsey's shores. It was the colour of the dull, brownish-green moss that grew on the great cliffs, moss clinging tenaciously to the rough granite, surviving the worst of the storms when the great grey waves roared like wild beasts with arched backs.

As Marie stood in the crowd, she hoped the men would be as strong.

At least her brother William was with her. Standing beside him in the sundrenched square, her wide brimmed hat shading her eyes, she prayed that they would be able to see

Abram one more time before he boarded the ship. She asked God to please let Abram be positioned in the march so that they could all catch one last glimpse of him.

She knew that, most likely, she wouldn't be able to find him amongst the five hundred men leaving the island that day.

But William, being so tall, and with his keen eyes, spotted him. Abram wasn't very close to them, but quite far from where they were huddled together in the bright yellow sunshine. At least, though, they were able to see him in the distance. She felt as cold, suddenly, as though she was in the root cellar beneath her kitchen, watching her Abram marching with his Regiment in his moss green uniform – a uniform, she found herself praying fiercely, that would withstand the terrible waves of the War.

William picked up Lorley and put her on his shoulders, her Union Jack held high. For a moment, Marie feared that her daughter would call out to her Papa, and she thought how torturous it would be for her husband not to be able to reply, nor acknowledge her in any way. But Lorley didn't say a word, as she moved her flag in a slow, graceful dance in the wide sky.

Now, as Marie reflected on that day in June, she wondered if Abram saw his daughter's tiny white arm, like one of the small gulls that flew by the sea.

She almost hoped not.

More than two months had passed since Abram left. The

Regiment had not yet been sent to France; the men were still training in England.

Without Abram, Marie felt truly lost. She felt fear deep in her heart, as if a sliver of glass had lodged there. The hope and the courage that had filled her whole being in those last few days with Abram seemed to have vanished.

Reginald and Herbert were working as hard as men in the fields, and even Lloyd and Randolph struggled along with their older brothers far longer than they should at their ages, although she knew that her two youngest sons would still run to the cliffs and the caves whenever there was a chance.

But she was afraid that even with her sons working as hard as they were, they wouldn't be able to keep the vineyard going without Abram.

If only, she thought, she could work in the fields like other Guernseywomen. Just on the farm next to theirs, Mme. Laporte, years older than she was, worked in the grapes from early in the morning until dusk. On the very day her husband left for the War, on the same ship as Abram, Mme. Laporte told her that she went straight home and began hoeing in the vines. Marie could easily imagine the Laporte farm that day. Mme. Laporte had worn her best church dress and hat to bid her husband farewell, a tub of a hat with roses clustered on the brim, larger than the rich soil of Guernsey could ever grow. And her dress, stretched taut across her large bosom and hips, was a brighter pink than the artificial roses on her hat. But Mme. Laporte said that as soon as she and her two sons returned to the farm, she got out of her good church clothes and put on her husband's shirt and overalls, and the straw hat he always wore in the sun. "No need," she said, "to ruin my complexion. I'm not going to throw away all those years of slathering cream on my face every night to end up as brown and wrinkled as a walnut. But," she continued, "I don't mind labouring in the fields with my sons if it means keeping the farm going for my husband, when he is fighting in the trenches." When she said that, patting her eyes with a handkerchief, she looked at Marie's hands, as soft as Easter lilies.

Marie, unlike Mme. Laporte and many of the other Guernseywomen, had never worked in the fields. Abram never wanted it, nor, truth be told, did she.

When she first told her Aunt Edith that she wanted to marry Abram Vidamour, her aunt thought she had lost her mind.

They were having tea in the sunroom in the grand home in St. Peter Port. She and her brother William had been raised there by their father and Aunt Edith, and then, after her father died, Aunt Edith had cared for them on her own. They were using the sterling tea set that, she knew, had been a wedding gift to her parents. When Marie was very young, she would hold the teapot in her small hands, and imagine her own mother gently pouring tea into a cup for her father, and think about her mother touching the gleaming silver. It had made her feel closer to the mother that she had never known, who had died giving her birth.

She had stared into the shiny surface of the silver when she tried to explain how much she wanted to marry Abram.

"But Dear," her aunt had said in her quiet voice, "he is a farmer, a prosperous farmer, I know, but he will expect a wife to do heavy work, in the fields, even. You don't have the constitution for it."

Her aunt had been terribly worried for her. And Marie

knew at the time that if her father had still been alive when she wanted to marry Abram, it probably would never have happened. He would never have believed that she could endure such a life.

But Aunt Edith had finally acquiesced, and lived long enough to see how happy her marriage was.

Now Marie stood in front of the large white enamel sink, staring out of the window at the grapevines, her worries about the farm churning within her. And even more, much more, she was filled with fear for Abram, yearning for him with all her heart. She stared at the bright, sunlit hedgerows, and thought, suddenly, how they guarded the rows of vines like crouching soldiers in emerald green uniforms – a green not like the dull khaki her Abram wore. His uniform was more like the colour of the mud in the ghastly trenches. Trenches that terrified her. She shook her head fiercely. She must be strong for Abram. For the children.

Too often these days, trying to hide the hot flickers of fear inside her, she worried that her words could sound as cold and barren as the granite cliffs. Sometimes, she feared that if the War went on for too long, she would be like a woman made out of stone, no longer able to feel anything at all, like Niobe in the Greek myth. It was strange that she had always remembered that story from her school days, about the woman who, in her great pride-filled love for her husband and her children, angered the gods. She was punished for her shameless boasting; the gods, in a single, remorseless lash of destruction, killed them all – except for Niobe, who, in her deep despair, could not stop the torrent of tears that fell from her eyes. And so the gods, annoyed and ruthless, turned her to stone. Now, Marie wondered if that story, which she first learned as a young girl in the fifth form of school, had stayed with her for so long because it would be her fate.

She shook her head a little. She had to stop herself from thinking that way.

Reginald walked into the kitchen as Marie stood there by the sink, finding it hard to move away and get on with her day. He looked very hot; she thought of the sun beating down on the rich, dark soil and the bright vines. There was very little breeze in the vines, protected from the wind by the hedgerows. But, she thought, beyond the fields, there were the glistening cliffs, and sparkling Rocquaine Bay beyond that. If only her eldest son could have been by the sea that day. Instead of toiling in the long rows of vines in the strong white sun, he could be running through the soft sand, the sea breeze blowing in his fine black hair.

He wiped his brow with his forearm, smearing some of the dirt on his face. He hadn't washed outside before coming into the house. "Mamma," he said, walking over to the sink beside her, pumping some water into the basin, "Herbert's working harder than I've ever seen him work." He began washing his hands, splashing some of the cold water on his face. "I can't believe how much help he was this morning. Between the two of us, we got an awful lot done."

She turned away, looking through the window again, at the rows of grapevines stretching towards the cliffs, and the bay beyond that, the blue of the sea today brighter than the sky, a sky so filled with light that it was barely touched with colour.

She saw Herbert at the outdoor pump, filling his hat with water, and then she watched him lift it high and pour it over his head, letting the ice-cold water fall down his back. His shirt, hanging loosely on his thin frame, would dry quickly in the sun that day.

Marie stared at the water pouring over Herbert's head, falling, falling so slowly, finally, into little droplets of water, everywhere. Like the tears inside her.

At least she wasn't yet Niobe. There were still the tears.

But the tears were for when she was alone, in the bed that felt too big without Abram.

A few moments later, Herbert walked into the kitchen, his wet shirt sticking to his lean frame, a bright smile on his face. "Ready to go back to work, Reginald?" he said.

Nodding quickly, Reginald said, "Have a drink first, Herbert," as he pumped some water into cups for both of them and handed one to him.

"Thanks," Herbert said, taking the water and gulping it down quickly.

"You're doing a good job," Reginald said, looking at his brother, respect in his eyes. Herbert smiled at his older brother's praise. Then Reginald held open the screen door, letting his brother walk through first. Before he followed Herbert, he looked at Marie, his eyes suddenly intense, and said, "We're going to be able to keep the farm going. Don't worry, Mamma."

Marie felt the love for her children surge within her – how, she said to herself, could she ever fear becoming Niobe?

I COULD SEE Lloyd and Randolph ahead of me. They were almost at the cliffs, racing each other. They knew that I was following them because Lloyd called out, as soon as he and Randolph began running, "We're going into the Creux Mahie. That's the biggest cave. Wait for us by the Giant's Toe."

I called back, "Okay, Lloyd," knowing that I could never catch them, but imagining, for a moment, that perhaps I could, that my legs would suddenly grow into the long and graceful limbs of a deer, that I would actually become a deer from the waist down, with a white tail that stuck straight up, and with sleek, brown fur – and above, not a young girl anymore, but a beautiful woman, with hair much brighter, as yellow as daffodils, that tumbled down my back.

I loved to imagine that, but I knew to keep such thoughts tucked inside of me. Mamma was working so hard, with Papa gone to win the War in France – I didn't want to make that worried look come back on her face if I could possibly avoid it.

Amazingly, though, she let me follow Lloyd and Randolph

to the cliffs, not seeming to mind so much anymore, at least not the way she had before, when I used to have to slip away as quietly as I could to catch up with my brothers. Now, Reginald and Herbert didn't go exploring in the caves at all, so busy with the vines that they had almost no time to do anything else. Even Lloyd and Randolph spent a lot of time working in the fields these last two months, since Papa left. But when Reginald told them that they had worked hard enough, to go have some fun, they would set off right away, calling to me wherever I was, usually in the kitchen with Mamma, or, when I was getting too underfoot, as Mamma said, in my bedroom reading. And when I heard my brothers call, "Lorley, we're going to the caves," I would drop whatever book I was reading, because even though I loved my stories dearly, I never missed a chance to follow my brothers. And I would run past Mamma, not saying a word but making sure that I gave her a bright wave.

Mamma knew where I was going; my brothers would have already told her. After the uproar over Bluebell Woods, I had promised to never wander off by myself. The rule, very carefully explained by Papa to all of us before he left, was that my brothers must always know exactly where I was at all times. This promise had, remarkably, given me the freedom to run after my brothers whenever I heard their call. I could still barely believe my good fortune.

Papa had quite a few talks with us before he went to the War, but the one he had just with me I held very close to my heart.

It was after we had all gone to the special church service at St. Saviour's. I was in my room, sitting on my big bed, staring out of the window. I couldn't see the cliffs from there, but I could see the woods at the edge of our property, bluish green that day, gleaming like velvet. Sadly, I couldn't see Bluebell Woods, either, over by the cliffs, and at that moment I longed to be there, lying in the flowers that I knew had magic deep in their petals. And I wanted to see the beautiful woman, who I also knew had magic inside her. I had seen it in her eyes. Somehow, I believed that she could help me.

Because as I sat there, I thought about what the Reverend said in church. And I needed powerful help.

Mamma had insisted that we all go to church that morning, even though it wasn't Sunday. The Regiment was leaving the next day, so there were special services being held all over the island. Our parish, St. Saviour's, wasn't as large as some of the others, like St. Martin's or St. Peter Port, where there were hundreds and hundreds of men leaving to win the War in France. But there were just over sixty from our church, I heard Papa telling my brothers, more than enough to fill our grey stone church. And even though it was a Friday, even families that didn't have a father or brother or a son going to the War went to church, leaving the grapevines and the tomato fields and the milk cows for a few hours. The bell in the high tower rang as the service began, something that usually happened only on Sundays, or during a funeral.

Rev. Pelletier gave the sermon, one longer than I had ever heard him deliver. Last Christmas, I had thought that he would never stop talking, when all that I could think about were the presents waiting for me in our front parlour, and the roast beef Mamma made on special holidays. Then, though, the sermon had washed over me, the words, somehow, losing their way, and everything that Rev. Pelletier said became little waves – I could almost hear them lapping on the shore of Rocquaine Bay.

But on that day before Papa left for the War, I heard every word of the terribly long sermon, and each hard word was deep inside me now, as if it had been chiselled in the granite of the cliffs. The Reverend usually had a voice as slow and creeping and wandering as the ivy that grew on the old oak trees. That morning, though, he had seemed a different man, waving his hands and crying that the brave men of Guernsey were ready to sacrifice their lives to defeat the terrible German foes. At first, I thought that, being so upset, he must be going to the War also, but then he said that he would pray for the Royal Guernsey Light Infantry every day that they were gone.

By the time the service was over I was very frightened.

The Reverend seemed awfully scared that the world was coming to an end.

It was all that I could think about as I sat on my bed that day, so afraid that I didn't hear Papa walk into my room.

But then I suddenly heard him say, "Lorley," and I felt his hands resting on my shoulders. I turned my head, and then he knelt in front of me, so that his eyes were level with mine. He was still wearing his church clothes, with his summer tweed jacket and high white collar, his cravat tied in a wide knot. His grey trousers were pressed, as always by Mamma, with a sharp crease, and his black leather boots shone with fresh shoe polish.

And with my Papa kneeling in front of me, I looked into his dark eyes, so afraid that I would never see him again, fearing that perhaps even the strongest magic of the silver woman in Bluebell Woods could not save us.

"I thought that the Reverend was never going to finish his sermon," he began, smiling at me, keeping one hand lightly on my shoulder, and touching my hair gently with the other, curling a strand around his fingers.

I nodded, looking intently at his face, suddenly afraid that I wouldn't remember what he looked like. I couldn't let myself forget a single part of him.

"Don't let him frighten you, Lorley," he said quietly, his face still smiling a little, his eyes calm, like the waters in the bay when no wind is stirring.

"But everything Rev. Pelletier said about the War was so awful, Papa. I don't want you to get hurt."

"You must not listen to that," he said. I searched his face. Surely, after what the Reverend said about the thousands of men dying in agony in the trenches of France, there must be fear somewhere deep inside of him.

I could not see even a flicker.

"Rev. Pelletier doesn't know what he is talking about – we're going to win this War, and I'm coming back to you, Lorley, and to Mamma, and to the boys. Don't be afraid, Honey. And don't be sad."

"I'll try, Papa, very hard." As I spoke, looking deeply into my dear Papa's eyes, I knew how hard it was going to be to keep my word.

But I had to do it. Somehow.

Then I closed my eyes, to say a quick prayer to help me find the way.

Strangely, all that I could see was a great swathe of bright blue.

At first, I thought it was the Blessed Virgin Mary's veil, unfurling in gentle waves in my imagination.

But then I saw in that brilliant, lovely blueness, the flowers. Bluebells in the woods.

And I remembered how they sang, so joyfully, filling my heart with love.

I opened my eyes and said, "Whenever I am afraid, or sad, Papa, I'll think about Bluebell Woods. I know that will help."

"Yes, Lorley, do that. Think about the pretty flowers."

I nodded my head. "I will, Papa. I'll remember how the bluebells sang to me that day –"

"What do you mean, Honey?"

"That day when I met the beautiful woman you said was called Mme. de la Rue. She asked me if I could hear the bluebells singing, and then I could, Papa." As I spoke, my words rushing out of me, I realized, suddenly, that I had never told anyone about what she said to me that day in the woods. And certainly nothing about the bluebells' beautiful song.

I didn't know exactly why I had not.

It wasn't the way I would have usually acted in my life – my life before I learned my Papa had to leave us to go to the War.

Before that, I could easily imagine telling everyone in my family about the love song of the bluebells. My heart would be overflowing with the wonder of it all, and I would want to share something so magical with them.

Perhaps it was the War that stopped me – the War had overtaken our whole world, and no one seemed to be acting the way they had before.

But now, telling Papa about it felt magnificently like the right thing to do, the War no longer pressing me into silence.

Papa said, his voice light and gentle, "And their song made you happy?"

"Oh yes, Papa, very much. I must tell Mamma and the boys about it, and Uncle William –"

But Papa began shaking his head before I finished speaking. "Let's keep this between us, all right?"

"But why wouldn't I tell Mamma and the boys and Uncle William?"

"I think it is best. It might worry Mamma too much."

I nodded my head. I mostly understood. Mamma would probably think my imagination was flying away from me again, the beautiful song lifting me too high into the sky, where I could get lost in all the endless blue. It would be a worry for Uncle William also and he already had too much on his mind caring for all his patients. And Reginald would definitely not be happy about me hearing flowers singing – and Herbert would most likely say I must have hit my head harder than he thought that day in Bluebell Woods. Lloyd and Randolph, though, wouldn't be upset, or at all worried, and they would try to believe me, but considering how the others in the family would probably react, what Papa said about keeping it between us made the most sense.

"I won't tell anyone, Papa," I promised.

"And you remember, Lorley, whenever you start missing me, and get afraid, and unhappy, let the bluebells sing to you. Do that for me."

I nodded, and I was about to explain to Papa that I couldn't just make the bluebells sing. That had only happened when I was with Mme. de la Rue in the woods that day. I could remember how they sang, and it made me feel a wonder that was light and lovely, like dapples of sunshine on my face, but it wasn't the same as actually hearing the bluebells singing. I believed that I needed Mme. de la Rue's magic sparkling all around me for that to happen.

But then, looking at my Papa, I knew that he shouldn't hear all that now. There wasn't time.

So I just looked into his dark eyes and kept nodding.

And saw love as bright as the bluebells.

As bright as all the magic that day in the woods.

And I was no longer frightened nor sad.

As I ran that day towards the cliffs, making my legs go faster than they ever had, I felt as if perhaps those deer legs really were growing out of me – my pale legs, as thin as twigs, snapped off neatly, beautiful, sandy brown legs with tiny hooves suddenly bursting out of me – all without missing a single step.

I knew it couldn't possibly happen – even the woman in Bluebell Woods didn't have magic strong enough for that. But I laughed to myself, thinking how such an idea would make Papa smile. For a moment, I thought that I actually would be telling Papa all about it that night, when he was kissing me good night.

I kept forgetting that he was gone. Perhaps it was because I was no longer frightened of losing him.

Not after our talk.

If my Papa said he was coming back, I believed him – more than I would ever believe the Reverend.

Or anyone.

Finally, I came to the edge of the cliff. Lloyd and Randolph were already on the beach, looking very small as they climbed on the rocks. They must have been looking for me, because they waved at me right away.

Then Lloyd called, "Come on and climb down! But take your time, Lorley!"

I knew that – if I rushed and fell, Mamma would put her foot down again and I wouldn't be going anywhere near the cliffs. I began climbing down where the slope was gentle, with little chance of falling, but I moved very slowly, just to show them how careful I could be.

Very few lichens, ferns, and brambles grew on this part of the slope. When I climbed down where the cliff was a little steeper, the sturdy hart's tongue, with their long, feathery fronds, were plentiful, and the lichens, especially the yellow and red, spread in a thick tangle wherever the ferns didn't. I could always hold onto the ferns to steady myself, and dig my heels into the lichens, as if it were a heavy carpet in brilliant hues.

On the gentle slope, though, where I was slowly making my way down, there was mostly moss, green mixed with brown. The mist could make the moss as smooth and slippery as one of the cloths Mamma used to clean the floors. Fortunately, there were outcroppings of rock on the cliff, as well, big fists of stone, some even the size of a fisherman's hut, and I could grab these rocks if, even on this gentle slope, I started to fall.

It was much lighter, pale grey rock, not like the deep brown and charcoal granite on the seashore, where the caves were. The rock, whether on the slopes or by the sea, was jagged edged, as if hacked out of the bowels of the earth with a crude pick, but there were smooth edges as well, polished by the wind and the water.

If I did have to stop myself from falling by hanging onto a rock, I would scrape my hands, though, as Randolph did all the time, racing Lloyd down the cliffs. He would go so fast that he would start to tumble a bit, but he would reach for one of the great chunks of rock, steady himself, and then run down the hill at breakneck speed. He easily beat Lloyd, even though his legs weren't as long, because Lloyd didn't seem to really like throwing himself down the cliff like that, even though I had seen him run hard with the older boys.

I looked down. My brothers were on the Giant's Toe, Randolph with his hand shading his eyes as he looked at me, Lloyd waving his arm at me.

I dug my heels into the moss, not looking at the boys, but at my feet. Even though this slope was the easiest way to get to Rocquaine Bay, I still had to watch myself. Staring at the ground helped.

At least there wasn't too much mist that day. With the sun still bright, the dark brown and green moss glittered with gold. I stopped for a minute to peer at it more closely, bending over and pressing my fingers into the soft ground, wondering if, perhaps, some of the gold might rub off on my hands.

Randolph called, "What are you doing, Lorley?"

I looked up quickly, waving, and cried, "I'm coming! Sorry!"

"Take your time. It's okay." Lloyd's voice wasn't loud, but I was used to his slow, steady way of speaking, and I could always seem to hear him, even at the cliffs.

Nearly at the bottom of the cliff, I took one last, quick look at the moss; I couldn't see the gold anymore. One of the few clouds in the sky happened to be passing over the sun, making the moss now more brown than green. And somehow it became the colour of Papa's uniform, the one he wore on the day that he left for the War. A rush of sadness came over me, but then I thought of him, kneeling in front of me before he left, and the waves of sadness, lapping inside me, went away.

Once I was on the beach, I ran towards my brothers almost as fast, I thought, as Randolph could.

Lloyd called out, "Easy, Lorley," but I wanted to be with them with a sudden, great urgency.

The turquoise waters of Rocquaine Bay beckoned me. I wanted to sit on the great boulder we called the Giant's Toe and gaze at the sea, waiting for my brothers while they explored the caves.

For some reason, the Giant's Toe made me feel safe, the way Papa always did.

Deep down, I believed there was magic in the rock.

I loved the sound of my shoes slapping on the wet sand. The sea was frothy – not as if it were about to storm, not with the sun so bright and nothing more than a few sparse clouds in the sky – but there was enough of a breeze to make the waves dance and swirl around the Giant's Toe.

My shoes were wet by the time I reached the rock, because the waves were strong enough that day to spread over the wide, smooth beach, glistening in the strong sunlight as the waves receded.

I climbed up the Giant's Toe, surprised that my brothers were still perched there. I expected them to scramble off the rock as soon as they saw that I was safely on the beach, calling to me over their shoulders to stay put on the rock until they were finished exploring. That was what had happened the last few times I came to the bay with Lloyd and Randolph.

But this time, they stayed near the top of the boulder, crouching where the rock was flat, worn smooth by the sea and the wind like polished linoleum.

"Don't slip!" Lloyd called, as Randolph leaned over, stretching his arm towards me as I clambered up the rock.

I did have to be careful. At least the sand that was stuck to my shoes helped me secure a foothold as I climbed. Once I made it to the throne, as we called the seat where my brothers were waiting for me, I would stretch out my legs and let the sun shine on my shoes. Now they looked as slippery as eels, but when I was so high up on the sun-drenched Giant's Toe, I could easily get them dry. Only in bad storms could the sea rush over the top, with waves that unfurled like the masts of great sailing vessels – there had been many terrible shipwrecks in these fierce waters. Just last year, not long before Christmas, there had been such a storm, and Papa and other Guernseymen had rushed to the cliffs to save the sailors from drowning.

When I finally joined my brothers, I saw why they hadn't left for the cave yet.

There were bundles of rags wrapped tightly around two long sticks. Lloyd had a bottle of something, and was very methodically sprinkling the thick liquid on the rags; Randolph was holding each stick in his hand, slowly turning them so that the liquid was spread evenly.

"What's that?" I said as I nestled close to them. There was still plenty of room, because the Giant's Toe was an enormous boulder on the edge of the sea. From my high vantage point, I could look all along the shore at the cliffs falling into the bright waters. And see, between the rugged ridges of granite and the aquamarine sea, the pale band of sand, lighter, even, than the soft brown sugar Mamma used for her fruit bread. The water that day was brilliant in the sunlight, shining like jewels, the cliffs like a rough treasure chest, lined with rippled brown silk, open to reveal the turquoise gems within.

The Giant's Toe stood out from the rest, separate from the cliffs. Perhaps at one point, in some terrifying storm, it had broken off. It was the same granite as the cliffs, although when I looked at it closely, I could see pink veins running through it, as if a hair ribbon had somehow been wound through the rock.

I couldn't figure out why everyone called it the Giant's Toe. Even for a giant, this rock was too immense to be his foot. Secretly, I always thought that this massive, jagged chunk of granite was his head. The flat part, where we now sat, did make him lopsided, for sure, but when I stood on the beach and looked at the huge rock, I could see a ridge for a very large nose, and a wide gap near the bottom that was a laughing mouth. And I didn't know how anyone could miss the recesses that looked like deep-set eyes, which shone with a light flickering in the depths of the rock, where the magic came from, I believed.

My brothers just thought it looked like a great, rough toe. I let them think that, but I hoped that as long as I could see the Giant's happy face and shining eyes, the magic would help keep us safe.

"It's paraffin, Lorley. Lorley, are you listening or lost at sea?"

They were used to my daydreaming.

Mamma, on those occasions when she became very

worried about it, said that my imagination was getting out of control, although more often she simply smiled and said I was lost in thought, with only a little crunch of worry on her face.

I smiled at Randolph and said, "Just looking at the Giant." Then, turning to Lloyd, I asked, "Why are you sprinkling that on the rags?"

"So they'll burn," Lloyd said, as he very carefully applied the lamp oil.

"We're making torches to take into the Creux Mahie. We'll light them right before we go into the cave," Randolph said, excitement in his voice that he was barely able to contain.

"Why aren't you using furze, like Reginald always does?"

"Smokes too much," Lloyd said, as he slowly, meticulously, sprinkled the oil on the rough rags.

When my older brothers explored the caves, they just gathered the furze that grew near the cliffs, tearing it out by the roots so that they could carry it by the thick stalks. But they had to pick the plants that didn't have any flowers, because the little yellow petals would burn very quickly and fall off in tiny sparks.

"Did Reginald say it was a good idea to use the paraffin?" The oil was making me nervous. It had a dangerous smell, noxious and powerful, oppressive in the fresh sea air. It didn't belong here.

Neither Lloyd nor Randolph said a word then, and I knew that Reginald didn't know a thing about these paraffin torches.

"We're just trying it out. Then we can tell Reginald how well it works," Randolph said lightly.

"Don't worry, Lorley. These torches will be safer than

furze, which smokes pretty badly. We'll be able to see a lot more than before," Lloyd added.

Randolph turned his torch, his arm raised high in the sky, looking at it carefully. Suddenly I wished that the tight wad of rags would burst into flight, like some strange seabird with great tattered wings, and fly away. And that Lloyd's would follow, vanishing in a scraggy flurry of feathers.

I ran my hand slowly over the rock, and then patted it gently, trying to find the right words, wishing that, somehow, the magic that I knew was in the Giant's Toe would help us.

"Maybe I should go with you. Reginald always says that there's safety in numbers." The fact was, as terrifying as I always imagined the caves to be, I was afraid to let my brothers out of my sight with their rag torches. I was used to them using furze – and it burnt quickly enough so that they were never able to stay in the cave for too long.

"You stop worrying now," Randolph laughed. "We're going to stay pretty close to the entrance, Lorley. We'll still be able to see the water and the sky, and with this bright sunshine today, it will be a lot lighter than it usually is inside the cave."

Lloyd nodded, smiling, his light brown eyes crinkling at the corners. "Just sit on the Giant's Toe and look at the sea."

"Pretend you're a pretty mermaid, okay," Randolph added, "and the time will fly by."

I had told Randolph, not long ago, that I often imagined being a mermaid when I sat on the rocks, with hair as bright as daffodils and eyes bluer than the sea. Randolph hadn't laughed at all, and said that he couldn't see a thing wrong with that. He and Lloyd, he said, pretended that they were pirates all the time.

Lloyd nodded his head after Randolph spoke, saying, "That's a good idea, Lorley. A mermaid. Sounds right to me," with no mockery in his voice. I didn't know if Randolph had told him or not, but it didn't seem to matter to Lloyd.

And I was thankful that Reginald wasn't there, because I knew he would not have thought that it was just fine to be daydreaming about being a mermaid – not when I was sitting on a great rock by the edge of the sea.

He would have worried that I would get so caught up in pretending that I had a fish tail sparkling like emeralds in the sea spray that, in a sudden rush of feeling all that mermaid splendour, I would dive headlong into the water.

Reginald didn't understand my imagination the way Lloyd and Randolph did. I knew that it worried him half to death, although Herbert, surprisingly, helped a little – because he just thought it was all silliness. If he had been with us right now, he would have told Reginald to just forget about it, that the only harm I'd do would be to start singing mermaid songs on the Giant's Toe and scare away all the seabirds.

But Lloyd and Randolph were more like me.

And because of that, I hated to see them go into the Creux Mahie, the largest of all the caves in Guernsey, with those torches, which would burn much brighter and for much longer than the furze. I was afraid that they would go too far, explorers on some wild expedition, pirates in search of a long-lost treasure.

For a moment, I was almost frightened enough to run back to the farm and tell Reginald, but then I looked at Randolph, his hazel eyes flashing with excitement, and even Lloyd's quiet brown eyes, bright with anticipation as

Randolph handed him a torch. And all that I could say, in a voice that was too small, was, "You'll be careful, won't you?"

"Of course we will," Randolph said. And then he added, with a wide grin on his face, "We can't leave you here for long, can we? You might really turn into a mermaid."

"No, we can't let that happen," Lloyd joined in, and I suddenly realized that I hadn't heard him sound this happy since before Papa left.

I nodded, but I couldn't smile back at them. I suddenly missed Papa, feeling a great yearning to see him. But it was not a sadness and a longing that made me feel empty inside. No, my painful heart felt as if it had grown too large in my chest, filling me to the brim.

Randolph waited until they had climbed off the Giant's Toe before he asked Lloyd, "How many matches did you manage to get?"

Lloyd pulled two boxes out of his pocket, holding them in his hand. "These boxes are really full – far more than we'll need. We'll take one box with us and leave the other one in the rocks with the paraffin."

"Why not bring the paraffin with us?"

"It'll just get in the way when we're exploring."

Randolph nodded his head. "We'll be able to go into the cave farther than ever before, farther even than we've ever gone with Reginald and Herbert. With the paraffin on the torches, we probably won't even have to light them again," he said.

"I don't think we will – it'll be so much better than the

furze torches. That stuff gets too smoky, and we always have to turn back sooner than we want." Lloyd looked up at the sky, a clear pale blue. "We're going to get a lot of light in the entrance of the cave today."

"We'll get them burning nice and strong, though, before we go in, don't you think, Lloyd?" Randolph said over his shoulder, as he led the way to the cave. He was so nimble on his feet that he could climb over the jagged boulders quite easily, even with the torch upraised in one arm as he tested how sturdy each piece of rock was before he stepped on it – but he and Lloyd had been over these rough slabs of granite ever since they were quite young, before Reginald allowed them into the caves. They would look for the crabs that lurked in the crevices of the rocks and, when they were fast enough, catch a few, although the crabs could move like lightning, disappearing into the rocks, suddenly invisible. Randolph would have his hands outstretched to seize the shell that was the same brownish grey as the rocks, being careful not to get pinched by the claws, long appendages that were as thick and as hard as the rough boulders. Mostly, the crabs managed to get away, and even when he caught one, Randolph always set it free – he didn't want to take the crabs from their homes deep in the tumble of rocks by the Creux Mahie.

Lloyd was right behind him now. "We'll light the torches as soon as we get close enough to the entrance of the cave."

Randolph nodded, climbing over the rocks. He saw a crab scuttle past his shoe as he stepped onto a jagged edge. For a moment, before he even had a chance to think about it, he was about to scoop it off the sandy ground – and then he remembered how much he always hated to see the little creatures captured. Trying to catch the crabs was just a game he played with his brothers, but it was one in which he, suddenly, didn't want any part. In his heart, he knew that Lorley was the one who had it right. If she caught a crab – and it would have to blunder its way practically into her lap when she was sitting on the Giant's Toe, with her mermaid face on, gazing out to sea – she would put it in a spot where she could watch it for a while, naming it as if it were a pet. And then she would set it free onto the rocks.

Lloyd saw the crab also, and he quietly watched it do its crooked dance over the rock before it vanished into the boulders.

They were now very near the entrance to the cave. Without saying a word, but smiling a little at his brother, Lloyd took out the matches, lighting the torch that Randolph held high in his arm. It caught fire slowly, not like the wild, hungry flames of the furze, flames that spread so quickly with bright orange tongues and then, after a fairly short time, died. All that would remain would be smoke, melding and smouldering with the grim cave walls.

Randolph was thrilled to see the paraffin torch burn so steadily, the flames nestled in the rags, like coals in the hearth at home. It would be almost as good as if they were carrying lanterns.

Lloyd handed his torch to Randolph to hold as he ignited the rags. It, too, burned smoothly, with little smoke, a globe of orange light, as if a bright sunset had somehow been bundled in the rags.

"We'll definitely be able to go farther into the cave than ever before," Lloyd said, in awe as he stared at the burning torches.

"I think we will," said Randolph, watching Lloyd stow the

paraffin and a box of matches in the rocks. Then he passed his brother his torch, and turned to stare at the cave.

Lloyd stood on a high slab of granite and looked back. He could just see Lorley, her face turned towards the sea. He called her name because he knew that she wouldn't want him to go into the cave without one more wave. At first, she didn't hear him – probably, he thought, with a little smile, dreaming of swimming down to the bottom of the sea with her mermaid hair streaming behind her and her long green tail flapping. He called once more, and then she turned and waved back at him, looking so tiny perched on the enormous rock.

The entrance to the cave had a low roof, not much higher than four feet. Although this was the largest cave in Guernsey, the entrance looked as if it wasn't much more than a shallow opening in the cliff, where you might take shelter from a storm. Long before Lloyd and Randolph began exploring the cave with their brothers, rocks had fallen from the overhanging cliffs, great chunks of granite, in what must have been a monstrous storm, and partially obscured the entrance – but they also formed a barrier, keeping the sea from rushing into the cave when the water was wild.

Randolph found it a bit tricky getting over the last stretch of large, jagged protrusions of rocks while holding a burning torch, but he could climb just about anything. And Lloyd was a great climber, too, and soon he was beside Randolph, crouching in the entrance way.

The sunlight streamed into the cave from the opening in the rocks, so it was hard to tell how brightly their torches would illuminate the cave, but Randolph knew that they would be much better than the furze. He thought of all the times he stood there with his brothers, trying to see through the smoke of their torches, their coughs echoing in the great chamber.

He nodded at Lloyd, and together, bent low, they began slowly walking forward in the tunnel that led to the main cave. It was strange, Randolph thought, how the tunnel always felt like a church. In places, it was so low that they had to drop to their knees, and, for Randolph, it was as if they were praying as they drew slowly closer, crouched as if in supplication, his torch held rigidly in front of him, his offering to the gods of the cave.

The gods, not the God who reigned in St. Saviour's Church. That would be a sin, to imagine God presiding anywhere except in the church. He thought of his parish church for a moment, with its bell tower so high it seemed to touch the clouds, and the light streaming through the stained-glass windows, as if sent from a heaven filled with rubies and sapphires.

The gods of the Creux Mahie didn't dwell high above, not with the St. Saviour's God. They were deep in the rock.

That day, as he and Lloyd emerged from the tunnel, rising from their knees and once again able to hold their torches high, Randolph felt, more than he ever had, that they were before the altar of some great gods who lived in the soaring granite walls before him.

In the main part of the cave, the ceiling was shaped like a dome and rose more than fifty feet into the air, as if a cathedral had been hewn out of the rough rock, thick walls rising in ridges and heavy veins, streaked with wide swathes of black, the granite like polished stone.

Standing side by side, Lloyd and Randolph were

spellbound by the sight before them. Their torches illuminated the cave more brightly than the furze ever had. As they slowly waved their torches, lifting them as high as they could, it seemed as if the cave had suddenly been lit with a legion of torches. The moisture on the walls that trickled down in thin, graceful rivulets caught the light and shone like votive candles flickering on the dark, deep walls. They couldn't see as far back as the end of the cave. Papa had told them that the Creux extended more than two hundred feet, but they could see the shimmering black granite in the lofty high ceiling, where the gods must surely be watching them, Randolph thought, as he gazed around him, awestruck.

He spoke to Lloyd, his voice hushed, as if he really were in a cathedral. "I can hardly believe it – I've never seen the cave like this." In the past, the furze would smoke so badly that the air would soon be filled with it, mysterious and magical enough that he could imagine the witches on the island brewing their strange concoctions in the murkiest depths of the cave. But now, with the darkness not thickened by smoke, he could see the steep walls of the cave better than ever before, the ridges of the dark stone looking like enormous tree roots, writhing their way up to the roof high above them.

Lloyd didn't answer him, but nodded, looking slowly around him, his eyes bright in the light of their torches.

Then he looked up, pointing towards the vaulted roof that was deeply shadowed, but even there, the droplets of moisture glistened, like faraway stars on a dark night. "Do you see the bats up there?" he asked.

Randolph felt his heart beat faster. Lloyd was right. He could see a few of them swooping slowly near the roof of the cave. He and his brothers were always trying to see the bats, but when four of them were in the cave with their furze torches filling the air around them with such heavy smoke, they rarely did.

"Let's see how far we can get to the end," Randolph said, as he began slowly moving forward, looking all around him, up at the roof, and then from side to side. Lloyd walked a little away from him, so that the light of his torch could illuminate more of the cave. Like Randolph, he found it hard to know which way to look.

There were more bats now. Randolph looked up at the roof, filled with perhaps a dozen of them, the high-pitched squeaking magnified in the vaulted chamber of the Creux Mahie. He reached out, touching Lloyd's shoulder, holding his torch up into the air. "Look how many there are now."

Lloyd stopped for a moment, reaching into the twilight air with his torch, and with his other hand he tried to count, but it was impossible. They could hear the growing cacophony of squeaks and clicks – more bats seemed to be emerging from the deep shadows of the walls – but they couldn't see them clearly enough in the gloom high above to know how many there were. Outstretched wings glinted in the light shining from the moisture that trickled down the ridges of the cave, sinister wings, swooping and diving as if searching for prey.

From the sound, and the great dark wings that now filled the dome of the soaring roof, Randolph thought there must be every bat that lived in the Creux Mahie there. And it was strange how much they sounded, in the great gloom of the cave, like the ticking of a clock, an enormous one, but one whose pendulum was going too fast, as though some demon was living behind the quiet clock face.

"They won't bother us – not with our torches," Lloyd said.

"I know," Randolph agreed, and he knew that his brother was right, but, deep inside, he wouldn't have minded if a few rogue bats came down from their lofty heights to fly near them. What a tale to tell Reginald and Herbert!

"You don't want to get too close to them. They can bite," Lloyd added quietly. Randolph didn't say anything, but he knew that Lloyd was right about that, too. Reginald had told them all the grisly details about rabies from bats, right down to foaming at the mouth and losing your mind – that was before you died a gruesome death, convulsing like a mad dog.

But Randolph would have loved to have been close enough to a bat to look into its evil little eyes, the spawn of Satan, according to some of the old stories told on the island.

They continued to walk forward slowly, deeper into the cave than they ever had before. Randolph kept hoping that Lloyd wouldn't say that it was time to turn back; he was thrilled with each step they took into the darkness.

Their torches were still burning as brightly as when they first lit them – not like the furze, that shrivelled too quickly into black cinders and a swarm of smoke. The cave, especially this one, the greatest on the island, was very dark, despite the yellow orange glow of their paraffin torches, but when Lloyd and Randolph held their torches very high, they could see more of the cave than ever before.

And then, moving with such slow, careful steps, it surprised them when they found themselves suddenly at the end of the cave. They stood in silence, staring at the sheer rock face before them, the dark stone with inky black veins twisting and writhing on the wall as if great snakes were entombed there, struggling to break free.

Randolph spoke first. "We made it. For the first time."

With his free hand, Lloyd reached out and touched his brother's shoulder, saying, "I'm glad we made it together."

Randolph couldn't see Lloyd's face clearly in the darkness, but he knew well the quiet smile that was in his brother's eyes.

"Me too," Randolph said, gripping Lloyd's arm. And then he yelled into the chilled black air of the cave, "We made it!" His words echoed in the great heights.

For a moment, he expected the bats to begin swooping in frenzied circles, as his words reverberated off the rock walls, but he could see their wings, still glinting in the darkness high above, move as slowly as ever, heedless of his wild cries.

Lloyd said, "We better head back. Lorley's waiting for us." Then he looked at his torch, and at Randolph's, saying, "They're burning as brightly as ever. It's hard to leave, but we have to get going." Randolph nodded, turning slowly around, and began walking back.

Now, though, he looked even more intently from side to side, peering into the darkness.

They were more than halfway to the entrance when he saw the tunnel.

If not for the rivulets of water trickling down the wall, and the angle of his torch as he held it in the thick darkness, the light catching the black stream, illuminating, for a moment, the tunnel, Randolph would have walked past it. They would have been out of the cave shortly, for they were only seventy feet or so from the entrance.

But in that instant, Randolph saw the gaping hole in the rock.

He and his brothers had always known that there were a myriad of tunnels branching off from the main cave. Even

Papa talked about it – how the Creux Mahie was like a heart, with arteries carrying the darkness deep into the bowels of the earth. Some even said that the tunnels and fissures bore into the very centre of the island. Papa said that was impossible, of course, but Randolph, although he would never disagree with Papa, didn't see why it couldn't be true.

He stopped and pointed at the tunnel, catching his brother's arm. "Look, Lloyd."

Lloyd stopped and peered into the darkness, holding his torch high in the air.

"It's the biggest opening to a tunnel we've ever seen – much larger than anything we've ever found with Reginald and Herbert."

Lloyd said, so quietly that Randolph could barely hear his words, "That's true. I can hardly believe it."

"Maybe it goes into another cave, one as great as the Creux Mahie."

"Someone would have found it by now."

"Who knows for sure?" Randolph said, the excitement rising in his voice. "Using furze torches, maybe no one ever saw it."

"I don't know." Lloyd paused, and then said slowly, "But we better keep going."

Randolph looked at the tunnel, the water trickling down the walls, glimmering in the darkness. The entrance seemed to be lit with a strange, unearthly power, beckoning to them.

Lloyd stayed where he was.

He didn't say anything as Randolph walked over to the opening in the rock, moving slowly through the darkness.

Randolph peered into the hole, holding his torch

outstretched as far as he could, but Lloyd could see that the light did little to dispel the thick blackness of the tunnel.

Looking once more towards the entrance of the Creux Mahie, Lloyd could just see the faint halo of white light catching the rocks that jutted around the opening.

But he turned and slowly walked over to join Randolph.

Peering beside Randolph, he held his torch to try to illuminate the opening, but the darkness was much thicker than in the main cave – it was like pressing your face into cold, heavy velvet. There was a low roof, not even three feet in height, and not wide enough for them to walk side by side.

"We can't go in there," Lloyd said, shaking his head. "Even with our torches, we can barely see anything. And we would have to go in single file. We couldn't even hold our torches together."

"You stay here. I'll just take a look, Lloyd. I'll be right back. Just think what we can tell Reginald and Herbert. And when Papa returns from the War, he'll know that we can be as brave as him."

Lloyd sighed, looking up into the enormous darkness. He could see, his eyes now more accustomed to the gloom, the bats gliding in slow loops high above, and he could hear their odd ticks. What a life, he thought, trapped in the Creux Mahie for all the days of your life.

Lloyd didn't know why he didn't just grab his brother's arm and run as fast as he could through the darkness.

And get them both out of the cave.

But instead, he said, "I'm going in with you. And I better go first."

Randolph smiled in sheer joy.

"But we can't go in very far. We have to get back to Lorley."

"We'll just take a look."

Lloyd nodded, already worried that they shouldn't be going into the tunnel at all.

"But I think I should go first, Lloyd. The roof is so low. It will be easier for me to see ahead. You'll have to bend over an awful lot."

There was some sense to that, and Lloyd nodded again as he said, "Let's get going now. We don't have much time."

Without saying another word, but with a smile that he couldn't keep off his face, Randolph stepped slowly into the tunnel. Lloyd walked behind him as closely as he could with his torch held at his side. The roof was lower than he thought. Randolph was right about going first because Lloyd, with his height, had to bend over so far that it was hard for him to peer ahead into the darkness.

And the darkness was far greater. Surprisingly, though, it was the earth where he walked that bothered Lloyd the most. Unlike the main cave, where the ground was fairly dry and sandy, like the beach on Rocquaine Bay, here it was slimy, slippery enough to make you fall if you didn't put each foot down carefully.

Lloyd was relieved that Randolph was going slowly, with one hand holding onto the rough wall of the tunnel. He did the same, although it felt as wet as the ground, like the rocks by the shore that were coated in sludge from the water. He wondered, for a moment, if the slime on the walls was dark green, as it was on the rocks by the sea, but in the deep darkness, he couldn't tell. He doubted it, though. Everything in this tunnel seemed to be intensely black – the cold, slippery stuff on the walls and underfoot.

He couldn't see how far the tunnel went. To Lloyd, though, as he put one foot slowly, so slowly, in front of the other, it seemed that it really could go into the very centre of the earth. It was getting darker the more deeply they penetrated the depths of the tunnel. They were both leaning over more and more as the roof sloped down.

"Randolph, we have to go back." His words, strangely, sounded muffled, as if there wasn't enough air in the tunnel, as if a thick wool blanket was held over his mouth.

"Okay. I guess you'll have to lead going back."

Lloyd was surprised at how readily his brother agreed. "Are you all right?" he asked, suddenly afraid that he had let his younger brother go too far. And he remembered how he had promised Papa and Mamma and Reginald that he would always watch out for Randolph.

"All this sliminess – I don't like it much."

"We'll be out of here in no time." And then Lloyd, reaching out into the black night of the tunnel, patted his brother on the shoulder and said, "Come on, let's go." He turned around and began leading the way out of the tunnel, walking faster than before, so anxious to get out of the dark, narrow hole, heedless of the slippery ground, thinking, instead, about the brilliant sky of Rocquaine Bay, about how he would breathe in great gulps of the fresh, salty air.

And then he fell.

He hit the ground hard, his limbs flailing.

Randolph, hearing his strangled cry of pain, rushed forward.

His brother's arm was outstretched, still gripping his torch, held upright. Randolph knelt down, holding the meagre light from his own torch as close to Lloyd's as he could, peering into his brother's face, and then his eyes moved over Lloyd's body, splayed on the wet ground, and he saw that his foot was stuck in a crack in the tunnel wall. "How bad is it?" Randolph asked, hoping, with a kind of desperation, that his brother would be able to twist his foot out of the black crevice that held him captive, do it very quickly. And they would flee this black tunnel and never look back.

"It might be pretty bad, Randolph. If I keep my foot still, it just sort of throbs, but –" and then Lloyd paused, breathing in short bursts. Randolph could tell that he was struggling as he said, "As soon as I try to move it, like this –" and then he tried and uttered a sharp moan.

"Look, I'll get your foot out. Just lie as still as you can – don't try to move." In the gloom, Randolph could see Lloyd nod his head, and he could hear him breathing in all the blackness. "I'm going to give you my torch to hold – do you think you can do that? You need to keep them both as upright as possible."

"I can, Randolph, I think so – my arms, though, feel –" and he swallowed hard and said, "weak, like I've been swimming for too long, all pins and needles."

Randolph put his hand on his brother's head, stroking his fine black hair. "It's going to be okay, Lloyd. I'm going to get you out."

He spoke louder than he needed to, kneeling on the damp floor of the tunnel. But he said the words with all his might, struggling to fight against the thick, awful darkness of the cave.

Lloyd said nothing as he listened to Randolph's brave words that seemed to get lost in the black night, like tiny pinpricks of light being slowly extinguished by the thick gloom.

And even though their torches were still burning, the darkness of the tunnel was getting worse.

Randolph peered hard, bending over Lloyd, trying to see how badly his foot was stuck. He clawed at the crack, hoping, with a raging desperation, that there was some loose earth that he could crumble enough so that Lloyd could release his foot.

Lloyd's entire foot had slipped into the crack, part of the ankle protruding, the pale skin ghostlike in the darkness. Randolph touched the ankle gently, and immediately, Lloyd's whole body tensed.

Randolph clawed harder at the rock wall, and some small fragments of earth fell off and then he clawed even harder, telling Lloyd to try to keep twisting his foot out of the crack.

"Keep going, Lloyd!" Randolph cried out, as he felt his brother's leg go limp again.

"Randolph – stop –"

"What's the matter? I can feel your foot moving – you're getting closer. Lloyd – you can do it!" Now Randolph was panting heavily, his cries sharp, like black knives in the darkness.

"Randolph – we're losing the light," Lloyd said, trying hard to keep the panic out of his voice, his words sputtering in little bursts. "The torches are burning out – you're going to have to go – for help."

Randolph looked at the torches then, still held by Lloyd, and he saw, with an awful pounding of his heart, that his brother was right. "But Lloyd, you've got the matches. I can light them again."

Randolph could hear Lloyd groping in the darkness. But then he stopped, and after a long silence, Lloyd said, too quietly, "They're not here. The matches must have fallen out."

"We'll find them, Lloyd. They must be on the ground." As he spoke, he took one of the torches from Lloyd and held it high, trying to find the box of matches, and Lloyd, too, searched as he lay on the ground, pressing his palm into the soft, moist earth.

But they were nowhere to be found.

Randolph suddenly cried, "Lloyd, try pulling again! Try hard!"

Lloyd heaved with every ounce of strength he had, his white ankle bleeding as it scraped against the iron grip of the rock.

"It's no good. I can't get my foot out."

That made Randolph dig into the wall even more, like a wild man. His brother's terrible words flew around him as if the bats from high above had found their way into the tunnel and were swooping over him.

"Lloyd, pull –"

"Randolph, the light's fading."

"I'll get you out. I can do it," Randolph said, as he looked at the torches that now shed much less light. And he clawed more furiously than ever for a few more frenzied moments, and then, with a feeling of despair that was blacker than the hell of the tunnel, he stopped.

"You have to leave me here and get help, Randolph –"

"No, Lloyd, I won't do that. I can't leave you here."

"You have to. While we still have light."

Randolph's head was bent as he stared at the torches' dying light, the rags burned almost to nothing.

Lloyd said, his voice dry and urgent, "Send Lorley to get help. And then you can use the paraffin and the matches I left in the rocks and get some furze to light your torch again. You can come right back with more light." With each word, Lloyd's voice sounded weaker, losing more and more strength, it seemed, as their torches grew dim, the monstrous, heavy darkness slowly smothering him.

"Lloyd, I don't want to do this."

"There's no other way."

After a long black pause, Randolph finally said, "At least let me leave you my torch, Lloyd – it has more light. It'll last until I get back."

Lloyd nodded.

Randolph bent over his brother, saying nothing as he embraced him, willing himself to be strong, to force his legs to run out of that tunnel.

He could see Lloyd trying to smile at him as he said, "I'll see you soon, Brother."

Then Randolph started to run, without looking back at Lloyd lying there, so alone, like a broken toy soldier. He knew he was being too careless of the slippery floor, knowing in his panic that if he ever fell and hurt himself, they would be done for – but he kept going at a breakneck speed, as if the black demons that surely lived in the horrible tunnel were chasing him.

chapter
five

I CLIMBED as high as I could on the Giant's Toe, and all that I could do was think about Papa.

When my brothers went into the cave, I was ready to be either an ancient queen or a mermaid. A beautiful queen in her great grey castle on the edge of the sea was my favourite – it was tried and true – but more and more, I had been saving it for the cliffs. Sitting on the Giant's Toe, gazing into the endless, shining sea, I almost always wanted to be a mermaid now.

And so I tried to release my mermaid dream. It was always inside me, fluttering, close to my heart, like an exotic bird with emerald feathers and a high yellow crest, waiting to be set free. And when I did, the feathers became my sparkling tail, and the bright crest became my long, golden hair.

But it wouldn't take.

My hair wouldn't stay in the bright mermaid curls tumbling down my back, but kept returning to my straight hair, as fine as the silky gold sand at my feet. And my tail kept disappearing, leaving me with nothing more than my plain white legs to stare at sadly. Every time I tried to bring her back, waiting for her to surface in one graceful swoop, as she always did, she would be there for just a few shimmering moments, and then she would disappear again in a single splash.

Because I kept thinking about Papa.

I told myself that I would feel better if I could pretend to be someone else. Even my brothers, before they went into one of the caves, often imagined that they were pirates, going to retrieve their buried treasure. At first, it had just been Lloyd and Randolph, waving sticks in the air as if they were brandishing cutlasses and sabers, but soon Reginald and Herbert joined them, with Reginald, naturally, declaring himself to be the Head Privateer.

I would wave at them, happy in my mermaid self by the magical sea.

But that day, it wouldn't work. I tried and tried, but fear for my Papa had come back. It overcame me, and all I could be was a lost girl missing my Papa.

As I longed for him, I looked at the sea, a brilliant turquoise that day. Closer to the shore, though, the water had a clear greenish tint, as if mermaids with their beautiful tails were gathered there just beneath the surface. The mist had lifted completely, so that the sky was especially bright, lighter than the water, and it seemed to go on forever.

We all knew that Papa would be leaving for France any time; no one really knew for sure when. I had heard Mamma tell Reginald that the little more than two months Papa had been in England couldn't possibly be enough training, but Reginald had reminded her that, as a member of the Militia since 1914, Papa already knew how to handle a gun. Mamma had just shaken her head.

I thought about Reginald, standing so tall and straight by the black stove in the kitchen, telling Mamma what a good soldier Papa was. I knew that was true, and it was a warm cloak that I wrapped around my heart.

But now, perched on the very top of the Giant's Toe, Reginald's words left me, and all I could do was feel fear for Papa. There wasn't room for anything else.

Staring at the sea from Rocquaine Bay on the west coast of Guernsey, I knew that I was looking towards the wide English Channel, the waters that everyone in my family always called the sea. And I also knew that it was just possible that Papa's ship might be out there, far away on the horizon, heading from England towards the War in France. And I suddenly wondered if perhaps, through some magic that I could not understand, he could see me.

So I lifted my arm high in the air and waved.

And as I did, I suddenly thought of Papa telling me to try to hear the bluebells singing whenever I became fearful.

I stared intently at the sea, wondering if, somehow, I might be able to see the flowers in that vast blueness, and perhaps even hear their song. But the only sound was that of the waves crashing against the rocks, sparkling blue thunder that sprayed plumes of white foam, like the feathers of some great seabirds.

So I didn't hear her coming or see her make her way down the beach.

She was standing in the sand, at the bottom of the Giant's Toe, gazing at the sea, when I saw her.

At first, I thought that she wasn't real; the silver woman

from Bluebell Woods couldn't be standing there on Rocquaine Bay.

And she looked so much like the ancient queen, who I often imagined myself to be, that I thought surely, she must be a dream.

In the bright sunlight that day, her long grey hair shone like silver, the strands moving in the wind like very fine argent chains, so beautiful that I was transfixed, thinking that I could hear them shimmering against each other, despite the sound of the sea all around me.

Her feet were bare, and her dress was made out of a simple cloth, with a low neck and a blue sash around her waist. It looked like the rough linen that Mamma used in the kitchen – but she wore it as gracefully as if it were a regal gown trimmed in ermine.

Then she lifted her head and looked at me, high above on the Giant's Toe, staring at me with eyes that shone with the same silvery light as her hair.

I began climbing down the rock to get closer. She stood very still, watching me, her pale, nearly colourless lips curved in a slight smile.

When I was close enough, on the rock just a few feet away from her, before she had a chance to speak to me, I said, "Are you called Mme. de la Rue?"

She nodded, and then, gazing at the sea, she said, "Always believe that he will come back, my little one."

At that moment, my whole world was silent except for the sound of those words coming out of her mouth.

And then Randolph's cries pierced the air.

We both turned towards the cave – and saw him running towards us like a wild thing, his face sick with fear.

I jumped off the Giant's Toe, heedless of where I landed in the sand, so close to the woman that I brushed against her. When my hand felt her bare arm, there was a coolness, like a dark fern in the forest, and her scent wafted through the air around me – it wasn't like the rosewater cologne that Mamma wore or like some of the heavy perfumes, as pungent as mothballs, that the ladies in her church group dabbed behind their ears. The scent that emanated from her reminded me of Mamma's spice cabinet, like ginger and cloves and vanilla, but stronger than all of them, stronger even than the smell of the rocks and the sea.

But all that lasted for a few seconds, and then, in a sudden panic, seeing the agony twisted on Randolph's face, I ran towards him.

"Lorley!" he cried, though I was still several steps away from him. "Lloyd's hurt, trapped in a tunnel in the cave." He was panting hard, his words coming out in one big burst.

His fear rushed inside me. "Did the rock slide?" I said, suddenly remembering the awful story of some men who couldn't get out of a cave when a slab of granite fell, blocking the entrance. I stared at Randolph, my heart pounding wildly.

"No – no – his foot's caught in a crevice, and I can't get him out. You're going to have to run for help," and then he looked at his torch, the fire gone, the rags shrivelled to almost nothing now, looking like a small piece of driftwood. "I have to get some furze quickly." And then he looked around with desperate eyes.

That was when he saw her, still standing by the Giant's Toe, blending into the granite as if she were somehow one with the rock. She wasn't looking at us, but digging through the large basket that hung from her arm. It was as pale as the dress that she wore, and I hadn't noticed it, but now I could see the sundry of plants, the long stalks and ferns, hanging over the edge.

He called out, "Can you help us, Mme. de la Rue?" And then he turned to me, saying, "Run, Lorley, run and get Reginald and Herbert, and tell Mamma!"

Lloyd stared at the torch, praying that he could keep the light.

He watched Randolph leave, disappearing into the darkness, with only his torch visible, bobbing in the distance, and then it, too, vanished. But he could still hear his brother's footsteps, the ground in the tunnel so damp and oozing that Randolph's shoes slapped softly against the earth as he ran. And then he could no longer hear the footsteps.

And there was nothing at all, except the thick night of the tunnel, and his own meagre light.

And it was dying.

For an awful moment he feared that Randolph had fallen, lying somewhere on the cavern floor, hurt and unable to move. But he told himself that surely he would have heard Randolph's cry; not hearing the footsteps must mean that Randolph had escaped the dark of this devil's tunnel, that he would soon get help.

It was when the footsteps died, though, that Lloyd wished, in a sudden panic even worse than when he fell and found that his foot was stuck in a crevice, Randolph was still with him.

He had never wanted his brother so much in his life. Terrified as he watched the light in his torch become little more than embers, the despair inside him darker than anything in the Creux Mahie, all that he could think about was that he needed Randolph, that he desperately wanted him back. Please God, he prayed, please God, his words like stones slowly sinking into deep black water.

He twisted his foot in the vise grip of the hard rock. He could feel his foot bleeding when he tried to turn it, scraping against the jagged edges, feel the sharp fingers of the awful gods of the rock who held him there, the gods Randolph had once told him about. The pain was piercing hot, a long, agonizing burn, like Rev. Pelletier's hell.

"Randolph! Come back, Randolph!" he called out into the darkness, knowing it was futile, his brother long gone, but he could not stop himself.

And his voice was so feeble, grown weak with fear and pain, that he could barely be heard. He didn't know what he would do when the light went out. And it seemed to be extinguishing faster now.

He would be lost, nothing more than one of the crabs that crawled in the rough boulders outside of the cave, crabs that were mercilessly captured by boys with careless fingers.

He was a prisoner now, chained to the rocks by the gods of the Creux Mahie, gods more horrible than he had ever imagined.

That made them twist his foot hard, desperate to escape. He was bleeding and he welcomed the pain fiercely, suddenly thinking that if there was enough blood, perhaps his foot could slide out of the rock and he would be free.

But then he had to stop, the agony too great – he lay there very still, as the rivulets of pain that convulsed his body slowly eased a little.

Lloyd told himself to look at the light, to think of nothing other than that his brother was coming back with Reginald and Herbert, with bright torches that would fill this horrible tunnel with a blazing fire, that the grim gods of the rock would loosen their grip on him, and recede back into the deep crevices of their awful kingdom, and let him go.

He told himself that he had to keep believing that, and hope began to glimmer in his heart again –

When his torch died.

It happened so quickly that, at first, he didn't understand the sudden enormity of the darkness.

But very quickly, the dying of the light screamed inside him.

It was as if the cruel gods of the rock were smothering him with a heavy, black, merciless hand, the darkness greater than anything he had ever experienced, a midnight so thick and suffocating that he could barely breathe.

He tried to call out his brother's name, knowing that it was useless but wanting him badly. His throat was so dry and parched that nothing came out but a faint, rasping sound, not enough for a single word, a sound utterly lost in the horrible blackness, a sound not any louder than that of a crab scuttling over the rocks.

In a great burst of panic, then, he struggled to free his foot, but the pain was too intense, the blood spreading over his ankle and dripping down his leg. He had to stop.

He felt great, heaving sobs rising from deep within him, but he was too exhausted – too lost and terrified now – to even cry.

Keeping his eyes shut tightly helped.

He told himself that his brothers would come, that he

would be liberated from this awful blackness, and he tried to still his wild beating heart, but his mind kept jumping from one fear to another, as though he was doing an agonizing dance on hot stones.

Then he thought of Papa.

And his mind slowed down a little, and then a little more, and he was able to stop his horrible dance, as he rested his mind on the image of Papa, going off to the War to save them all.

He could hear his father's voice, talking to him before he left, telling him to be strong and brave. Papa said the words with a smile on his face, but there had been a deep intensity in his eyes.

His Papa needed him to be courageous.

The trenches of France were worse than this black tunnel.

His Papa would not panic.

He could imagine his Papa trapped in some narrow, mud filled trench. And he, knowing that a soldier, a soldier with the strength and loyalty of Randolph, Randolph the Lionheart, was on his way to rescue him, wouldn't see monsters in the dark; he would not see these great, gruesome gods of the rocks.

No – he knew that his Papa would never stop seeing the light, long after his torch died.

***

I started to run towards the cliffs as if in a trance, in some kind of spell, not really believing what was happening.

The silky sand flew around my ankles as I sped towards the cliffs. But at the base, where the rocks jutted like clenched grey fists, I stopped. I had to – I had to look back, and make sure that it wasn't all some strange, horrible dream, that my mind had not finally fallen over the edge, an edge more treacherous than any cliff face in Guernsey.

Mme. de la Rue was there. She had pulled furze and what appeared to be two stones out of her basket. Striking one stone against the other, she quickly lit the furze.

Randolph was talking to her, gesturing with his hands, looking back at the cave and then at her. For a moment, he left her to scramble among the rocks, where he picked up the can of paraffin and a small box that I figured must be matches. But Mme. de la Rue shook her head and must have told him that she didn't need any of it, because he left the paraffin and matches in the rocks, and then quickly returned to her. She handed Randolph her furze torch, and then she gathered more furze and lit two more torches as Randolph continued to talk to her. I couldn't hear what he was saying, for I was too far away and the waves were crashing with a greater force now, filling the air with their fresh thunder. I saw her then nod her head and reach out, giving him another furze torch and then hold her hand over his head. It looked as if she were about to cast a spell on him, and I gazed, barely able to breathe, wondering what magic she really could conjure. But then she touched his shoulder, and even from the darkness, I could see that it was gentle, a caress.

And then they both turned their faces towards me, and Randolph began calling my name, waving his arm, beckoning to me.

I hesitated, puzzled, and then Randolph called again, "Lorley, come back! Hurry!"

Randolph began talking before I reached him, saying,

"Lorley, you're going to have to go into the cave with us." He held his brightly lit torches high in the air.

I should have been horrified.

But strangely, I was calm.

I didn't know what had happened to me, but I suddenly felt brave enough to walk into a pit of writhing, snarling devils if it meant saving Lloyd.

And helping Randolph, whose face looked as if something with sharp teeth and claws had lunged at him.

"You have to go into the cave far enough so that you know which tunnel we take to rescue Lloyd. I'm going to scrape the wall with a big V so that you will know for sure where we are. As soon as you see us go into the tunnel, run home as fast as you can to get help. Can you do that, Lorley?" Randolph spoke very quickly, handing me a torch as we began walking towards the cave, and I nodded my head with as much force as I could. Mme. de la Rue was already a few paces ahead of us, her long grey hair falling down her back, the grey rocks and the light blue sky forming an aura around her, like the haloes I had seen illuminating the saints.

Staring at her back, feeling braver, amazingly, than I ever had in my life, ready to stare into the red eyes of any devil waiting for me in that cave, carrying a brightly burning torch as casually as if it were a loaf of fruit bread, it suddenly struck me, like a lightning bolt from heaven, that she must have cast a spell over me.

There was no other explanation.

I no longer felt a single prickle of fear as I followed the beautiful, silvery woman, now so close that I could touch her long skirts falling behind her as she climbed over the rocks, moving so gracefully, as though she was doing a dance – and I felt as if everything that was happening was the most natural thing in the world. Surely, I told myself, some deep magic had penetrated my skin.

We were almost at the entrance of the cave. I looked at Randolph, silently making his way over the rocks beside me, and I saw his eyes on my torch.

"Hold it steady, Lorley," and then he reached over and put his hand over mine, straightening my arm so that the burning furze was upright again. I hadn't realized how much I had let it slowly tip down.

"We'll save Lloyd. Don't worry," I said, speaking quietly.

He nodded, his face determined, his lion heart in his eyes.

And, as the three of us crouched down to crawl through the black entrance of the cave, I prayed that the silver woman's light and magic would be strong enough to conquer whatever waited for us in the darkness.

Lying in the tunnel, as if trapped in a nightmare, but knowing with an awful, dull awareness that he was awake, he twisted his foot, rotating it ever so slowly, but no longer really believing that he could escape from the rock. He couldn't stop trying, though, despite how futile the obsessive twisting and turning seemed. He tried not to even think about it – he just did it, as jagged bursts of pain ran up and down his leg.

And then it was, when he was lying in the dark earth, the musty reek of the rock walls filling his nostrils, exhausted, fatigue hanging on him, greater than anything he had ever experienced, that his foot suddenly slipped loose from the rock.

At first, he didn't believe it. He could not believe that the rock gods had released him.

This had to be some foul nightmare that had ensnared his brain, some devious trick of the gods, casting him into this twilight sleep and making him believe that he was free, their cruelest joke of all.

But then he opened his eyes wide, staring hard into the darkness, and he knew that he was awake and alive and that his foot had somehow twisted out of the rock.

He touched his foot, lightly. In the thick darkness he couldn't even see his own hand, but he ran his fingers gingerly over the torn skin on his ankle, feeling the sticky blood and the scrapes, the shredded skin, but he couldn't find any deep gashes. That was good, he told himself.

And he knew what Papa would do.

Right now, Papa could be in France, in some black trench, alone, and lost, and hurt, struggling to get back to the other soldiers. Papa would not lie in the darkness, thinking about some demonic gods in the rocks. He would crawl, with every ounce of strength he had left, and keep crawling until he found the other men.

So, Lloyd began to move, very slowly, on his hands and knees. Then he tried to crouch in the low tunnel to get out of the tunnel faster, but jolts of pain shot up his leg, and he had to fall back down. But that was all right, he muttered to himself. It was all right. It was better crawling very slowly, feeling the rock walls on either side of him, inching his way towards the main cave.

He didn't think that the tunnel branched off into smaller ones. Some did in the Creux Mahie, some formed a maze so intricate, Papa had told him, a labyrinth that could trap you forever, like a writhing nest of snakes, tunnels with rock walls that suddenly fell away into treacherous drops of fifty feet or more.

He told himself that if he crawled on his belly and kept his hands on the rock walls on either side of him, he could make it.

As long as he was moving in the right direction.

It was hard to be certain in the absolute darkness of the cave.

What if he was dragging himself slowly away from the main cave? What if he was nearing a precipitous drop into some great abyss?

But he kept moving. It was what Papa would do.

The cave was much darker than I expected, a greater darkness than I experienced the time I stumbled into the other cave looking for my brothers. It had been much smaller, with a broad entrance that allowed the sun to pour through the opening in a wide splash of light. When I had peered into the blackness, though, I saw a devil, clinging to the rock with his long claws, watching me with hungry, cunning eyes.

And in my great babyish fear, I had run out as if Satan himself were snapping at my skirt.

Now, though, the spell that had surely been cast over me had woven courage into my heart, and I stared into the cave, knowing that I could do my part.

Randolph and the beautiful silver Mme. de la Rue moved quickly ahead of me, advancing into the cave.

I stood very still, and I found that, as my eyes grew more

accustomed to the darkness, I could see more, the deep midnight of the cave becoming a twilight, the thick, jagged rocks and the walls, with their cracks and crevices, and the soaring roof, slowly emerging in the gloom.

"Lorley!" Randolph said, calling to me. "Wait right there. Don't take another step into the cave. Watch us, watch our torches. You'll see me scratch a V into the wall before we crawl into the tunnel. As soon as you do, run home to get help."

"I can do that, Randolph," I said, my voice echoing in the great cave. As I called out to him, I saw how the woman's silver aura shone as if she were floating in a dark sky.

I watched their torches bob as they descended into the cave. I stared hard at their light in the thick darkness, hearing Randolph's footsteps in the still silence.

Mme. de la Rue was as silent as a star in the night sky and suddenly seemed very far away.

It was not long before the eyes of the devils were on me. They surfaced with fiendish speed from the deep crevices where they lurked.

The spell that the beautiful woman had cast was torn away, as easily as if the demons were ripping butterfly wings from my shoulders.

I was terrified.

All that I wanted to do was to run out of the cave, to scramble over the rocks to the sea, to gaze into the sparkling, sun-kissed waters, and hear the waves crashing against the shore.

In that moment, I believed that I had never wanted anything so much in my life.

Randolph and Mme. de la Rue seemed terribly far away from me now.

And the devils seemed so close.

But I told myself to stay very still, that the black fiends who inhabited these rock walls would leave me alone as long as the silver woman was in the cave.

And I tried not to look into the cave. I didn't want to see the long, wicked faces of the fiends who dwelt there, to see their leering eyes glittering in the darkness.

I looked, instead, at the torches, concentrating as hard as I could on their movement through the cave, but even then, the awful thought came to me, one that I could not wrestle out of my mind once it took hold, that perhaps devils had leapt from the rock walls onto Randolph and Mme. de la Rue, digging into their necks with their horrible razor-sharp teeth, with such demonic speed that there was no time to cry out in agony.

Perhaps the silver woman's magic wasn't as powerful as I thought. After all, the spell that had given me a brief burst of courage hadn't lasted, but had been swallowed by the black heart of the cave.

But I told myself that their torches were steady and strong – surely no ambush had occurred.

I cried loudly to them, "Are you all right?"

"Yes! We're almost there," Randolph called back, his voice strong. "Keep watching us, Lorley."

I stared harder than ever, finding a bit of courage, finding a few shards left from what had shattered. I thought of Lloyd, waiting for Randolph to come to help him, lying there so alone, staring into the darkness of the narrow tunnel, listening for footsteps coming to save him, and hearing nothing except the trickle of water that ran in slow rivulets down the rock walls – and the long hiss of the devils living in the tunnel walls, their malicious mouths grinning as they watched Lloyd suffer.

And that thought was the worst of all.

I knew that I would rather have every demon in the cave breathing over me with their foul breath, inching towards me with outstretched claws, than to have them lurking in the tunnel with Lloyd.

I looked up at the roof, praying that somehow the rock walls would loosen their grip and open wide, and let the bright sky fall into the cave and vanquish the darkness. I peered upwards, yearning for such a miracle.

It was then that I saw the great winged creature flying above me, a demon let loose from the rock walls, with wide, leathery wings, swooping towards me.

I tried to scream, but no sound came. I felt my torch fall from my hand, and then the darkness engulfed me.

Long fingers were stroking my forehead.

They couldn't be the hands of a devil. They were cool and lovely, slightly wet, as if they had been dipped in the sea. They were pressed gently on my temples, across my forehead, and then both palms rested on my cheeks.

I slowly opened my eyes, thinking that I was at home, in my big bed, with my Mamma helping me wake up, the morning sun shining through the high casement window in my room. Then I saw that the light came from a torch, and I could not understand why Mamma would be standing over my bed in the middle of the night with a flaming bunch of furze.

But then I smelled the musty air, and I felt the hard, damp rock beneath me, and I opened my eyes wide, about to cry out, remembering in sudden horror that I was in the cave.

The soft fingers pressed on my mouth, and I heard Mme. de la Rue whisper, "You are safe, little one. You fell and bumped your head, but you will feel better soon."

"Have you found Lloyd? Where's Randolph?"

I struggled to stand up, but her hands, quite strong, stopped me, pushing back gently on my shoulders. "Rest for a moment. Take a few deep breaths."

"But are they all right?"

"Yes, yes – we will go to them in a moment."

My head felt as if the darkness all around me had found its way into my brain, making everything difficult to understand.

But then I felt the beautiful silver woman gently raise me to my feet, holding me close, and I could smell the warm, spicy scent of her skin and her hair, so comforting, for a moment, even overpowering the foul air of the cave.

"Come and see your brothers."

I felt my legs moving, slowly, her arm wrapped around me, almost carrying me as we made our way through the cave.

At first, I was leaning against her, holding onto her so tightly that my face was buried in her skirts. She held the furze torch with one arm and kept her other hand around my shoulders as we walked.

As I nestled deeper into the rough cotton of her skirt, I felt as if I could stay like that forever. And I knew that I wasn't supposed to think that she was the Blessed Virgin Mary who had come down to earth to help me – but walking with her in that cave, I couldn't stop myself.

I raised my head – and found that, just as she had said, my head was clearing. The mist behind my eyes was gone, and when I looked up at her, I saw, in the heavy darkness all around us, her eyes staring upward, as if gazing into heaven, just like in the holy picture.

It was at that moment that I heard the bat wings, flapping high overhead, and she patted my shoulder, saying, "Don't worry. Our fire will keep them away."

I felt immediately reassured, and I looked away from the great roof, and stared into the darkness before me –

And it was then that I saw the other torch, and I saw Randolph, kneeling beside Lloyd.

Filled with a sudden, wild burst of joy, I broke away from her. I wasn't very far from them, and, heedless of the demons surely lurking all around me, I began running towards my brothers as fast as I could.

"Be careful," she said, and she was soon right behind me. I felt my heart throbbing. All that I wanted to do was to see Lloyd.

He was sitting, leaning against Randolph, his legs splayed apart. His eyes were closed, but he opened them when I drew near, and in the gloom of the torchlight, I could see his small, gentle smile.

A smile just like Papa's.

chapter
six

MARIE SAT AT THE LONG, oak table, running her fingers over the broad surface, the deeply grained wood smooth and warm to her touch. When Abram first showed her the farm where his family had lived for over three hundred years, the large, two story house made from wide, brown granite slabs, rising in the green fields like a high sandcastle, Marie knew that she wanted to live there with Abram Vidamour as his wife.

Now she sat in the kitchen of that farmhouse, gazing through the casement window at the bright green vines and hedgerows. In a few spots, the glass was so thick and wavy that the leaves looked more like the sea, lapping slowly towards shore.

And then, as so often happened these days, her thoughts drifted ever more deeply into the past. She could not seem to stop herself – but she would have no more fears about becoming the tragic Niobe, as she had in the past few days. No, she would dwell on happier thoughts.

Her brother William was at Trinity College in Dublin studying medicine when she met Abram. She had attended a dance at the St. Saviour's Parish Hall, with Aunt Edith trundling along at her side as chaperone. Most of those at the dance were country people of French descent, from families like Abram's, who had lived on the island for centuries.

Sometimes she wondered if she would have ever met Abram if her parents had not died. Quite probably she would never have attended a French country dance. Growing up in St. Peter Port, her life had revolved around the English speaking community; of course, many of them also knew Guernésiais, the dialect spoken by the rural people, for they used this French often in their businesses. Her father, in his shipyard, had employed many labourers from the country, and she still remembered how the dialect had flown off his tongue, as if he had been born speaking the language. She had been told that her mother could not speak any Guernsey French, which was understandable, considering her childhood spent in England. But she and William, at the insistence of their father, had both learned to speak the dialect. She smiled a little when she remembered how proud he had been when they acquired the language so quickly.

At least she had her father until she was fifteen. William had been seventeen years old when their father died, just finishing his secondary education and about to start university. She thought about how wonderful he had been, delaying going away for over a year until they had everything settled, helping Aunt Edith in their large house in St. Peter Port. William still resided in that house, even though it was really too big for him, being a bachelor with no children to fill the seven bedrooms. But Marie was thankful that he had never sold it, that high, three story house constructed of narrow wooden planks, a house that looked like one of the ships that her father's company once built, tall and proud, hovering on a hill as if anchored at the dock, ready to set sail. With its narrow gables and shiny green shutters, it was distinct from the stone houses in Guernsey.

That house, as bright in her mind as the white and green wood, as fresh as if it had just been painted in her memory, would always make her think of her father – although now, at thirty-four years old, she realized that she had lived more than half of her life without her father. She had never known her mother, for she had died when Marie was an infant, so there had never been anything real about her – nothing more than a still and distant figure, a painting done with very delicate brush strokes, a ghost grey palette, barely there.

She was thankful that William was visiting today. It always helped to see him. She hoped that he would be able to stay for dinner, a thought which made her get up from the table and check on the potage that was simmering on the black stove. She lifted one of the cooking plates to check the fire, remembering what a difficult time she had with this farm kitchen when she and Abram were first married.

It was one of the arguments her Aunt Edith had used when she pleaded with her not to marry Abram. Marie could still hear her saying that she would be slaving away in front of some great beastly stove making stews for field hands, telling her that it was not at all how she had been raised, that she didn't even know how to cook.

Marie had refused to acknowledge that any of this would

be a problem – and her aunt, when she finally saw the farmhouse, had been somewhat mollified, because there was a lovely front parlour, and a dining room with a grand china cabinet, and five bedrooms upstairs, some with antiques that had been in the Vidamour family for generations.

When they were first married though, her aunt had proven to be correct about her cooking. Marie was an utter failure in the kitchen. Truth be told, Abram made most of their food in the beginning, after eating her burnt offerings for the first few weeks of their marriage. But Abram, who was a very patient man, and a very good cook, taught her to actually love making food for the family. She smiled now to think how, initially, the stove had completely defeated her, glowing in the corner like some fiend with mocking red eyes. For years she had jokingly referred to it as the devil from hell. But then, not long ago, she had noticed Lorley staring at the stove with a peculiar look on her face, and Marie had resolved to be more careful with her words. She didn't need to stoke the fires of her little girl's imagination – they were burning far too brightly as it was.

She lifted the lid of the heavy pot, breathing in the thyme and the bay leaves, the aromatic, soothing spices blending with the ham and beans.

"The potage smells delicious," William said as he walked through the door.

Startled, Marie turned quickly, surprised that she hadn't heard his car driving up the lane. The cars on the island were creating a ruckus in the countryside, making so much noise that the dairy farmers protested that these tin cans should stay in St. Peter Port, where they belonged. Poor M. Collinette, who had the largest herd of milking cows on the west shore of Guernsey, claimed that all the grinding and growling dried up the milk.

But William's car, because he was a doctor, was tolerated, even by M. Collinette, especially after the farmer had that awful bout with rheumatism. Her brother used one of the new medications developed in England to treat him and the farmer felt so much better, moving like a spring chicken again, he told everyone in St. Saviour's. After that, William could have driven past M. Collinette's precious caramel coloured cows with a dozen Model T Fords, and the farmer wouldn't have minded. Quite the opposite – now, when he saw William driving down his lane, the farmer took off his straw hat and waved, calling out, "Good day, Dr. Moore!"

Her brother had been one of the first Guernseymen to buy a car, having it shipped from England just before the War – ostensibly to make it easier for him to make house calls to his rural patients – but Marie knew that, really, William would have had a car even if he had chosen to work in their father's shipbuilding business, sitting at a desk all day in one of the offices.

"I didn't even hear you coming," she said, as she rushed over to him, embracing him. "Did you drive your car?"

But then, peering over his shoulder, she saw the car parked in the yard, the black paint as rich and dark as licorice, gleaming in the sunlight, the elegant leather upholstery the same tawny gold colour as the spokes in the wide wheels. It was such a beautiful car, the large headlights shining like the crystal in her china cabinet.

"I thought that I would take the boys for a ride when

they're finished in the fields," William said, as he sat down at the oak table.

"They would love that – but are you sure you have the time?"

"I can make the time." And then he looked at her, his eyes intent, so caring that Marie was afraid that she might start crying, something she couldn't allow herself to do.

"How are you doing, Marie?"

"I'm managing, William. For the sake of the children. Some days are harder than others. When I am alone I dwell too much on the past. It makes me miss Abram so much that sometimes I think I can't bear it." Then Marie turned away from him. Moving back to the stove, she picked up the heavy percolator. "Would you like some coffee, William?"

"Yes, thank you," he said quietly, and when she turned back to him with the mug in her hand, she looked at him, and felt a sudden rush of love in her heart.

Smiling at him, her eyes bright, she picked up the pitcher of cream, saying, "Fresh from the Collinette farm."

"You know how much I like Guernsey cream," he said, a wide smile on his face again as he patted his slim middle.

"You could drink a gallon of this cream and never gain weight," she laughed, feeling some of the tension easing out of her shoulders, and poured a dollop of the heavy Guernsey cream, rich and yellow, into his cup.

She sat across from her brother, gently placing the mug on the table. "Is there any news in St. Peter Port about the Regiment?"

He took a quick sip before replying, shaking his head. "Nothing, Marie. I heard that some letters arrived on the last ship from England. I hoped there would be one from Abram."

"Perhaps a letter is on the way. Do you know when they will be going to France?"

"Soon, Marie," he said, reaching out and taking her small hand in his. "They could be on the ship now."

She looked into his clear blue eyes, and at his fair hair, so blond in the afternoon sunlight. "I don't know what I would do without you," she said.

"Marie, you know that you can always count on me. And whatever happens, you and Abram will get through this."

She looked down at the table, at the grain of the oak, staring at the golden brown waves that seemed never to end. And she said, speaking slowly, "I have to believe that, William. But I get lonely, and scared, missing Abram so much. And then I start worrying, about Abram soon in the trenches, and about you, too, being sent to France, and then I fear that I won't be able to stand it."

"Marie, I don't think it's time to worry about me yet. You know when my time comes to serve, I will, but I'm being kept home for now because of the shortage of doctors in Guernsey," he said. Then he looked at her, and smiled, his eyes very kind, saying, "Please try to stop worrying."

"I will try, William, I really will," she said. "I just pray that the War will be over soon."

She got up and unlatched the window, opening it wide. Gazing at the cliffs, she thought how beautiful they were in the light, as clear as if they had been painted with a very fine brush. The mist had lifted, the moss and the ferns and the lichens a rich green and gold tapestry.

She was about to turn away and go back to the table, when she saw Lorley. At first, she thought that her little girl was alone, but then she saw Randolph, right behind her. She peered through the open window, looking for Lloyd, and saw nothing but the cliffs and the wide, light-filled sky. And then, appearing, it seemed, out of that pale blue sky, was a woman carrying Lloyd.

She turned to her brother, saying, "Lloyd's hurt. Some woman I've never seen before is with him."

William got up quickly from the table and was out of the door before Marie had a chance to say anything else. She followed him, her eyes fixed on the children as she made her way towards them, holding her long skirt above her ankles, cursing the heels on her shoes that were too high for running. She could see that Lloyd was hurt, because there was a wide bandage wrapped around his foot and, despite his dark complexion, his face seemed pale.

But even in the distance, she could see him trying to smile at her.

Randolph's face was quite different. Though she was still several steps away from him, she could see the pain in his eyes, as though he was the one who was injured, yet she saw no sign that he was hurt.

Finally, she looked at Lorley, walking closely beside the woman, gazing all around her with a face that Marie could only describe as one filled with wonder.

Mme. de la Rue had known exactly what to do. Randolph held the torches while she looked through her satchel, removing some strips of cloth and a small bottle. The glass vial looked like something the apothecary in St. Peter Port would sell, but I knew that it must contain a potion that the beautiful silver woman had conjured herself. I wondered if it would glitter like fireflies when she poured it on Lloyd's foot, or, perhaps, illuminate the whole cave, the bats screeching when the blinding light hit them.

But I knew deep down that couldn't happen; if she had possessed such magic, she surely would have unleashed it as soon as we entered the Creux Mahie.

She was kneeling very close to Lloyd, the cloth strips resting on her skirt, the vial placed on the rock beside her as she continued to look in her bag. I saw that the large, loose satchel, one I had not even noticed her carrying, for it had been concealed behind the basket that held her plants, appeared to be made of the same rough cotton as her skirt. But then I saw that it was actually leather, very old and creased, as pale as the sand on Rocquaine Bay. With her long arm, she searched for something in it, and I thought how magical the bag seemed, endless, like the horizon. She finally pulled out another bottle, larger than the first one, with a brown cork protruding from the narrow aperture.

I looked up at Randolph and saw the wonder in his eyes, the very same wonder I could feel tingling throughout my whole body.

I couldn't stop myself from whispering to him, "Do you think it's a magic potion?"

Randolph didn't answer, but remained very still, his eyes transfixed on the woman. I could tell that she caught my words, also – words softer, I thought, than dandelion fluff on your face, but somehow I knew that she heard, and I saw a slight smile on her face.

She uncorked the smaller bottle, and the scent of cloves filled my nose, reminding me of Easter, when Mamma stuck the little nuggets of spice on the ham like pins on a pincushion. The scent of cinnamon also wafted over me, much stronger than anything I had ever smelled in Mamma's kitchen. Very slowly, the silver woman tipped the bottle, shaking it a little, so that several droplets were released into her other hand.

"What is it?" I muttered, the words, unbidden, falling out of my mouth, like the strange, aromatic liquid.

"Wood Avens," she said, without looking up, her eyes fixed on Lloyd.

I shuddered, looking at the shredded skin on Lloyd's foot. His ankle was the worst, like a fleshy bone that the butcher sold for stew. The wounds seemed to have stopped bleeding; dark brown rivulets ran in jagged streaks down his foot, and they looked crusty and sticky, but no fresh bright blood was oozing out of the deep scrapes.

Before I could catch myself, I gasped when she pressed her hand, filled with the strange ointment, directly on the wound. Her movements were very gentle, almost hypnotic, and when her hand touched Lloyd's awful, lacerated flesh, he flinched – but for just a moment, and then some of the pain began easing out of his face as she held her hand on his ankle. It was as though she was in some green meadow and not deep in the Creux Mahie, that she was simply resting her hand on a patch of sweet clover.

"Why don't you use the cloth?" Randolph asked, no longer fearful at all.

Nor was I – even though I was crouching on the floor of the most sinister cave in all of Guernsey, with, no doubt, a nest of devils, swarming like wasps, clawing through the rock walls ready to lunge, incisors dripping with blood from their last kill. I couldn't be afraid, not with the silver woman beside me, who, I now believed with all my heart, was more powerful than anything in the cave.

As I watched her, gently pressing her hand onto Lloyd's terrible, torn flesh, his foot one awful wound, she looked at Randolph briefly, not seeming to mind his question, and said simply, "The heat of my hand makes the ointment more potent."

And then she began chanting, in a language that I didn't understand, words that I had never heard before, words that sounded like the rich, spicy scent of her skin.

The pain was melting away from Lloyd's face as the chanting continued. I looked at her, kneeling beside my brother in that great black cave, feeling her silver aura flowing around us all.

I don't know how long the chanting continued, her voice so light, the song of an angel. But as soon as that thought came into my mind, strangely, so did Rev. Pelletier. And I knew that if he could see with his little, squinting eyes right into my head, he would most likely tell me that my thought was a sin. This woman, he would say, was not now, or would ever be, in the realm of angels.

But as I crouched in the Creux Mahie, letting the sound of her chanting sway over me like Easter lilies, the pure white lilies that the Reverend placed on the altar on the feast day, her voice, as quiet as it was, seemed to fill the whole cave. And the devils, lurking in the rock walls, shrivelled and sank, grimacing, deeper into the stone.

As the chanting continued, I knew that the Reverend was wrong.

In Bluebell Woods, she had become the Blessed Virgin Mary. And here in the Creux Mahie, she had become a silver angel. Mme. de la Rue was a magical being, with more than one beautiful face.

But I didn't think that the poor Reverend, if he ever met her, would see any of that beauty. Sadly, with his tiny, fearful eyes, he would miss all of the magic, and probably see nothing more than a woman with long, grey hair.

***

When the chanting ended, the last note lingering in the darkness like a slowly fading star, she opened the other larger bottle and told him to drink. "Slowly," she said. "Take little sips."

"What is it?" Randolph burst out then.

"It's tea," she said quietly. "Green tea from plants that I grow."

Lloyd looked at Randolph, smiling. "It just tastes like grass. It could use some Guernsey cream."

After a few more slow sips, he tried to stand up, but his leg buckled immediately. She caught him in her arms, effortlessly, as if she knew full well that was exactly what would happen, and then lifted him, cradling him as if he weighed no more than her leather bag.

"I can help carry him," Randolph said.

She shook her head, saying, "You take care of your little sister. And rest your arms. You are carrying too much already."

And even though Randolph wasn't carrying a single thing besides his torch, his other arm hanging loosely at his side, I knew what she meant.

Because it wasn't really his arms, which were always too full, but his lion heart.

I took Randolph's hand, squeezing it, and he squeezed back, and we followed her out of the cave, into the brilliant sky and sea.

I felt as if I were being transported into another world, everything more beautiful than it had ever been before.

And I couldn't help believing that Mme. de la Rue's magic made the sky and the sea so heavenly bright, and made the great blue light sing inside me.

She knew the way to our farm. None of us thought to tell her, but after we climbed the cliff, taking the gentlest slope, following her careful steps over the mossy rock, she began immediately walking towards our fields.

I couldn't wait for Mamma to meet her.

She would see the magic in the beautiful silver woman. How, I thought, could she not, with so much wonder swirling all around us?

I saw my Uncle William first, running from the farmhouse, down the path that ran between the fields towards the cliffs. Mamma was behind him, but she couldn't keep up – his long legs were moving in great strides, while she was holding her long, full skirt bunched in her hands.

For a moment, they both looked so young, looked so

much, somehow, like me and Randolph, running to the cliffs and the caves.

But then Uncle William, so tall, was leaning over Lloyd, and all thoughts of him as a young boy vanished. He took Lloyd out of Mme. de la Rue's arms and laid him gently on the soft grass, deftly unwrapping the bandage. The smell of the ointment she had rubbed on his ankle was suddenly quite strong, pungent in the air.

He turned to her, saying, "What did you put on his foot?"

"Wood Avens," she said quietly.

Uncle William didn't say anything, but continued to carefully examine the awful, torn flesh on Lloyd's ankle. Then he looked at Lloyd, lying there, propped up on his elbows, and said, "How much does it hurt?"

"Not too bad at all, Uncle William. Ever since she," and he looked, with a quick smile at Mme. de la Rue, "put the ointment on, it hasn't hurt too much."

Mamma arrived and put her arms around Lloyd, holding him close. "How are you? What happened?"

Lloyd said, "I'm fine, Mamma –"

Randolph quickly interrupted, saying, "We were exploring a tunnel in the Creux Mahie, and his foot got stuck in a crevice."

I burst in at that point. "And Mme. de la Rue rescued us. She made more torches and used her magic on Lloyd's foot."

I smiled at her, but she wasn't looking at me. Her eyes were staring into the distance, at a grove of willows shining in the strong sunlight.

Turning, then, to Mamma and Uncle William, I waited for them to shower her with great 'thank yous.' Mamma would most likely leave Lloyd for a moment to take the silver woman's hands in hers.

But Uncle William continued to examine Lloyd's foot, and Mamma said only, "What is that smell?"

"Some ointment that she used," he said, cocking his head slightly at Mme. de la Rue.

"Do you think it has done any harm?" Mamma spoke the words quite softly, kneeling on the rough grass, so close to Uncle William that her words were not much more than a whisper in his ear. But I could hear her, and I looked up quickly at Mme. de la Rue, certain that she heard what Mamma said as well. But she was gazing at the trees, as still as a beautiful stone statue.

I looked at Randolph, waiting for him to tell them all how she had rescued us, but he was staring straight ahead with unhappy eyes, and he did not seem to be listening.

And Lloyd had shut his eyes, now utterly exhausted from his ordeal, no longer paying much attention to anything.

Uncle William shook his head at Mamma. "I don't think she's done any damage. We'll get him back to the house right away and clean the wound properly."

For a moment, I didn't know who he was talking about, and then I realized, with a sudden, awful feeling in my heart, that he meant Mme. de la Rue.

My words tumbled out in a rush. "She didn't hurt us at all! She saved us, leading us back into the cave, shining like a star, making the devils scurry back into the rock walls."

Uncle William continued to examine Lloyd's foot, but he said, quite sternly for him, "Lorley, what's this about the devils?"

Before I had a chance to answer, Mamma said, "Dear,

don't say such things. You know there aren't really any devils."

"But I could feel their eyes on me, Mamma! And Mme. de la Rue's magic made her glow, with this silvery haze shimmering all over her."

"Lorley, that's enough," Uncle William said firmly. He muttered something to Mamma that even I couldn't hear, and then looked at me, saying, "Where did you get these ideas about devils?"

"They've just always been there," I blurted out, and I looked at the silver woman, her gaze still fixed on the trees.

And my Mamma and my uncle were both staring at her as well, and I could tell by their expressions that, despite what I said, they believed that she had filled my head with such things. The truth was that the only thing that she had filled my head with was the beautiful sound of the bluebells singing.

Then I thought very hard, and I suddenly remembered – that all of my ideas about devils did come from somewhere – from Rev. Pelletier. He loved to describe the fates of sinners, who were sent to live with the devil for eternity. His stories about hell never failed to scare me to death.

I was about to tell them that when the beautiful silver woman looked at us, her eyes resting gently on Lloyd, and Randolph, and me. Then, with a soft smile on her face, she turned away and began walking towards the small grove of willows. She covered the ground quickly, her basket and satchel over her shoulder, and then slipped into the trees, a grey shadow flickering and then melting away.

We all watched her go, no one saying a word. Suddenly, I felt like running after her to catch up with her and hug her around the waist and bury my head in her rough skirt. I wanted to take her hand in mine, so that she would know how thankful I was for all that she had done for us that day.

And in that moment, I could imagine her taking me in her arms and lifting me high above the ground, where I would shine in the silver light of her halo.

It didn't take them long to get Lloyd settled in his bed, and for William to pronounce that his brave nephew was going to be just fine. And for Lloyd, as soon as Reginald and Herbert came rushing in from the vines, to tell them what had happened.

At first, Marie felt such relief.

But it was short-lived – because as she listened to Lloyd, she realized that the strange, silvery woman had been extraordinary. Quite simply, Mme. de la Rue had saved her children. She didn't even want to think about the terrible harm that could have come to her children if the woman hadn't appeared on the shore when she did.

Yet, over and over, she saw her walking into the trees alone. The truth was that now, as she listened to the whole story, she realized how badly she had treated the woman.

Lloyd did most of the talking while Randolph sat close to him on the bed, unusually quiet. As he finished his story, with Mme. de la Rue carrying him out of the cave, Reginald said, looking at Randolph, "You did well."

Randolph shook his head and said in a quiet voice, "I shouldn't have wanted to go into the tunnel in the first place.

It was all my idea. I'm just thankful that Mme. de la Rue was there."

William spoke then, saying in a stern voice, "All of you should stay out of the tunnels. They're treacherous, with holes that plummet hundreds of feet."

Marie was grateful that her brother was with them. Of course, it was important to stress the awful dangers of the caves, and William, though strict about such matters, was never unkind. She should have been able to do all that herself, but at the moment she wasn't thinking clearly.

She knew it was because her heart was so uneasy now whenever she thought about Mme. de la Rue. She could not get the image of that tall, strangely beautiful woman out of her mind, seeing her again and again walking quickly towards the trees, her long grey hair shining in the sun, a radiant mirror that seemed to cast light all around her.

And over and over, Marie asked herself why she hadn't run after the woman, to catch her before she disappeared into the trees. Why didn't she fall on her knees and thank her? Even before she knew the complete story, there was good reason to give thanks to the woman.

Instead, she had stood silently and let the woman just walk away, without offering a single expression of gratitude to her.

And the more Marie thought about it, and visualized the woman in her pale, roughhewn dress, her hair flashing in the sunlight, she started to see what Lorley saw – a silvery glow around the woman.

She shook her head, telling herself not to have such thoughts. This talk about witchcraft and magical powers was foolish superstition, still told by some of the old country people and embellished over the years throughout rural Guernsey. The boys had heard the stories, and they were as intrigued by it all in the same way that the tales about Guernsey privateers from long ago made their eyes sparkle with excitement.

She quietly left the bedroom to make some coffee. Reginald and Herbert left also, to return to their work in the vines. Randolph and Lorley remained with William by Lloyd's bed, watching him as he fell asleep. The tea that William had made him drink, prepared by Marie, was strong chamomile with a drop of laudanum. William had produced the vial from his black medical bag, telling Marie that the amount of the drug that he was giving Lloyd would do nothing more than make him sleep for the rest of the day. Marie had been uncertain about the medication, thinking that the chamomile tea would be enough, but William assured her that the minute dosage of the drug would give Lloyd the restorative sleep he needed.

William walked into the kitchen as she was pouring the strong black coffee into mugs. "He's sound asleep now, resting comfortably, the other children monitoring his every breath," he said, sitting down.

"Thank you, William. I don't know what I would have done without you," she said, joining him at the table with the steaming mugs. Quickly, she added a generous dollop of cream to his coffee.

"I'm glad that I was here. Lloyd hasn't sustained any serious injuries – the ankle looks pretty messy, but there is no real harm done to the foot."

"But there was so much blood –"

"All flesh wounds – nothing that I could even stitch. He'll just have to keep it very clean."

"Thank you again. I'm just not myself with Abram gone."

She paused then and said, speaking very slowly, "And I can't stop thinking about that woman, getting all sorts of crazy ideas – even wondering if she does practise a kind of white witchcraft."

"You know that's all nonsense."

"I know Abram would laugh at such foolish talk – but he knows who that woman is, William. He said her name is Mme. de la Rue, who lives in a cottage on the South Shore. Country people say that she concocts all sorts of strange drinks and ointments."

"Marie, some of the old women on the island do that, and actually, their brews can have a placebo effect."

"What do you mean?" Marie found her brother's presence so comforting. Talking to him like this reminded her of when they were younger, still living in the large house in St. Peter Port. When William came home on holiday from Trinity College in Ireland, he would be so enthused about what he had learned that term in Medical School, describing his scientific studies in intricate detail. She couldn't follow a good deal of it; unlike her brother, she did not have the mind for it, but she loved seeing his face light up as he talked passionately about medicine.

"Placebo is a recognized phenomenon, from the Latin, meaning, 'I shall please.' The patient believes that something will heal him – say a bunch of weeds that this Mme. de la Rue boils in her soup pot – and feels better as a result."

Marie smiled. "Like the broth Aunt Edith made when we had colds – it had such a horrible taste."

He nodded, his handsome face creasing into a wide grin, saying, "That's right. I think she had the cook add cayenne pepper and fish oil – but no dandelion weeds or lichen roots, like the country women use."

Marie laughed at that, and for some reason, the sound of her merriment in the quiet kitchen made her think of Abram, and of all the laughter they had shared sitting at the long oak table. She grew quiet then, and her brother reached out and touched her hand.

"Try not to dwell on things too much. I know it's very hard on you – but the children need you more than ever."

She nodded. "I know. I resolve each day to try to be stronger." She paused for a moment, and then she said, "William, regardless of whether Mme. de la Rue's medicines are truly effective, I should have had the presence of mind to thank her. I should have acknowledged her kindness."

William shook his head. "Marie, do you think it would have really mattered to her? I hear about these old women on the island from time to time. They think they are healers. Trust me, they are a strange bunch; some fool around with stuff that can cause serious harm, while others are downright soft in the head. That woman is probably lost in her own odd, little world. You have no idea what I see sometimes in the hospital –"

"But has this Mme. de la Rue done anything that you've heard about?"

"Not her, specifically, although more often than not, the patients don't tell us who they went to see. There are maybe half a dozen old women who claim to be able to heal every ailment known to man. They all seem to live on the South Shore, in cottages that are not much more than hovels."

William paused and said, "But in fairness, as I said, I've never seen anyone who told me they had specifically been treated by this Mme. de la Rue." And then he ran his hand through his thick blond hair and sighed, saying, "But I shouldn't have spoken to her the way I did. You're right, Marie. And she should have been thanked for going into that cave after the children, whether it would have mattered to her or not. But please stop blaming yourself for that. I'm the one who should have expressed some gratitude."

Marie looked at him, putting her hand lightly on his shoulder for a moment. "If she hadn't helped the children when she did, it could have been much worse. Lloyd would have been all alone in that cave –"

William broke in, saying, "Believe me, I know. He could have been lying there for a long time, waiting for Randolph to get help. And with Lorley there as well – God knows what could have happened."

"I want to go to the South Shore to thank her, William, I really think that I must."

William was shaking his head before she finished her sentence. "Marie, you can't go there. You know Abram wouldn't want you to do that. I've seen how strange some of these old women get –"

"Mme. de la Rue isn't frightening at all. I know she's different. But honestly, William," and she stopped for a moment, thinking about the woman, her shining grey eyes, and her radiant hair, and said, "I think she is a true healer." And the more she thought about her, all that she could see in her mind's eye was a dove, with soft grey feathers extended in full flight.

"Marie, you can't go there."

William then looked into her eyes, and said, "You have the kindest heart of anyone I know, Marie. And I do regret how I treated Mme. de la Rue – but you have to let this go."

"What possible harm could it do, going to see her?"

"Not very long ago, I went to one of the cottages where an old woman named Dugas lived. At one time, she was renowned for her séances. Country people, mostly, went to her, swearing she was able to bring back their loved ones. Her cottage was on the South Shore, so far from any road that I had to walk through the woods for a half mile or so to get to the place. A farmer's lad up there who delivered provisions to her every month said that the woman seemed to be very sick. The lad's father – you know him – Cecil Roget –"

"Oh yes, he's a friend of Abram's, a nice fellow."

William nodded his head, taking another drink of the strong French coffee. "He's a good man, Marie. He was worried about this Dugas and asked me to check on her."

Marie looked at her brother fondly. "That was kind of you, William."

He shrugged and said, "I just hoped that it wouldn't be too late. Roget said the woman had become almost a complete recluse. He hadn't seen her for a while, but, as I said, his lad would see her about every month –"

She interrupted quickly, "So Cecil wasn't afraid of letting his son go there by himself?"

"Marie, he's as trusting as you are. He felt sorry for the old woman. She didn't want to see anyone though, other than the boy. Even people who wanted her medicine," and William shook his head when he said the words, "waited for a long time in the yard outside her cottage, but she wouldn't come out for them, either, and eventually they went away. And, of course, the séances had stopped some time before that. The yard, if you could call it that, was in terrible shape, overrun with plants gone to seed, and noxious-smelling weeds. The vines that grew on the cottage had spread to the ground, mixing with the thick stalks of the overgrown foliage. It looked like a nest of snakes, really. And the vines were infested with mice, big, fat things that were feasting on something in that undergrowth. I could feel them scampering around my ankles when I made my way up to the cottage."

"You must have wanted to turn back."

"Marie, the place was so deserted that I feared this Dugas was dead. Or suffering badly. And I called to her, standing in the doorway – although what passed for a door was a piece of leather, crudely cut, hanging there. The vermin that lived in all those weeds had free reign in the hovel."

"That poor woman, living like that, William."

He let out a long breath, shaking his head. "And it was much worse inside. Poor Dugas was lying, wrapped in a thin cotton sheet, on a straw mattress strewn on the filthy floor, and I mean filth. There was rotting food in some of the pots on the hearth, and foul-smelling herbs, and grime that looked as if it had been there for years. Marie, the yard felt cleaner than that hovel – the scat from the mice and other animals was everywhere. There were cats, several of them, sitting as still as stone on the rafters. The poor woman was barely conscious. She was emaciated and suffering from pneumonia. I managed to get her to the hospital in St. Peter Port, but she only lasted a few days."

"That's so sad, William. I'm thankful, at least, that you found her before she died."

He looked at her, his eyes very serious. "You see, surely Marie, why I don't want you going to see this de la Rue."

"But she's not like that, William. I know."

"Marie. Think of Abram. And the children. They need you now more than ever."

She agreed then, reluctantly, knowing that her brother was right about Abram – he would never want her to go to the cottage. He would tell her to leave well enough alone.

But she knew that she would not be able to get the image of Mme. de la Rue out of her mind.

The image of a beautiful grey dove, wings spread wide in a shining silver sky.

chapter
seven

A LETTER FROM ABRAM ARRIVED.

Lloyd collected the post that day from the mailbox at the end of their lane.

And almost immediately, he came running back to the farmhouse. "Mamma, a letter from Papa has arrived from England!"

Marie dropped the knife she was using to chop vegetables, letting it fall with a clatter onto the heavy wooden cutting board. She rushed to her son standing in the doorway. Putting her arm around him, she held him close as he handed her the letter. "It feels heavy, Mamma."

She nodded, looking down at him. More than a month had passed since the awful accident in the cave, the scars now hard, jagged lines. Marie checked it every day, and Lorley often managed to be at her side when she did. As it healed, and the flesh slowly melded, the torn skin knitted together into bright, angry red ridges, Lorley finally said one day, "It looks like a devil's claw grabbed his foot."

Marie had stared at her little girl, wishing such thoughts never entered her mind.

Then she had knelt down, and looked into her eyes, saying, "Lorley, you know I want you to keep ideas about devils out of your head. It's not good to think such things."

"Yes, Mamma, I'll try my best," she had said, in a solemn tone.

"Try to think of angels instead, Lorley. Promise Mamma." And Lorley had nodded earnestly, and Marie hoped that dancing angels with their snowy wings would fill her little girl's head and keep the devils far away.

Thankfully, there had been no more talk of devils since then, and now, when she looked at Lloyd, she felt certain that the incident in the cave hadn't had any lasting effect on him.

There were to be no more excursions into the caves, of course, not even with Reginald and Herbert. William had stated that very clearly, telling them all that their Mamma had too much to worry about to have them wandering into treacherous caves.

She looked at the letter, about to open it, and then caught herself, telling Lloyd, "Go get your brothers in the vines – and Lorley – in the flower garden with the freesias and lilies. I want to read Papa's letter with all of us here."

As soon as he left, running as fast as ever, his fine black hair glinting in the sunlight, Marie sat in the wicker chair by the stone hearth, holding the letter close to her heart.

She knew, of course, that many people would have handled the envelope since Abram put it in the post, but she felt the thin paper and liked to think that she was the first to touch where Abram's hands had been.

Bowing her head, she breathed deeply, trying to catch

Abram's scent from the letter. It was foolish, she knew, but she couldn't help herself. Turning over the letter, she saw that it was postmarked more than two months ago, at the end of July.

Many other Guernseywomen had already heard from their husbands, and brothers, and sons, and Marie had been alarmed when no letter came, but William said repeatedly there was no need to be concerned – no harm could come to Abram in the camp outside of Canterbury, England where the Regiment was training. It was wartime, and the mail delivery was erratic. William told her, though, that soldiers from English towns who were already in the trenches in France were able to send letters home, some arriving at their destinations faster than letters sent from one end of Guernsey to the other. Marie was incredulous that such a thing could happen. She had feared that when Abram's Regiment was finally shipped to France, he would never be able to contact her – but William assured her that it would be possible.

It filled her with a new kind of hope, one that lightened the despair that dwelt in her heart since Abram left. She thought of Lorley and her devil clawing at Lloyd's foot; the sad truth was that too often, she felt as though a devil was clawing at her heart, bleeding despair, a despair that she had to fight against every day. The angels she urged Lorley to imagine doing their golden dance on her heart, were exactly what she tried to imagine within herself.

Sometimes it helped.

But lately, it had been more difficult keeping the darkness at bay. She told herself that it was only natural, each day passing slowly, with no letter from Abram.

She worried, though, that it was more than that –

because ever since the accident in the cave, it had been worse, and she feared it was because she hadn't thanked Mme. de la Rue for saving her children. Sadly, the angels wouldn't dance very long inside her now – no more than a few steps, then vanishing as quickly as hummingbirds – no more than a flash – the despair bleeding more strongly than ever.

She had to find this Mme. de la Rue; it was weighing too heavily on her heart, and her soul.

It didn't take long for Lloyd to bring everyone into the kitchen. It was a particularly hot October day, the dark purple grapes dusty in the bright sunlight, the leaves a paler green, with some yellow around the edges, as if some of the sun's gold had stayed there.

Reginald and Herbert, with their swarthy complexions, had become even darker after their summer in the vines. They had always helped their Papa, from when they were Randolph's age, but they had never had to work these long hours, bearing such a heavy burden.

"Boys – please have a drink," she said.

Reginald walked over to the pump by the sink and quietly filled an earthenware mug with ice cold water, handing it to Herbert. Then he filled his mug to the rim and gulped the water down.

The rest of the children came running into the kitchen, sitting at the long oak table, eager for news of their Papa, their eyes fixed on her. She was about to open the letter, and then she paused, looking at them all, thinking about Abram, the father of five children, soon to be sent to France to fight in the trenches.

It all seemed so horribly wrong to her. She wished, often fiercely, that she could be like the other Guernseywomen whose husbands had gone off to the War. They all seemed so proud of the sacrifices their husbands were making, believing fervently that going to battle was the only thing that could be done. It seemed to be so simple for them, the only possible answer, like an arithmetic question done on a slate with a piece of chalk.

It wasn't like that for Marie. She inwardly raged against the War. She didn't believe in it for a moment; it seemed to her to be pointless, not worth taking Abram away from her. And when such thoughts possessed her, she felt the despair so heavy within her, the devil clawing her soul as if it were a bone, digging deep into the marrow.

Her eyes fell on Lorley, sitting close beside Randolph, her small white hand resting on her brother's arm. Her little girl seemed filled with such hope, as if the angels were singing inside her, and it lightened her heart.

She began reading:

Dear Marie and Reginald, Herbert, Lloyd, Randolph, and Lorley,

What a long way to start a letter, I know, but I can't begin without mentioning each one of you. I think about you always, trusting that you are well.

Here in Camp Bourne, we believe that the War will be over soon.

Perhaps I will be home in time to harvest the grapes.

So many of the letters have been delayed, but others

arrive faster than seems possible. I received one from you just yesterday, and it had been postmarked at St. Peter Port almost a month ago; and yet a letter arrived for the fellow in the tent beside mine who has been here less than a week.

Receiving these letters is the very best part of my life here.

Reginald – Mamma writes that you are doing such an excellent job in the grapes. She is so proud of you, and so am I. To think of you, at fourteen years of age, doing the work of a man, of someone twice your age. You remind me of your grandfather, who could work harder than anyone on the island.

And Herbert, I am awfully proud of you as well. Mamma tells me in her letter that you are out in the vines every day with Reginald. And you were right about the training here in Camp Bourne. It is not too hard. You knew what you were talking about when you said that the years of hiking and climbing cliffs have kept me in good physical condition. I have no trouble keeping up with the younger fellows. Some of them are even a bit slower than me.

I am also so happy to hear, Lloyd and Randolph, you are doing your fair share – more than your fair share Mamma writes, and being good boys and keeping out of trouble.

And I am thankful to hear how well you are doing, Lorley. Mamma tells me that the stories, the fairy tales, and the book of the Arabian Nights that we used to read together, you are now able to read on your own. When I return, you can read to me, and I will be the one whose eyes get heavier and heavier and slowly fall asleep – but I won't be the Sleeping Beauty that you are, not with the big, black moustache I have now.

How I miss you all, but we must be strong. I tell myself to keep my head down and keep going. And I think of you, and hold you all so dear. I love you with all my heart.

Be good to your Mamma,

Papa

When Marie finished reading the letter, the kitchen was very silent. Only the clock in the front parlour could be heard ticking. And to Marie, it seemed as if there was too much silence between each tick, as if the heavy quiet that had descended upon the house had spread to the clock, slowing it down, engulfing it in the stillness.

Then Randolph said, "A letter doesn't seem to be enough. We miss him too much."

Lloyd, his hands spread out on the old oak table, looking more pensive than usual, said, "Randolph's right. But it's good that Papa says the War will be over soon."

And Reginald, moving towards the pump for another mug of water before going back to the vines, said, "We'll have to see about that. I bet some of those younger fellows he mentions aren't much older than me." With that, he looked at Herbert, and they left, Reginald looking as though he was ready to do the work of ten men.

Randolph, leaning back in his chair, said, looking at Mamma, "I'm glad that Papa thinks I'm staying out of trouble." Lloyd stared down at the table and nodded at Randolph's words.

Mamma smiled at them both, her eyes especially kind.

"You are working very hard, just like I told Papa. Run now and help your brothers before suppertime."

Only Lorley remained, still sitting at the table, gazing through the large window, where the rows of grapes, and the cliffs, and, at the very edges, a ribbon of turquoise sea, could be seen. Marie didn't think, though, that her little girl saw any of it. "What's wrong, Lorley? Isn't it nice to hear from Papa?"

She shook her head. "I don't know, Mamma. Somehow, Papa sounds different. And I'm frightened for him."

Marie was quiet for a few long moments, and then said, "Try not to worry. Papa means it when he tells us that everything will be fine."

"I guess so, Mamma."

Lorley looked at her, as if she wanted to say more, but then she got down from her chair and walked towards the screen door, moving very slowly, as if she were in the Creux Mahie again, and not sure of her next step.

After Mamma read the letter from Papa, I wanted to run to the rocks by the sea, to sit as high as I could on the Giant's Toe, far past the throne where we usually sat, to get as close to the top as I could. To somehow escape the sadness of missing my Papa.

I wanted to stare out to sea, to gaze into the shimmering horizon, where the sky and the water blended into a pale blue haze, and call to my Papa – and somehow bring him home.

If only, I thought, with a great yearning, I could fly. I would perch on the very peak of the Giant's Toe and then glide through the air and find Papa's ship heading to France, or, if he hadn't left England yet, fly to him there.

But I couldn't even climb down the cliffs on my own – not without my brothers, and they were all too busy.

I looked down at my legs, and I held my arms out at my sides, so pale and thin – more like spindly branches on a birch tree. It suddenly seemed so silly to imagine flying, with these arms and legs, flapping in the air, my dress like a wisp of cloud in the wind. The only part of me that would look like a bird at all would be my hair ribbon, and that was too pink to be any bird that flew over Guernsey.

I had wanted to tell Mamma how sad the letter made me feel, but I couldn't. She knew that something wasn't right with me, but I couldn't tell her. Since Papa left, her eyes and mouth were still soft and smiling, as always, but it seemed as though her face was cross stitched into place each morning, as carefully as her needlework, a beautiful, happy face in a neat oval frame. I didn't want to tell her anything that might make that face unravel into a jumble of loose threads.

And it wasn't just Papa's letter. I was afraid that if I stayed in the kitchen any longer, that I would tell my Mamma about what had happened the night before.

I didn't want her to ever know anything about it.

It would frighten her too much.

The night before my Papa's letter came, I had not been able to sleep.

I had been thinking about Mme. de la Rue, longing to see her again. Every time I closed my eyes, her beautiful silver hair rippled so brightly that I could not fall asleep in the glow of silver.

Finally, I rose from my bed to gaze at the trees that spread before my window like a dark green blanket. I hoped that if I imagined lying in that deep greenness, my dreams would come.

It was then that I heard Reginald and Herbert talking in their room down the hall. I could not make out what they were saying; they were speaking too quietly, but I knew that the low rumble was their voices, a rumble almost as deep, now, as when my Papa spoke.

The deepest voice, though, the one I knew was Reginald's, sounded agitated, at times more like a far, faraway roll of thunder, and that worried me.

I wondered that Lloyd and Randolph hadn't awakened. From my room, though, I could hear their deep, rhythmic breathing, and I knew they were exhausted from working in the vines all day. I doubted, also, that Mamma, who slept with her door shut, could hear.

I felt as if something was very wrong, that my big brothers were in trouble of some sort. And I realized in that moment how much I feared for them and, most especially, for Reginald. Ever since Papa had left for the War, Reginald had a light in his eyes that I did not understand. It frightened me – though I could not understand that either. How, I thought, could I ever be afraid for someone as big and brave as my brother, Reginald?

But I was.

And that made me leave my room to try to hear what my brothers were saying.

If I hadn't been so fearful for Reginald, I would never, ever have done such a thing.

Trying to be as silent as the deep green trees I had been gazing upon, I left my room and stood behind their door. Pressing against the heavy oak panel in my white nightgown, I shed all my quiet greenness and imagined myself shimmering all over, until I felt as if I nearly disappeared, like a ghost. Then I peered into the room through a long, thin crack in the door frame.

Reginald was talking. He was still in his work clothes, pacing in front of the window. Both casements were wide open, so that the dark blue draperies unfurled wildly in the night air, like flags high on a mast.

Herbert was sitting on the bed, removing his shirt, but very slowly, as though he was taking off his clothes underwater, floating beneath the turquoise waters of Rocquaine Bay.

I couldn't remember ever seeing Herbert move so slowly. He always seemed to be hustling to keep up with Reginald, who, though only one year older, was bigger and stronger. Herbert was a tall lad as well, the tallest in his class he had proudly told us all the past year. But then he laughed and said that every time he grew a few inches, Reginald seemed to leap ahead by twice that.

Reginald wasn't moving or talking slowly. He paced in front of the window, the curtains nearly enveloping him at times, but he didn't seem to notice. Combing back his thick, shiny black hair with his fingers, he said, "I tell you, Herbert, now is the time to enlist. I'm big enough to fool a recruiting officer."

"How are you going to do that, Reginald? You're only fourteen," Herbert said, his voice a hoarse whisper.

Reginald's words had been whipping through the room like a riptide, though even with his wild words, he kept his voice low enough so that he would not wake our Mamma.

But to me, his words still roared in my ears, because I was terribly frightened by the thought of my big brother Reginald leaving us to fight in the War. How, I thought, at only fourteen, could he ever manage to do such a thing?

"Listen, Herbert," he said, "if I go to a parish that's far enough away from here, like Vale, I think I could get away with it. I've been told that they don't ask for birth registries most of the time."

Herbert finished taking off his shirt, letting it fall onto the bed. He looked at Reginald and, after a long pause, said, "Then I'm going with you."

I looked at Herbert's white, rigid face, far more ghostlike than I was, hovering by the door in my pale nightdress. And I had to grip the door with both hands, as if my fingers were carved out of white stone, because all that I wanted to do was run into the room and throw my arms around my brothers, begging them not to go to the War.

Then Reginald said, "Herbert, you know I can't let you do that."

"Why not? I'm only a year younger than you – and even though you're bigger and stronger, I can still hold my own. And you know that, Reginald. I couldn't get the better of you in a fight, but I could whip most lads your age and older."

As I listened, I felt as if some phantom who looked like Herbert had slithered through the walls and taken his place.

Because this person did not sound like Herbert.

Not only did he never boast about fighting, I had never seen him hit anyone. Not that I had ever seen Reginald strike anyone either, but I had heard sharp bits and scraps of stories my brothers told each other about Reginald having to fight someone. They always stopped talking, though, when they realized I was within earshot.

"Herbert, what are you talking about? You're not like that, and you know it."

"I'm not going to let you go without me. We have to stick together. We always have and always will."

"I know. But Mamma can't keep the vineyard going with only Lloyd and Randolph." And then, staring hard at Herbert, he said, "You're not ready."

Herbert stared back at him with eyes just as hard. "You're not going without me. You can try leaving before me, but I'll be right behind you."

Reginald looked at Herbert, then, for what seemed like a very long time, as I took more slow, silent breaths than I could count.

"Herbert don't do this. I need to go when I still have the chance. The recruitment officer up in Vale right now is especially lax, but they say he won't last. Don't follow me."

Herbert's voice became even quieter. "Reginald, you've got to think about this some more. Listen to me. Lads like us get killed, and then they can't be found. It's as if they had never been there."

"What do you mean, they disappear?"

I was listening so closely that I wanted to call out the same question. How, I thought, could poor dead soldiers lying on a battlefield just disappear? All that I could think was that it must be Jesus, with his kind brown eyes and gentle hands, lifting them straight up to heaven. He must be moving faster than a flash of sunlight so that no one could see him doing it. He would know that they had already suffered too much and needed heaven right away.

But as Herbert continued, I knew, sadly, that wasn't what was happening.

"Their bodies are either never found, or they can't be identified. You weren't there when Uncle William told me and Lloyd about it. It was just a few days ago. He saw Lloyd reading some poetry for school. When he saw that it was war verse by Rudyard Kipling, he shook his head and said it was a tragedy what happened to the man's son."

"What?"

"Uncle William said that Kipling believed his son, John, should serve his country, but the lad was so shortsighted that he was rejected by the Navy and the Army. But Kipling was so desperate to have his lad fight that he asked the Colonel of the Irish Guards, who happened to be a friend of his, to accept his son. And the Colonel obliged. John was only seventeen at the time. He trained for a year, and just a few days after he turned eighteen, he was sent to the trenches. Just what his father wanted."

Herbert paused for a moment, looking down at the floor. He finally said, "Poor fellow didn't last a month, Uncle William said. He died charging a hill. But they couldn't find his body, Reginald. Now, Kipling goes to every field hospital in Europe. He just can't stop hoping that his son is still alive. Uncle William said lads in the trenches disappear like that all the time – and can't be found. And our uncle told both me and Lloyd about other horrors in the trenches."

Reginald was silent.

"Some lads don't last a day, I've heard. They stick their heads up, and a sniper's bullet gets them. Even worse, though, is this mustard gas the Germans are using. They hurl these canisters that spew noxious gas into the air. Lads suffocate to death, screaming for their mothers. And if it doesn't kill you, it blinds you. Burns the skin off your body. It's bad, Reginald. Worse, I think, than we can even try to imagine."

As I listened, I didn't have to worry about being quiet. What Herbert said was so frightening that I couldn't move. The thought of the young lads in the trenches, crying for Mammas who could no longer help them – but it wasn't just what he said that made me very fearful and very sad. It was the look on Herbert's face as he talked about the War.

Never had I seen his face, which was so often wreathed in a smile, so terribly afraid.

Reginald stopped pacing and gripped Herbert by the shoulders. "I know it's bad. Believe me, I do. But I can handle it, just like Papa. But it's not your time yet," he said. His voice was still very low, but each word punched into the room like a fist. "You've got to stay here." As Reginald spoke, he sounded so like my brave Papa, and it made me miss him even more.

"I tell you, Reginald, I won't let you go to the trenches alone. If you go, so will I. Nothing's going to stop me." As Herbert spoke, his words sounded every bit as fierce as Reginald's, fierce and frightened, and I could tell from the look on Reginald's face that he knew Herbert meant what he said. When Herbert's mind was fixed on something, he never changed.

Then all at once Reginald let go of Herbert, and turned away, staring out of the window. Reginald's broad shoulders, usually as stiff as a crossbow, seemed to bend forward, and his whole body softened.

When he had been raging about the War, he had been like a genie from the Arabian Nights suddenly exploding into the air. But now, it was as if the genie had vanished.

And I said a quick, fervent prayer to Mme. de la Rue, hoping that her sparks of magic could keep that genie buried deep inside Reginald.

Then Reginald said, "I can't go then."

And, speaking even more quietly, "I know you'll follow me to Vale, and if I get in, so will you." Reginald paused, and then he said, "I can't risk that. I can't do that to Mamma and Papa. I can't do that to you."

I felt much of the fear leave my heart.

Mme. de la Rue must have heard my prayer.

Her silver light now a bright shield, saving my brothers, stopping them from going to the War.

Herbert was silent. And then he rose from the bed and put his arm around Reginald.

And at that moment, I suddenly realized Herbert's lion heart was as mighty as Reginald's.

Perhaps, I said to myself as I returned to my room, even more.

Remembering all that had happened the past night, and now thinking about the letter from Papa, all that I wanted to do was to go to Bluebell Woods and lie on the flowers and rest my head on the dark blue petals. I could never be a bird, but lying in those woods would feel as if I were sleeping on a piece of deep blue sky.

But I could not go to Bluebell Woods, so I told myself that I must try to spend the day reading my books, and staring out of my bedroom window.

And tell myself not to be afraid, and not to be sad.

And dream about the bluebells singing, and dream of my Papa.

Marie waited until the evening, when everyone was in bed, to read the other letter from Abram. It was tucked in the envelope also, but Abram had written 'For My Dear Marie' on the outside of the carefully folded page.

She had wanted to read it throughout the long day, but she couldn't risk any of them seeing it – and Lorley had been in and out of the house, looking as if she wanted to say something, staring at her with such big eyes, but then she finally went into her bedroom to read her books. But when Marie checked on her, the little girl was sitting on her bed, a book propped open on her lap, staring through the large casement window, not reading a word.

At the time, Marie believed that her small daughter was simply missing her Papa so badly.

The truth was, if Marie hadn't been so busy with her household chores, she would have done exactly what Lorley was doing – and stared out of one of the mullioned windows of their farmhouse, thinking about Abram, imagining him coming home to her, walking down the long laneway, home forever from the War.

But she had to wait for her children to be in their beds before she could do any of that. When she finally heard Reginald and Herbert shut the door to their room, she got into her bed, always so empty now without Abram, to read the letter.

And so she began reading with anxious eyes, her brow furrowed.

Dearest Marie,

I think of you and the children constantly.

Without all of you, I don't know how I could get through this.

I pray that my letter to the children sounded hopeful – I can't tell you how many times I rewrote it, trying to find words that were truthful, but still concealed what I am really going through here in the camp.

It is not the physical demands. Most of the Guernseymen, especially those of us from the farms, are used to hard labour – and we are as strong as the men from England.

But many of the officers, if you can call them that – have never seen a battle, but have enough money and influence to buy themselves a rank – and they treat us with ill-disguised contempt.

And they have such little skill. I wouldn't care about their arrogance or their silly self-importance – if they knew how to train soldiers for the Front. But I tell you Marie, they have no idea. I am thankful that I already knew how to fire a gun and keep it in good condition, because what they're teaching us here is so woefully inadequate.

Marie, I fear for some of the men who will soon be

leaving the camp to go to France. Some of the boys, only a few years older than Reginald, don't know much more than how to march in their uniforms and pack their rucksacks.

And there are stories, Marie – about men being sent to the trenches in France, poorly trained and ill-equipped – who die so quickly – they don't last long fighting.

A fellow told us the other day about soldiers from the training camps getting to the trenches in the evening – and dead before breakfast the next day.

Before anyone knew their names.

I try to help some of the young fellows with their guns – not that I am such an expert, but I'm trying to do what I can.

They remind me too much of our sons. God help them.

At least, Marie, it is the summertime, and it has not been too wet. There are not enough barracks, so most of us sleep in tents, and when it rains, the ground turns into a sea of muck. Some joke that at least the ankle-deep mud is preparing us for the trenches.

Marie, I almost didn't send this letter, because I know my words are grim. But I fear for my countrymen. Opening my heart to you helps me keep going.

Always know that I love you. I see your face when I close my eyes at night, and when I wake in the morning. It is your love, and our children, that will get me through this.

Yours Forever,

Abram

Marie stared at the letter, touching it lightly, the paper so fragile, like the powdery wings of a moth, and she imagined the paper becoming dust in her fingers if she held it too roughly. Never could she remember missing Abram more. She longed to take him in her arms, to stroke his forehead and cast all the demons away.

She wanted him to come home to her.

She wanted him here, in their bed, where she could wipe away his fears.

And her own.

Because she had never been so frightened. For all of them.

She didn't know how she would ever sleep that night, thinking of Abram, and his fears for the young Guernseymen, and of what was to come –

But she forced herself to close her eyes and try to sleep.

And she told herself that she must get up early in the morning and greet her children with a smiling face – the sadness and fear must be buried deep inside her.

She would imagine a sculptor, carving bright eyes and a joyful mouth on her face, smoothing the wet plaster over all the pain.

The smiling stone woman.

For Abram.

That night, she dreamt that she was in the forest, completely alone. She wondered, as she moved very softly in her bare feet, where her children were, and it troubled her greatly that she couldn't remember where she had left them. But she kept moving – because the one thing she did know was that she had to keep going through the forest to find Abram.

She looked at her feet, shining white against the dark

underbrush, at the sharp twigs protruding like rigid claws, and the heavy roots rising from the earth, like the thick, sinewy arms of a beast. She couldn't understand why her feet weren't bleeding as she walked over the spikey ground – and then she realized that she could not feel her feet, and when she reached down to touch them, she found that they had turned into cold, white marble.

She could still walk, but it was as though she was wearing very stiff shoes – and she even laughed, a little, at that, but the sound of her laughter in the enormous, silent woods was more like a cry, as if she really had hurt herself. She touched her feet again, the white marble very cold, and then, lifting her skirt, she saw that her legs were stiffening, streaks of marble slithering up from her ankles.

She was suddenly terrified that soon a film of marble would cover her entire body, paralyzing her, that she would be lost in the strange, soundless forest forever, a small, pale statue that no one would ever find. A grave without a name.

With her stone feet, she began walking faster, now desperate to find her way out of the forest, heedless of the long branches that lashed against her face and the ferns that swept at her skirts. At least, she told herself, she could still feel her legs. And then, as the heavy branches hit her, she saw that the once deep green leaves were now black. Looking up, she saw that the entire forest, the bark, and the branches, and every single leaf, were all black, as black as the Creux Mahie.

And then she saw that she was no longer in the forest, but in the great cave, lost, deep in the earth, afraid to take a single footstep, surrounded by a darkness so great that she feared if she breathed too deeply the blackness would rush inside her and she would dissolve into the cave.

Somehow, she stumbled forward, knowing that at any moment she could plunge into an abyss, step off a ledge into a black emptiness, but she had no choice other than to keep going, holding her hands out in front of her, in a gruesome parody of an embrace.

And then her hands touched the rock, the hard rock wall, and she clung to it; it was something to hold in the darkness.

She pressed her face against it and closed her eyes, and began praying that she could still, somehow, find Abram.

And when she opened her eyes, and looked at the rock in the darkness, she could see little glimmers of grey, not much more than sparks.

But they spread, and soon shone before her, a smooth expanse, almost a mirror.

And as she gazed deeply into the shimmering surface, a surface so suddenly beautiful, she saw the face of Mme. de la Rue.

She awakened before dawn. She knew what she had to do.

Lying in bed, she could see the woods. Usually, the mullions in the window etched the expanse of green into small squares, but before going to bed she had opened the window wide – so that upon awakening, she had a clear view of the woods.

The trees were as beautiful to her as the sea. She loved to walk in the forests of Guernsey, on the paths where the trees, their frothy green leaves forming an arbor overhead, melded their high branches together like dancers in an embrace.

As a young girl growing up in St. Peter Port, her father's

large house had been on a hill overlooking the sea, and in some rooms, the turquoise water and sky seemed to fill the whole space, as though the house was a high rock surrounded by the water and the cloudless sky.

She loved that the deep green woods, on the edge of their property, were so close, and gazing at those woods, she experienced the same wonder as she had as a young girl gazing at the sea.

That early morning, in the moonlight that still fell on the trees, the leaves were darkly green – beckoning her.

And as she gazed through her window, she knew that she had to go to the woods on the South Shore, woods much thicker and darker than those she looked upon now, and find Mme. de la Rue.

To thank her for saving her children.

It was the right thing to do; she knew that now in the deep green heart of her being.

She needed goodness to save Abram.

***

By the time I finally fell asleep, my dreams came quickly. Strangely, though, I lost my Papa's face in those fragments and shreds of nighttime. All through my scattered dreams, I never ever stopped trying to find him, sometimes as a bird flying over the sea, but mostly as a little girl wandering endlessly through a dark woods, looking for him with every slow step I took.

By the next morning, I felt as if I had become a jumble of sad, loose threads.

But I forced myself out of bed, and I untangled my hair as

best as I could and tied a ribbon in it – a lopsided one, but at least Mamma would see that I had made an effort. I tried to fix a smile on my face, because I didn't want Mamma to see how sad Papa's letter had made me. I told myself firmly that I must, as I walked down the back stairs, the narrow steps that led straight into the kitchen, try to have a happy face, like the puffins by the sea.

Everyone was already in the kitchen, Mamma in her place at one end of the long table, the chair at the other end empty – Papa's chair. They were about to begin eating, and I slipped quietly into my chair beside Lloyd and Randolph.

"Lorley – you slept in this morning. Good for you – you needed a good rest," Mamma said, and she reached over the table, patting my hand.

I looked at her and saw her smiling face, her beautiful, smiling face, her face before the War, her real face, that had somehow, it seemed, emerged now from the oval frame.

For a moment, I thought that perhaps she had received the news that Papa was coming home, that perhaps the strange War in France that was taking him so far away from us was over.

"Has the War come to an end?" The words were out of my mouth before I knew it. Seeing Mamma so much happier, I thought that surely some change had occurred during the awful night that had just passed.

A shadow crossed her face, briefly, and she shook her head, saying, "Not yet, Lorley. But soon, Dear."

Reginald, at the other end of the table, his chair as close to Papa's empty one as possible, was eating an enormous breakfast, several slices of bread and butter and three eggs on half of the plate, the rest of the dish filled with sausages. His appetite, now that he was working so hard on the farm, had become even greater than before, and even before the War it had always been something of a wonder to me. It was almost like watching a giant eat breakfast. A giant, I thought, remembering two nights past, who had somehow been tamed by Herbert – with the help of Mme. de la Rue, I fervently believed.

He swallowed a mouthful of bread quickly and said, "Lorley, Papa's Regiment will be in France any day now. We'll beat the Germans."

Herbert joined in, saying, "It could take years, though. Reginald and I will be going then." He didn't look up from his plate, one almost as big as Reginald's. He kept eating, more slowly than his older brother, and his thoughts seemed very far away, not at all on the mound of sausages he was trying to get through.

"You're right about that. They're going to need us," Reginald said.

Mamma said quickly, "Don't even think that. The War will be over long before you boys are eligible." I was sure that Reginald and Herbert had a lot more they wanted to say about it, but they said nothing.

Then I looked very closely at Mamma, seeing the struggle in her face, as if the thought of her sons going to the War was pulling her, still and unhappy, back into the oval frame. But she didn't let it happen. And I, as upset as I had been that morning, as frazzled as the poor lopsided ribbon in my hair – that Mamma's eyes had fixed on briefly – found myself feeling a little better.

She sat, then, looking at each of us, at Reginald and Herbert quietly finishing what was on their plates, their eyes fixed on the remnants of their breakfasts. And her eyes stayed on Lloyd and Randolph a little longer, who were looking at each other, feeling, like me, I could tell, that something important was about to be said, sensing the change in Mamma as I did.

Finally, with a last look at me, she said, "I am going to Mme. de la Rue's cottage. I must thank her for what she did in the Creux Mahie."

Everyone was silent for a moment, although I wondered, for a few extraordinary seconds, if the sudden surge of happiness in my brain was stopping me from hearing anything.

But it wasn't that, of course – everyone had stopped eating and was looking at Mamma, not saying a word.

Reginald finally spoke, putting down his cutlery, pushing aside his plate. "Mamma – you can't do something so dangerous. I promised Papa that I would look after you. You can't do something like this."

She shook her head, saying, "Reginald, there's nothing to worry about – that woman isn't harmful. Why, in that cave –"

Reginald was about to speak, but Herbert jumped in, saying, "There are all kinds of stories about the weird women on the South Shore. Uncle William told me about this old hag named Dugas, who –"

"I know all about that poor woman. Your uncle has never heard anything troubling about Mme. de la Rue. And," Mamma said, pausing for a moment, looking through the wide kitchen window at the cliffs, "I wouldn't believe anything bad about her anyway."

Herbert was about to say something, but Reginald said, "Mamma, that woman is as strange as they come, believe me.

Some fellows, John and Robert, from St. Martin's tried to go to her cottage once, hiking through the woods to get there –" Reginald stopped talking then, looking around the table, waiting a few minutes before he continued. "When they were still quite far from her house, she suddenly appeared, as if from nowhere, they said. They were walking, and heard something in the trees, and then, she was just there, in front of them, standing on the path. John said she was about six feet tall, with scraggly grey witch hair."

"What did they do?" Randolph asked.

"Well, they ran as fast as they could out of there. Robert said that he looked back once, and she was waving her arms, clawing at the air as though she was crazy. And he said her eyes were like a wild animal's."

Mamma listened, her eyes calm. "But she's not like that, boys. I know that."

"'There are other stories, Mamma," Herbert said quickly. "She makes potions – people know about them all over the island. I've been asking around about her. They say she's descended from a line of witches."

Mamma shook her head, saying, "You know those tales about the witches are told by the old country people. I've never believed any of it."

"Mamma," Reginald said, "they burned witches in St. Peter Port. It's in the history books. Rev. Pelletier knows everything about it. He can go on for hours."

I looked at my eldest brother. There were so many questions I wanted to ask him.

But it was not a good time to interrupt. What was happening was too important.

"Those horrible burnings happened all over Europe and in

America, too, but that was hundreds of years ago." And then, looking directly at me, Mamma smiled a little, saying, "There is a long tradition of natural healers on the island. Those old women on the South Shore who are supposed to be witches are eccentric, for sure, and some think that they can cure ailments, but it's no more than that."

Mamma's voice was very calm, her face still the same as it had been before Papa went away. Reginald's face, though, was more upset than ever, looking the way it did when I had run off to Bluebell Woods. He said, "Mamma, you know Uncle William doesn't want you to go. And I think that woman is even crazier than the rest."

Lloyd and Randolph had been listening very intently, saying nothing, but so absorbed in the conversation that they had barely touched their breakfasts. Then Lloyd said suddenly, in a much louder voice than he usually used, "She's not crazy, and she's not evil. But," and he paused, and then said, almost as if he were talking to himself, "I know that she can do magic."

"I do, too," Randolph said quickly.

I was about to agree wholeheartedly, but I didn't have the chance because Lloyd's words flew too quickly from his mouth.

Pushing back the fine black hair that fell over his forehead, his eyes on Mamma, he said, "Something happened in that cave that I've only told Randolph about." He paused, looking at his brother beside him, who nodded slowly, and his eyes told Lloyd to continue. "There was no way that my foot should have finally come loose the way it did. I had been trying so hard, and then when I lost the light, I tried harder than ever, but I couldn't get my foot to move, not even an inch. And when finally, exhausted in the darkness, feeling as if maybe I was never going to get out of the cave, my foot just came loose." He looked at all of us and said, "I swear that I wasn't even trying when it happened."

"Lloyd and I believe that it happened the moment I crawled into the cave with Mme. de la Rue," Randolph said.

Mamma was about to speak, but Randolph continued, his hazel eyes bright in the sunlight that was shining through the wide kitchen window. "I really believe that it had to have been Mme. de la Rue's magic. Lloyd and I talked it all over –"

"I don't believe it," Reginald said, staring at my brothers.

And Herbert, pushing his plate aside, said, "That's about as strange as it gets."

Mamma said quickly, "I don't think any of this is so strange." And then she looked at each of us again, her eyes finally coming to rest on Lloyd and Randolph. "It was Mme. de la Rue's beautiful goodness that saved Lloyd."

"Mamma – I don't think so –" Reginald began.

But Mamma stood up, shaking her head at my brothers. "No more. No more about witches and magic. Mme. de la Rue is a good woman who saved Lloyd. And I'm going to thank her."

My heart was bursting with a surge of sudden happiness. It was as if the sunlight pouring through the window had filled me up from my toes to the top of my head. I felt as if I must be as bright as a daffodil.

But I also knew that, for once, my Mamma was wrong. Deep in my heart, I believed that it was Mme. de la Rue's magic that saved us that day in the Creux Mahie.

chapter
eight

MY MAMMA DID NOT WASTE any time.

Less than a week after she made her announcement at the breakfast table, she was on her way with Uncle William to see Mme. de la Rue, driving to the South Shore in his beautiful car.

And I was sitting in the backseat with Lloyd and Randolph beside me.

If I hadn't believed in magic before, this turn of events truly would have made me believe in the power of all things magical.

But here we were, all five of us in Uncle William's car, driving to the South Shore on a road that was never meant for an automobile. With its wide leather seats, its silver fenders that ballooned in front and behind, mirrors that flashed in the sun, and enormous tires as white as clouds, his car seemed impossibly large for the narrow, winding road.

But even the plainest cars – without all the beautiful ornaments, with tires that were so much smaller, like plain walking shoes compared to the flamboyant tires, the big, fancy dancing slippers, on my uncle's car – were too large for the road that we had to take to the South Shore.

If my Uncle William hadn't been such a good driver, able to ease the car over the dirt road, manoeuvring it over the ridges, the uneven ruts in the earth, we would have got stuck – the sparkling car in the emerald green forest buried like a pirate's treasure chest deep in the woods. There was an old stone wall covered in a thick tangle of vines, a tapestry of velvety greens and browns, so close to the road that I wanted to reach out and touch it. On the other side, there was no wall, but only trees with great, grey trunks rearing their heavy green branches into the air, their powerful roots protruding from the ground, making the road even more difficult to navigate.

The back of my uncle's head looked very unhappy. I thought about sharing that, quietly, with my brothers, but I didn't think that even they, who could understand me so well, would know what I meant.

But my uncle had such a cheerful face; the dimples in his handsome face seemed always ready to burst into a grin, and his normal, everyday happiness was such that I could see a smile even when he had his head turned away from me.

And on the rare occasions when he was not cheerful, I could tell, somehow, before I looked at his face; one glance at the back of his head, at the smooth, blond hair growing over the collar of his white shirt, told me how he was feeling.

On that day, as we drove slowly towards the South Shore to find Mme. de la Rue's cottage, Uncle William was definitely not happy. The forest, so powerfully green, and all the magic such emerald beauty promised, seemed unable to lift his spirits. He didn't want anything to do with witches or magic – he called it hogwash whenever anyone mentioned it.

He said it quite a few times when Mamma told him her plan to see Mme. de la Rue.

The very day she made her announcement at the breakfast table, Uncle William came to the farm – which was no surprise, because he visited frequently, and ever since Papa had gone to fight the War, he came even more often.

Sitting at the table, Uncle William looked at Mamma for a long moment after she told him that she needed him to drive her to the South Shore to thank Mme. de la Rue. And then he said, leaning back in his chair, "But what for, Marie? There is no reason on earth to see her."

"But there is, William. I know it. It's the right thing to do," Mamma said, her eyes fixed on him intently. I was the only one with them in the kitchen, sitting on the wicker chair by the hearth, as quietly as if I were a cat perched on the pillow. Both seemed to have forgotten that I was there.

"That's hogwash, Marie. Absolute hogwash. That old woman is as eccentric as they come. And I'm not entirely certain she isn't deranged. You've always been too trusting, Marie. You know that. And remember, this woman doesn't want any visitors – unless it's to sell them some harmful, or, at best, useless potion made from crabgrass and moss."

Mamma paused for a moment, looking down at her lap, at the pale silk gathered there in tiny ripples. I wondered if she was, like me, trying to imagine what a drink made from crabgrass and moss would look like, or taste, and I couldn't help shivering a little.

"No, William – I don't see it like that at all," she said, her voice as soft as if she were saying a prayer. "With Abram in the War, I feel that if I don't do what I believe is the right thing to do, something might happen to him."

I moved too quickly then, tucking my legs underneath me, and Mamma turned, looking at me, a little surprised, and then turned back to Uncle William.

"It doesn't work that way, Marie," he said, his voice very quiet.

"But I believe it does, William," Mamma said with great feeling. "And I don't believe Mme. de la Rue is deranged or in any way harmful. I've asked the ladies in my church group about her, and some have heard that she is a healer. And William, before you say anything," and Mamma paused as Uncle William began shaking his head, about to interrupt, "I know that some of the others on the South Shore call themselves healers, too, like that poor Dugas woman. And they call themselves white witches, and they wave their arms crazily in the air and claim to have magical potions. Mme. de la Rue is not like the others."

"Marie, let's be clear. It's not medicine. It's hocus-pocus foolery."

By that, I was sure he meant that it was hogwash.

I was still curled up on the pillow at that point, trying to make myself as small as possible.

I didn't know anything about white witches, but to me, they sounded comforting, somehow. I pictured old women in long, pale gowns, flickering in the moonlight like white candles, brewing potions and peppery teas that helped people. I could imagine Mme. de la Rue in white, when she was making her medicines. She would take off her dress, leaving it in a little silvery puddle on the floor, and underneath would be a gown as white as the gulls that flew over Rocquaine Bay, as white as angel wings.

And although Mamma said that Mme. de la Rue was not one of these white witches, I wondered if perhaps she was. It made me feel almost desperate to see her.

I began dreaming about Mme. de la Rue in her white gown, conjuring spells that swirled like fireflies into the air, and I stopped really listening to what was being said for a few moments. It wasn't hard not to hear them; Uncle William's voice, even when he was angry – and he was most definitely angry about seeing Mme. de la Rue – was still low and quiet. To me he always sounded as though he was sitting at the bedside of a patient, offering comforting words in his soft-spoken, caring way, as calm as though he was reading them a bedtime story.

Mamma's voice wasn't loud, either – it never was – but when she said, "And I'm taking Lloyd and Randolph with me," her voice rang loudly in my ears, and I stirred out of my reverie as if knitting needles had suddenly pierced my warm, woolly daydream.

"No, Marie, that is a very bad idea –"

"William – they have themselves convinced that some sort of witchcraft freed Lloyd's foot. I want them to get that idea out of their heads and simply thank the woman for her kindness."

"Marie, it's one thing for us to go there, and I guess that I do understand why you want to do this. I know how it will help you cope with Abram gone, believe me, but the boys thanking her is nothing short of ludicrous, absolute –"

I was sure that he was about to say hogwash, but Mamma

spoke too quickly. "It's important, William. As important as me going there, and I want them to see that she is no witch."

"I'm not at all convinced that she's as harmless as you think. Just because the ladies in your church group haven't heard anything doesn't mean a thing, and I don't believe that Mme. Laporte would consider this Mme. de la Rue to be so harmless." I glanced at Mamma, and I could see by the look on her face that Uncle William was right about that. "But, Marie, none of them really know. They've never gone near any of those women on the South Shore. And I don't think it will end any notions of witchcraft in the boys' minds. Quite the contrary, I think."

"William, please try to understand –"

When I heard Uncle William say, "And I suppose we're taking Lorley as well?" my heart leapt inside me, and I could no longer sit curled up in the chair. I jumped off the wicker seat, smoothing my dress quickly.

But before I had a chance to say a word, Mamma looked at me again – with such a surprised look on her face – I could never, in my life, remember her forgetting so often that I was there – and then turned to Uncle William saying, "I know you don't mean that. She's far too impressionable."

I opened my mouth to protest, knowing that this was somehow about my imagination getting out of control again, and so I paused for a moment to say a fast, fervent, silent prayer to Mme. de la Rue, holding a picture of her in my heart, her silver halo glowing all around her, asking her to help me find the right words, and then I said, "Please let me go. It would help me enormously, too. I need to visit her just as much as everyone else does."

"Little pitchers have big ears," Uncle William said, looking at Mamma.

I had no idea what he was talking about, but I glanced at the large earthenware pitcher Mamma kept by the sink – and I imagined a pair of soft, white ears sprouting from the sides of the brown clay – and thought how they would look like small lilies growing there, and rather pretty, but I still didn't understand what that had to do with me.

"I've said too much, William," Mamma said, and then she got up from the table and knelt before me. She held my face in her hands, and then absently touched the bow in my hair, that I knew must be cockeyed – more like a baby bird clinging to the side of its nest, but she didn't try to straighten it, and said, "Dear, get the idea of going with us to see Mme. de la Rue out of your head."

"Please, Mamma," and I began praying very hard, letting the silver halo shine in my mind.

"No, Dear," Mamma said, shaking her head.

Then Uncle William said, with a small sigh, "You might just as well, Marie."

And so I came to be riding that day in the backseat of my Uncle William's car with Lloyd and Randolph.

I couldn't stop looking at the trees because their heavy green branches hanging over the road, almost touching the roof of the car, were so beautiful – a sky filled with bright, shiny leaves, as if we were driving into the very heart of the tree, deep inside the trunk. I wondered if perhaps that was where Mme. de la Rue really lived – I imagined a latch in the thick grey bark, and when I pulled on it, a door appearing, etched in the tree. Stepping through it, I would see, deep in the darkness below, a long, narrow spiral staircase that seemed to go endlessly down into the earth. It would be hard to descend the stairs of roughhewn stones, uneven, sloping downwards, and slippery from the moist earth. It wouldn't be dark, though, like the Creux Mahie, because the steps would shine like starlight – and as you came closer and closer to her house, at the bottom of the stairs, the glow from these rooms would illuminate the winding corridor of tiny, crooked stairs.

And when I imagined her house deep in the earth, I kept seeing a light grey mist swirling on a smooth, white floor and immense chairs encrusted with silver filigree and bright jewels. I shook my head a little at that because I suddenly realized that I was getting all the stories about what heaven looked like mixed up with Mme. de la Rue's cottage. There could not possibly be clouds swirling underneath the ground, or enough room for all those thrones I imagined.

"What's wrong, Lorley?" Randolph whispered.

I looked at him, tearing my gaze away from the trees. I hoped that I hadn't been shaking my head too hard, so lost in my daydream that I wasn't even seeing the leaves anymore, but only the strange, shining staircase and rooms filled with floating clouds.

"What do you mean?" I asked, feeling a bit desperate, knowing full well that if I acted too strangely, I could still be stopped from seeing Mme. de la Rue – although I wasn't sure what they could do with me at this point. They couldn't very well leave me in the car while they traipsed through the woods to Mme. de la Rue's cottage, but still, I didn't want to take any chances.

"You were shaking your head, back and forth," he said very quietly, so that Mamma and Uncle William couldn't hear.

"I kind of fell asleep, I think," I said, and it was pretty much the truth. Perhaps the trees, as we drew ever closer to Mme. de la Rue's cottage, were casting a spell on me with their clear, green light.

"Be careful, all right, Lorley?"

I nodded and stared down at my black walking boots. They reminded me of the iron shoes they nailed on the horses' hooves. Uncle William had insisted that we all wear our sturdiest boots because he had been told that it was quite a hike from the road to the cottage. Even Mamma had put on a pair of thick boots, so unusual for her, and they looked odd with the pale pink dress she wore.

I hoped that fixing my gaze on my boots would keep my daydreams at a distance, weigh them down with heavy soles.

But I knew that I couldn't keep them away for long, because we were in Mme. de la Rue's magical land now, and I was certain that I could feel her gazing down through the bright green leaves, even when I wasn't looking.

***

Marie was thankful that the children were so quiet – even Lorley, who was staring hard at her boots. She wondered what was going through her little girl's mind as she looked at her black laces.

Sitting snugly in the back seat, with Randolph on one side and Lloyd on the other, Lorley seemed as happy as if she were going to a party. She was wearing her best dress and white stockings, and although she had been a bit dismayed to learn that she had to wear her chunky boots with the thick soles, she had complied readily enough, not wanting anything to stop her from going to see Mme. de la Rue.

The truth was, Marie herself had cringed a bit when she put on her own walking boots. They felt so heavy on her feet, and she wasn't sure how well she could make her way through the thick woods to the woman's cottage. But when William arrived that morning, he said that she would be grateful to be wearing the boots when they were hiking through the underbrush, and she shuddered inwardly, thinking of the dark leaves, as heavy as ropes, the stems writhing over the ground, the mice and the snakes that lurked there, silently, ready to flash into such swift life.

At first, when he arrived, she thought that he was angry with her for pressuring him to take her to the South Shore – as he silently took the coffee she made for him, his eyes avoiding hers.

She said, then, "Thank you, William, for doing this for me. I know you don't think it's the wisest thing to do, but I really do appreciate you going along with it."

"Marie, it's fine, really," he said quickly.

"But I know how busy you are – that I'm taking you away from your work to do this."

He shook his head, still not looking at her, and after a long moment of silence, said, "You know I want to help you in any way I can, Marie. Going to the South Shore isn't the issue."

"But what is it, William?" she said, but before he answered, she suddenly knew.

"The Royal Guernsey Light Infantry is in France now, Marie."

"But they can't be in the trenches yet?"

"No," he said, shaking his head slowly. "I don't think so. Abram isn't fighting yet."

And then he looked at her, his eyes carefully exploring her face, knowing that he had to tell her everything. "Marie – I will be going soon – perhaps within a month. They're in desperate need of doctors."

"But there isn't really anyone else to do the surgeries here – except Dr. Monet, and he's over seventy now."

"Paul Monet said he can manage. The fact is, Marie, that many of the English doctors have been in France for too long, and they need to return home."

She looked at him, and the silence filled the room; only the clock could be heard ticking, and she wished, suddenly, that she could take the long, golden hands, hands that were moving too quickly on the stark, white face, and push them back, and back, far enough back so that the War had never begun, and Abram was home with her.

But the clock kept ticking, and there was nothing else to do but to keep going, the clock uncaring as it etched the seconds, and the minutes, and the hours, scratching tiny black lines on a wide, empty canvas.

She shook her head, willing herself to let such thoughts go, just as she told her small daughter to do when her mind seemed to become such a whirling dervish. Looking at William, no longer hearing the thin golden hands moving, but instead turning towards the bright yellow light shining through the kitchen window, she said, "We'll wait to tell the children."

Standing by the stone hearth, William stared at her, and she knew he was most likely thinking how fragile she looked – like a china figurine that had fallen off one of the high shelves on the mantel but had somehow remained intact. He had told her that before. Then she said, sounding surprisingly strong, "And William, thank you for taking me to the South Shore today. It's what I need to do, more than ever."

Now, after driving in the car for a short while, she felt her spirits rising. Perhaps it was being in the green loveliness of the woods. It was incredible to her that, after hearing what William had to tell her that morning, only a few short hours ago, she could feel any happiness at all.

But she did. And the closer they drew to the cottage, buried deep in the woods, the better she felt.

It was as if, somehow, the strange, silver woman could draw hope from the deep green leaves and pour it into her heart.

The road ended in the sea.

As the dirt road narrowed, becoming not much more than a path winding through the heavy woods, it seemed as if our car would soon be able to go no farther. There was no longer a stone wall beside us, but only trees with thick, black trunks, their branches extended like mighty antlers high overhead, their leaves no longer bright green the way they had been when we were first on the road, but much darker, as though this part of the forest was older.

Here the ferns grew in wild profusion, spreading in plumes and flourishes against the heavy bark of the trees, like great waves crashing against the rocks, arcs of sea foam cascading on the shore. With their long fronds caressing the black bark, the deeper darkness of the trees made the ferns, the only flash of colour in the darkness, seem even brighter.

And beneath the aged trees, everywhere there were moss covered stones and vines with twisted leaves that streamed over the ground, vines that seemed to go on forever, like an endless labyrinth.

I tried to peer deeper into the forest, knowing that no bluebells could be among these trees. There wasn't enough light, but I hoped that surely, in these woods, some flowers must grow – perhaps something with long, silver petals, and leaves that stuck out like stars – just beyond my vision.

I found it hard to believe that I was drawn to the dark woods so much. Usually, I would be frightened. The thought of the Creux Mahie still terrified me; our black stove could still have a devil lurking there if I looked at it the wrong way.

But not these woods. I could not stop gazing into the darkness, for nothing in these twilight woods seemed completely still. Everything seemed to be moving ever so slightly, even though there was no wind. Deep in my heart, I thought it must be Mme. de la Rue's magic flowing through the leaves and the ferns and the rocks.

Truly, Mme. de la Rue felt very close, like the silver flowers that I couldn't quite see.

And then our car suddenly burst out of the dark woods into a great expanse of sea and sky.

And it seemed as if we must have driven over the cliff.

For a moment, I believed that Mme. de la Rue's magic had taken over our car and done exactly that. Being in the middle of the back seat, I couldn't yet see that our car was simply very near the edge of the cliff. So, for a sliver of time, I revelled in thinking that Mme. de la Rue's magic was working on us now – like a sudden gleam of silver blue – like the flash of a hummingbird in a lilac bush.

Mamma uttered a short cry, and I knew that she, too, had the feeling that we were suspended in midair between the sea and the open sky, in a space filled with dazzling light.

And Uncle William, who had seemed so burdened all day, now smiled widely and said, his eyes taking in the beauty all around him, "We're almost there."

Lloyd was staring up into the sky, and then down, and I leaned over Randolph and saw how the edge of the steep cliff fell precipitously down, to the shore strewn with heavy rocks. Both my brothers seemed mesmerized by what was before them. Randolph could only have had more happiness on his face if our car really had driven over the cliffs and was flying through the sky.

"That's a tight space, Uncle William," Randolph called out, peering through his open window, looking over the side as far as he could.

"Be careful, Randolph," Mamma said, turning in her seat, reaching out her slender arm, holding his shoulder.

I reached out also – my arm, like Mamma's, looked very white against his dark shirt and trousers, and we would have been powerless to stop him from falling out of the window if he had stretched out too far. But the opening wasn't wide enough for someone even as wiry and agile as Randolph to get through. It made my heart lurch a little, though, especially when I pressed against his shoulder to look at the cliff face that fell so sharply to the rocks below, as if it had been gouged out of the earth with a heavy knife.

"How are we going to turn around?" Randolph said then, and I suddenly imagined my uncle trying to drive backwards through the woods, and it seemed like something that could only happen in the strangest of fairy tales.

"There's enough room," Uncle William said. "When we get out of the car, you'll see that we're not as close to the edge of the cliff as it seems."

Mamma looked out of her window, and then at Uncle William. "That's a sheer drop – almost three hundred feet."

He nodded his head as he stopped the car, pulling on the brake with a long screech. "It is, but when we get out, you'll see that there's a stone wall, and at this part of the cliff, the incline isn't quite as bad before it drops off to the sea."

He turned to us in the back seat. "But get out carefully. You children are used to the cliffs in St. Saviour's, but here on the South Shore, they're much steeper."

Randolph had his hand on the door, and he looked ready to burst out of the car.

Lloyd, though, leaned over me and, putting his hand on Randolph's arm, said, "I'll go first."

"Yes," Uncle William said, "You get out with me, Lloyd, and you, Lorley, take my hand. Randolph, you stay beside your Mamma."

It was at that moment that everything seemed not completely real, as if I were in a dream and I couldn't quite wake up, even though I kept trying to surface from the light waves of sleep lapping over me.

How could it be that my Uncle William, with my Mamma, had driven me, with my brothers, to this place on the island, a plateau on a rock face that dropped dangerously to the sea?

And it was all because Mamma wanted to see Mme. de la Rue!

Up to this point in my life, such things would have only happened in my storybooks.

It was hard to believe that Mamma was even letting us get out of the car here, I thought. And then, as the bright light filled the car, and I knew that I couldn't be dreaming in so much sunshine, I wondered if something had happened on that ride through the dark woods, if Mme. de la Rue had cast a spell over Mamma and Uncle William.

I got out of the car, taking the large, warm hand of my uncle, looking into his face as deeply as I could, trying to see any signs of magical power that had taken root there, but I saw only his smiling face. That was startling enough, considering how unhappy he had seemed when we began our journey.

I looked all around me, standing on the high plateau, a rock balcony overlooking the sea. On the edge of the precipice, there was the stone wall, high enough to stop me from tumbling over the edge, and even our car would have had a hard time driving over it, so Uncle William was right when he said that it was safe.

But the wall seemed so insignificant on the cliffs, where the magnificent rock plummeted into the sea. The granite formed deep ridges at the bottom, where even the moss and the lichens couldn't grow, the bare rock clawing at the water as if a great grey beast truly dwelt under the cliffs, reaching for its prey in the turquoise sea.

On the sheer, majestic rock face, the wall was nothing more than a ruffle. It looked as if it had been there for a long time, and it was sturdy enough, for on this great height, there was only the wind to wear it away. The wall, made of shards of granite, sticking into the sky like a snaggle-toothed mouth, its jaws gaping open, could never be touched by the foaming sea far below. But somehow, it still reminded me of something built as a lark one summer day, like a sandcastle on Rocquaine Bay, something you left behind for the sea to slowly wash away.

"This is beautiful, William. I have never been to this part of the South Shore," Mamma said, as her gaze swept over the cliffs and the strange rock wall.

"It's a very isolated part of the island. There are no beaches, and the cliffs are too treacherous to climb without special gear," Uncle William said, holding my hand firmly in his own. I knew that there was no way that I could take even a baby step closer to the wall, even though I wanted to touch it, to feel its sharp rock teeth, to pretend that it really was a wild beast sleeping in the sun with its mouth wide open, to dare to touch its ferocious jaws.

"Who do you think built this wall, and the road through the forest?" Mamma said.

Uncle William shrugged. "I have no idea. I first saw this when I came to see that poor Dugas woman. Perhaps your Mme. de la Rue did." He said the words lightly, and I knew that he didn't really mean it – although as his words washed through my mind, it all seemed to make perfect sense to me.

I could easily imagine her, standing on this grey rock, her feet bare, her long, beautiful hair falling past her waist, looking as if she herself had just emerged from the cliff face, the hard surface of the granite shimmering suddenly and releasing her from its depths. And she would use her magic to build the wall, her good magic, magic that kept people safe from plummeting to their deaths.

Mamma looked as if she, too, thought it was possible, because she smiled only slightly, and then gazed at the sea and then high into the sky, in one long sweep. I looked, too, at the brilliant expanse of turquoise light, where the sea and the sky seemed to almost become one.

I understood the need for a wall. The water and the sky were too beautiful, beckoning you forward to float in that soft blue world. Uncle William was squeezing my hand particularly hard. Like Mamma and Papa, he seemed to know what dangerous thoughts could dance in my head.

When I looked at Randolph, I knew that he felt exactly as I did. Standing beside Mamma, his whole body looked like a coiled spring ready to fly into the air – not that he would ever get as carried away as I could, but I knew that it was taking all of his willpower not to let go of Mamma's hand and lean far over the edge.

But he stayed close to Mamma, his hazel eyes filled with the sky and the sea – he knew that she needed him to be beside her.

Lloyd didn't need anyone's hand to hold him back. He stood beside me, looking at the high cliffs, his large, quiet eyes staring intently at the gleaming rock slashed from the earth, rising so impossibly high from the sea.

"Where is her house?" he said, turning to Uncle William.

I suddenly felt as if I really had been flying, like one of the seabirds over Rocquaine Bay, my feathers like white icing in the sky – Lloyd's question brought me back to earth with a little thump, and I was no longer a lighter than air bird, but a girl in heavy walking boots once again.

I could feel Mme. de la Rue's presence here as much as I did in the woods. More than ever, I could see her building the stone wall – it just seemed to be something that she would do one early morning, slowly, carefully, piling the rocks in the grey dawn, and then disappearing into the trees, her work done.

Uncle William pointed at the forest, to the heavy woods that grew almost to the edge of the rock face. "I was told that her house isn't too long a trek into the woods – on the edge of the cliff, they say, to the west from here," and he pointed towards the dark, thick forest, the trees so close together, their branches melding together, deep green draperies that would shut out the light from the sky.

"Is there a path through the woods here?" Mamma said, as she stared at the trees.

"That's what Rev. Pelletier told me. The only path I knew was to Dugas's hovel, to the east of here."

Mamma wrinkled her brow, saying, "How would he know, William?"

I looked at my brothers, waiting for them to explain that Rev. Pelletier knew more about witches and devils and just plain evil than anyone in Guernsey, it seemed. I could tell by their eyes that they were about to tell Mamma that when Uncle William said quickly, "The man has made himself something of an expert on these so-called healers."

"I have heard that," Mamma said, and looking at the cliffs and the forest that spread all around us, said, "But I can't imagine him coming here."

Uncle William shook his head. "Oh, he hasn't. He just seems to spend a lot of time talking to people who have."

Lloyd and Randolph were listening intently to everything Uncle William said; they would want to tell all this to Reginald and Herbert. I felt relieved to learn that Rev. Pelletier had never actually been in this place. It would be too much for him – he was very tall, but so awfully thin; his wrists, when he waved his arms delivering a sermon, were like twigs with all the bark stripped away, the bones protruding, looking as if they were about to burst through his parchment skin. The thought of him, with his spidery legs and stooped shoulders, and his shiny black suit, trying to drive on that winding road and make his way through the forest, was troubling. He would get himself hurt, possibly tumble right off the cliff, his long legs spiralling in the air like some crazed seabird.

Uncle William, still holding my hand tightly, looked at Mamma and the boys and said, "You stay together. I'll lead the way."

Then, with one last look at the car and the strange parapet of rock jutting out from the forest, we turned and walked into the heavy woods of tall oaks, sycamores, and elms, on a path so narrow that it was barely there.

I glanced back at Mamma, and, for the first time that day, I saw fear on her face.

Uncle William must have sensed it, because, suddenly turning around, he said, "Are you sure you want to do this?" His voice didn't sound frightened at all – his whole mood seemed to have lightened with each hour that passed that day.

Mamma hesitated, and I knew she was struggling now –

and I wanted to cry out, "But it's Mme. de la Rue. Don't be scared!"

But then Mamma's face looked calm again, and she said, "I need to do this, William."

The forest was not quiet. I wasn't sure what animals lived there, but I could hear things scurrying through the underbrush. I could imagine their tiny brown feet with razor-sharp claws, sinewy tails whipping behind them, teeth too large for their furry mouths. And I feared there must be animals, even more dangerous, near me that didn't make any sound at all, but lay silently in the thick ground cover – or, perhaps, stood poised in one of the tall trees, watching us pass through.

Now, and I couldn't quite understand it, Mme. de la Rue felt very far away.

I wondered if my uncle was going the wrong way. I knew, after all, that Rev. Pelletier could get things mixed up terribly sometimes.

"We stay on this path for about a mile, not much farther, and then we should be at the house." Uncle William's voice was quiet, as if he didn't want to disturb whatever lurked in the woods.

No one spoke, but then Randolph said, "It's getting steep. Her house must be up pretty high." His voice was low, like Uncle William's. I turned around to look at him and saw how intently he was staring into the woods, which were growing darker and thicker with every step we took. He was walking very close to Mamma, and Lloyd was on her other side, and I could tell that both were trying to protect her.

Nodding his head at Randolph, Lloyd looked up at the trees that grew so high into the sky, the leaves blending together, a heavy dark green veil filtering the light, filling the woods with long shadows. He said, his voice hushed, like Uncle William's, "I've heard that she lives on the highest point on the island." He spoke quietly, his words trailing off, and the forest seemed to grow louder.

I peered into the woods all around us. The path was getting quite steep, the trees seeming to move closer and closer together as if they were forming a phalanx, their branches poised, like soldiers in their green uniforms, ready for battle.

And I suddenly realized that I hadn't thought of my Papa yet that day. In the excitement of seeing Mme. de la Rue, my mind so full of the beautiful silver woman, I had stopped missing him that morning. At that moment, I was thankful for the dark woods to hide my shame.

I looked back, then, at Mamma, at her face as she trudged along in her heavy boots, her dress as pale as a butterfly in the dark woods. Her eyes seemed very far away. And I knew, I knew somehow from that one glance at her face, as if I had Mme. de la Rue's magical powers, that all she was thinking about was Papa. And that, for some reason that I could not understand, she was doing all this for him today.

The path became even steeper, as if we were climbing a cliff.

No one was talking now. The trees on either side of us

were dense, and the sounds in the underbrush were growing louder. Whatever creatures dwelt there, I thought, must be very large.

And it was not just my imagination – of that, I was absolutely sure. Even Uncle William, now, looked around sharply whenever he heard a noise in the woods.

I told myself to stare straight ahead, to think of Mme. de la Rue at the end of all this, waiting for us in an aura of silver light, a star high above the dark night of the forest.

And then there was a rush in the trees right beside us, and a creature leapt onto the path, arms reaching towards us, arms like long sharp hooks.

No one screamed. We stood, motionless, under the immense trees, the branches swaying slightly. Nothing else moved. Even the animals in the underbrush were suddenly quiet.

The woman who stood before us was still now – except for her eyes, which darted over each of us, never resting anywhere for more than a few seconds, like an animal trapped in a cage. Her eyes were dark mirrors, reflecting the colour of the trees all around us, full of the black forest. I couldn't look away, and so I watched with a dreadful fascination as her dark eyes slowly became colourless, milky white, like porcelain, as they rolled back into her head.

I looked at the old woman, so tall, at the great tangle of grey hair hanging over her shoulders like stringy rags. And at her torn dress, and her arms covered in long scratches, and the bright, fresh blood smeared on her forehead – or perhaps it was flowing there from another gash – I couldn't tell.

Her mouth was clenched in a grimace like one of the animals in the underbrush, teeth as brown as rat's fur, lips not much more than cracked red lines, veins that were bleeding out. Suddenly, she opened her jaws very wide. I saw a tongue like a long tail slithering around her teeth, and then she stuck it out of her mouth in a jagged scream.

And as the awful sound filled the woods, as if the dark branches, too, were screaming along with the terrible creature before us, I felt only a great sadness.

Because surely some black curse had befallen Mme. de la Rue, and the creature before me was what had become of the beautiful silver woman.

chapter
nine

ABRAM WATCHED the other men in the trenches scribbling on sheets of paper in the dusk, trying to catch the last of the light.

Ever since the sergeant announced that the men would now be able to send letters home, Abram had thought of little else.

It had only been a few days ago when Sgt. McCauley, holding a package of pristine writing paper, waving it in front of them as they sat pressed together in the trench, had told them, self-importantly, that the British Army had a system in place for delivery of the mail. He had paused after he spoke, waiting, perhaps, for cheers from the men.

Fool, Abram had thought at the time. The sergeant had a ridiculous moustache, no more than a licorice strip on his upper lip, carefully, ludicrously trimmed. Abram wondered how long McCauley would be able to keep that moustache, living in the trenches, in the long, narrow holes carved out of the earth – the dry earth, thankfully dry, at least for now. The powdery dirt, he knew, was better than the mud, but it caked their faces and their hands and their uniforms and found its way into their mouths, and their eyes. That was the worst – because you could spit it out when the fine earth was in your mouth, but when it was in your eyes, you could do very little. Your hands were too filthy; when you rubbed them on your stinging eyes, it just became worse.

So, how the sergeant tended his little strip of moustache, Abram had no idea. He wasn't a Guernseyman, but an Englishman from London, assigned temporarily to their trench. To show them how to manage, he said. They couldn't wait to get rid of him.

When he had stood before them with the writing paper, Abram had stared at the pompous little man, and at the shining white package so incongruous in the filthy trench, with a kind of wonder.

At first, the thought of sending a letter to Marie and the children had filled him with a kind of joy he hadn't thought was possible in the trenches.

But the initial euphoria was soon replaced by the awful truth that he didn't want them to know anything about the hell that he was living.

The hell of fighting just to stay alive in the trench. Like a great grave, the trench snaked through the earth with the other rows of trenches, a cemetery without headstones, open to the merciless sky. It was filled with writhing, faceless men, all desperate to survive the shrapnel and the bullets and the shells and the gas.

But then, the more he thought about it, and agonized over it, he realized that if he could send a letter to Reginald and Herbert only, one that Marie and the rest of his children wouldn't see, he would be writing it at that moment, filling the bright white paper with all the horrors, the black ink flowing from his pen like the blood of dying soldiers.

Because that was what his life was now – seeing men die.

And he wanted his eldest sons – so desperate to fight in the War, the War that they thought was all glorious men, valiant in battle – to know what it was truly like – so that they would never dream again of being soldiers.

He knew that he would not be able to find the words that could express how awful it really was, but if he could be certain that Marie and his other three children would not see the letter, he would do the best he could to fill those pristine, absurdly white pages with the filthy truth of the War.

He would start with the rats, the brown rats, and the black rats, that infested the trenches. Strangely, it was the brown ones that grew so large, many the size of cats, grotesque things that gorged themselves on the corpses; they especially liked the eyes and the liver. And the rats ballooned in size; their fur grew luxuriantly thick.

Yes, he would tell Reginald and Herbert that, and he would also explain, not sparing them a single detail, that the rats would never run out of food because already there were hundreds and thousands of corpses in No Man's Land, and so many, hundreds, were added each day, that even though a single rat, he was told, could produce nine hundred offspring each year, the brown rats would never be hungry.

And it was so easy for them. They barely had to dig with their yellow claws, claws as long as fingers, because the graves were so shallow, a thin layer of dirt covering the faces of the dead, not much thicker than the cloth that the mothers of the dead boys used on their kitchen tables.

There was no time to bury them in real graves; their

shovels were needed for the trenches. So, they had to leave the dead blue eyes staring, sightless, through a patina of dirt, to the rats, who fed on them as if they were ripe berries.

He shook his head, telling himself that he dare not go that far.

But then he thought, if it stopped his sons from wanting to fight in the War, shredded those dreams as mercilessly as the rats tore apart human flesh, then he would write about such horrors and send the letter, and pray that the rest of his family would not read his words.

He wanted to believe that the War would end long before Reginald and Herbert were old enough to fight. But, God forbid, if it didn't, he had to start warning them now. About the putrefying corpses in No Man's Land. How they filled that great sea of despair, the islands of corpses growing higher and higher, the maggots swarming like obscene fish. And how they needed fresh young men to fill the ranks, younger and younger, like Reginald and Herbert. Yes, he had to warn them.

Because it was dangerous, very dangerous, to arrive at the Front with dreams of valiant battle shining in bright blue eyes.

Abram had already seen what happened to them.

Some didn't last a single day.

He would never forget the boy from St. Martin's Parish in Guernsey, the LePage boy, who had proudly told him that he had turned eighteen that very year. Abram had tried to help him as much as he could in the training camp. There the boy's shining eyes made Abram fear, badly, for the lad. And then, seeing the boy's clumsy hands as he tried to fire a gun properly, Abram didn't know how he was ever going to manage – but he improved a little in those few short months.

But he didn't last a single day.

He didn't keep his head down.

They had all been told, again and again, to resist peering over the parapet of the trench into No Man's Land. Strangely, and Abram had felt it, you wanted to look, to see with your own eyes that still, desolate, quiet space between you and the enemy, to try to see if the Germans were really there.

The LePage boy did that, his baby blue eyes wide when the Sniper's bullet hit him in the neck.

Abram wasn't close enough to him to hold him while he died, but Royer was beside him and cradled him in his arms, pressing his hand against the soft, white neck, powerless to stop the great gush of blood.

Before they buried him, Abram managed to get one last look at the boy's face, and he saw then how light the boy's beard was, barely there, not as heavy as Reginald's.

Now, as he thought about the warning he must send to his eldest sons, he told himself that nothing would be too awful to tell them. And the longer he wrestled with it in his mind, the more certain he was that he must risk mailing the letter.

He had to tell them about the soft white neck, with its scarf of blood.

Reginald couldn't stop thinking about what Uncle William told him before he left that morning.

His uncle was going to the War in France, most likely in the next month.

Reginald could barely stand it.

Here he was, almost fifteen years old, and as tall and strong as the lads who were fighting in the Royal Guernsey Light Infantry in France, like real men.

And he was working on the farm, day after day after day, while the War was being fought, the War where the brave men were doing their part.

While he was picking grapes, other Guernsey fellows, no more than a few years older than he was, were fighting in the War. Some of them could even become heroes. At least they had the chance, and he believed a chance like that probably came once in a lifetime. He twisted off a ripe cluster with his quick, deft hands and carefully placed it in a bushel basket. He could not remember ever feeling so unhappy with his life.

As he looked at the darkly shining grapes, at the vines that had always held a kind of wonder for him, he realized, suddenly, how much he hated them now. Last year at this time, when he stood on the back porch with Papa, looking at the grapes, purplish-black and as soft as velvet, the gold-edged leaves curling in the sun, he had promised Papa that he would always take very good care of the farm.

Now, after hearing that Uncle William was going to the Front, he felt, just as he had a few short nights ago, that all he wanted to do was leave, leave these rows and rows of grapevines behind and fight in the War. It was where he belonged.

He couldn't stop thinking about the night when he had been determined to leave and enlist at the recruitment office in Vale. He still struggled mightily with what he had finally decided to do. If not for Herbert, he knew he would have left for the War that night.

But he had stayed behind.

He was deeply unhappy, and now, knowing that Mamma and the children had gone to the South Shore to see that de la Rue, he felt even worse. He didn't agree with any of it.

Despite his Uncle William's assurances, he believed that those old women who lived there were dangerous. Strange stories about them abounded on the island. Farmers who went to the South Shore for cures came back with such queer tales about these women, living in their odd, dilapidated cottages, making freakish potions from inedible plants and, some even claimed, from the vermin that dwelt in their houses.

It was Rev. Pelletier who said the old women were descendants of the witches from four hundred years ago, when they burnt witch hags at the stake in St. Peter Port. Without a doubt, the Reverend told Reginald and the other St. Saviour's boys, these cunning women worshipped the devil, dancing in the woods stark naked, their hideous wrinkled skin exposed, hair hanging to their knees like long, grey weeds, writhing in the woods like reptiles. Reginald did not really believe they were witches. But he believed they were evil.

That morning, as soon as his Uncle William arrived, Reginald tried once more to dissuade him from going to the South Shore, telling him, again, about the weird old women. But he had barely begun recounting all the horrors that Rev. Pelletier had shared when he stopped, suddenly aware that his uncle didn't seem to be listening to him at all. And he also saw a great sadness in his face that he had never seen before.

"What's wrong?" he asked. "Is it about going to see that de la Rue?"

His uncle looked at him, staring at him with solemn eyes, and shook his head.

"Because, Uncle William, you know that you don't have to go."

"No, Reginald, it's not that." And that was when his uncle told him that Papa's Regiment was in France now and that he, himself, would be leaving for the Front, most likely within the next month. "They need doctors – they're desperate, Reginald."

"But don't you want to go?"

His uncle shrugged his shoulders then and, looking at the vines, his voice sounding very far away, said, "It has nothing to do with wanting to go – I have to serve, there is no doubt in my mind about that – but I worry about leaving you all – your Mamma will need you more than ever, Reginald."

He nodded his head, looking down at the ground, at the soft brown earth on his shoes. He knew that he had to stay on the farm and work harder, even, than before. But at that moment, the horrible feeling descended on him, a suffocating heaviness, an awful realization, that his life was surely passing him by, that his chance to really prove himself, to fight for his country, was never going to happen, that his life would be as quiet and as ordinary as the purple grapes falling into the bushel basket.

He felt the morning sun on the back of his neck, his shirt collar already moist. Slowly, he took out his handkerchief, wiped off the sweat, and said, his voice flat, "You know I will look after Mamma and the children."

But his uncle seemed to know exactly what he was thinking because he said, "Reginald – I know how much you want to be part of the War."

"It will be over before I ever have the chance, Uncle." Try as he might, he couldn't keep the bitterness out of his voice, and he hated sounding like that, but he couldn't help it.

His uncle, though, looked at him kindly, putting his arm around his shoulder, and said, "It is a very bad War, Reginald. There's unspeakable suffering in those trenches, so many, many innocent lives lost."

Reginald pulled away from him, saying, "But that's why I want to fight, to do my part."

His uncle shook his head, saying, "You can't imagine the suffering, Reginald. Believe me, I hope and pray that the War will be over before you and Herbert ever have to serve."

Then his uncle walked into the house to get Mamma and the children to go to the South Shore.

Reginald had wanted to shout after his uncle, "I know all about the suffering – about the rats and the lice and the mustard gas. And the corpses, I know about the smell of the rotting flesh – I know about all of it, and I know that I can fight." He said nothing, though.

But he prayed that he would have the chance to be as brave as his Papa.

Always like his Papa.

chapter
ten

THE WOODS BEGAN MOVING AGAIN.

I looked away from the creature before me.

And saw a flash of bare shoulders and a tangle of grey hair in the thick leaves beside us.

The black trunks of the old oaks, sycamores, and elms were as heavy as the masts of great ships, the enormous branches swelling like sails high above – but around the trunks, dense bushes grew, with narrow, prickly leaves so that the forest was a nearly impenetrable wall of dark sinister green.

But I saw the wild burst of grey hair and the bare shoulders as white as the bones Mamma used for the potage. It was no more than a slash of a knife, the leaves moving apart so swiftly, the way a snake can suddenly appear by your feet in the long grass, and then vanish – a single moment of time that is there and gone in an instant.

I turned to Uncle William, to see if he had seen it, too, but he was still staring at the cursed creature before us, his eyes fixed on her terrible mouth, on the rat's tail tongue, stiff and awful as she screamed and screamed.

Then I heard the leaves rustle very suddenly on the other side of the path. Again, the movement was so quick, serpentine in the dense leaves, and gone in an instant, but I saw a swish of grey hair and, this time, a long neck.

My Uncle William was still transfixed on the creature before us, and when I looked back at Mamma and my brothers, they, too, were staring straight ahead.

I wanted to cry out, "There's more of them," but I couldn't make any sound come out of my mouth, nor could I move my legs. It was as though I was in a dream, helpless and paralyzed, as the world around me became a long scream.

I was desperate to let them know that there were more, desperate to try to save us all from what was swarming in the trees, a woods haunted and alive with possessed creatures.

But even in my horror, my mind dizzy with fear, I thought, with such great sorrow, what an almighty curse had befallen Mme. de la Rue, to transform her into all these crazed creatures lost in the woods, to shatter her into so many pieces.

A wild rustling in the woods made me turn around, and in that moment, long, filthy fingers, like gnarled roots, like tubers from deep in the ground, parted the thick green bush. A face jutted through, crazed, hunted eyes, worse even, than the creature who still stood before us screaming with the black trees – worse because the face suddenly before us vanished in an instant – a head without a body, there and gone so quickly, moving with a speed that couldn't be human.

Not without the power of black witchcraft.

Everyone saw the face, and Mamma cried out, "William – the children –"

He reached out and held us all close, still gripping my hand, his other arm around Mamma and the boys. And he said, his voice loud, fighting the screams of the poor creature before us, "Get away!"

As still as death now, the creature's milky white eyes closed. The only movement was in her mouth, jerking spasmodically as the scream slowly died into a long, low growl.

Glancing quickly at my brothers and at Mamma, I saw their bright eyes as they stared at the creature, a strange mix of fear and pity on their faces, as though a wounded animal was before them.

But at that moment, another creature jumped onto the path, landing on all fours, her bare feet clawing at the dirt path as if she were about to lunge at us like a wild beast. There were torn remnants of a rough tunic on her back, but not enough of it was left to cover her withered breasts and skeletal, ghost white legs.

Mamma looked as though she was about to scream – as the poor crazed creature, crouching on her hands and knees, her tangled grey hair dragging in the dirt, began crawling towards us.

Uncle William let go of us then, moving me very close to Mamma, and stood in front of us on the path, saying, "Stay calm. I won't let them harm you."

I looked at him, not knowing how in the world he could think that. We were in a woods nearly as dark as the Creux Mahie, with two terrible, possessed creatures before us, clearly cursed by some awful black sorcery, one of them moving closer and closer, inch by inch, and my Uncle William was telling us, in a voice now as quiet as if he were reading a story to us, that everything would be fine.

Next, I thought, feeling utterly lost, as if I had fallen into a world that didn't make any sense at all, my uncle would be tearing off his tweed jacket and white cravat, revealing that he was a witch also, ready to wield his magic to protect us.

Because at that point, I was ready for anything. Seeing these poor, demonic creatures, that surely had to be the remnants of beautiful Mme. de la Rue, I found – and this was perhaps the greatest shock of that day – that my fear was vanishing, not much more than a curl of grey smoke inside me, and I was being filled with a tremendous, tired sadness.

For Mme. de la Rue.

And what had happened to her.

Uncle William began walking towards the poor creatures, one arm raised before him, saying in a measured tone, "Stop. Stay where you are."

The one who was crawling kept moving, dragging her rough hands and feet in the dirt, looking at Uncle William with blank, uncomprehending eyes.

And the other one began screeching again, like a great wounded hawk, as if Uncle William had struck her with a quiver of arrows.

It was at that moment, despite the agonized, pitiful screams and Uncle William's commands, telling the creatures before us to stop, that I heard the voice.

A voice that I couldn't quite believe.

Because I had heard it when the bluebells began singing to me.

The silvery voice of Mme. de la Rue.

I looked up and saw her on the path far ahead.

I knew that it was the beautiful radiant woman – as I gazed in wonder at the luminous halo of hair falling over her shoulders.

In her long blue dress that fell past her feet, puddling on the forest floor, she appeared to be floating towards us, like the Blessed Virgin Mary coming down from heaven to save us all.

Marie saw her on the path right after Lorley.

She had been looking at her small daughter, at Lorley's eyes as she stared at the poor women before them, seeing the fear and, despite the horror of the screaming, the sadness there – too much for someone so young.

And then she saw Lorley's eyes open very wide, filled with a sudden joy and wonder, and Marie looked and saw the woman.

It was Mme. de la Rue. Even though Marie had only seen her once, she knew. With her grey hair falling past her waist, a shimmering veil that cast a silver aura around her, she moved, as she had when Marie last saw her, like an ancient queen through the forest.

In the distance, Marie couldn't see her face clearly, it was still too far, but she knew that her eyes would be as tranquil as the sea in the early evening, a light pearl grey.

The poor, terrible creatures were both screaming now, their voices coarse, ragged edged, their throats raw. They were very ill.

Marie wanted to try to comfort the aged, demented women, but they were in such a frenzied state that she knew she didn't possess the strength, and she also knew that these old women, tortured and senile, could be quite dangerous – more to themselves, than others, she was certain, but she had to keep the children away from them.

Lloyd, Randolph, and Lorley would think that they had walked into a coven of crazed witches, the suffering old women before them in the throes of some demonic possession. What these lost souls were doing, running like wild animals through the thick woods, Marie could not fathom, but she knew that the strange, silvery woman moving towards them, seeming to glide over the forest floor, was going to help these poor creatures.

William was watching Mme. de la Rue make her way down the path also – as he advanced towards the old woman still crawling pitifully in the dirt, his arms raised to restrain her.

"Please don't touch her! She will be too frightened," Mme. de la Rue called out, and at the sound of her voice, both women slowly stopped screaming and then became motionless, as if in a trance.

She heard Lorley whisper to the boys, very quietly, but Marie could hear what she said clearly, in these woods that were now as still as though some great magic really was at work: "She just cast a spell over them."

And Marie had to admit that it seemed that way – because it was nothing short of remarkable to see these old women suddenly become as quiet and meek as lambs, as if a sorcerer's wand had been swayed over their rough, grey heads, soothing their ravaged minds.

Then Mme. de la Rue was with the ragged creatures, like a soft veil falling over them, saying words Marie couldn't quite hear, but the sounds floated in the quiet woods, as gentle as a caress. Slowly, she raised the one on the ground to her feet, and held the other one close to her side.

William was watching intently, as he lowered his arms. Finally, he said, "Do you look after these women?" And Marie could hear the respect in his voice.

Brushing some of the dirt off the old woman who had been on all fours, keeping a tight hold on the other one, she nodded, looking quickly at William as she said, "Yes, ever since they became ill – I've had them live with me. It's been a while now."

"Do they run off like this often?" he said.

Marie saw Mme. de la Rue look sadly at the old women before she answered. "They never used to – it just started happening recently. I'm going to have to be more careful when I leave to gather my plants."

The old woman, who had been the first to appear, began moving restlessly, her face twitching, and Marie feared that another fit was about to seize hold of her. Quickly, Mme. de la Rue reached into a pocket in her long skirt and pulled out a vial. With one deft movement, she poured several drops of an oily substance into the old woman's jerking mouth.

"Laudanum?" William asked quietly.

Mme. de la Rue held the old woman's cheek, gently closing her mouth and stroking her throat. Marie could see the woman slowly swallow, and it seemed as if the tension that had been coiling in the poor creature's body was gone almost immediately. Then Mme. de la Rue did the same to the other old woman, who was becoming agitated as well.

"Stronger than laudanum, but from the *Papaver somniferum* plant."

Marie looked down at her children, who were gazing, spellbound, at Mme. de la Rue. It was as if they were all watching a play where a beautiful sorceress reveals her power. And what had happened that day did feel as if they had travelled to a fantastical land of magic and witchery.

But what surprised her even more was that now, as she watched Mme. de la Rue, an arm around each of the old women, begin slowly walking up the path, as gently as if she were cradling them against her breast, motioning them all to follow her with a slight nod of her head – what was really most surprising, was how beautifully real it all was.

I couldn't tell if a spell had been cast over me or not.

I did feel as though I was tingling all over, that the halo shimmering around Mme. de la Rue was all around me, too – but I didn't feel as if I had become silver. I felt that surely I must be pink, as pink as the petunias that looked like bright kisses in Mamma's garden. Or I could even be yellow and white, like the wild daisies by the cliffs, my face beaming in a blaze of sunny petals.

Slowly walking up the path to Mme. de la Rue's cottage, my brothers and I were behind Mamma and Uncle William – and that, in itself, made me feel as if surely some great magic was at work. For them to let go of our hands and let us follow them through these wild woods was hard to believe.

But then, with Mme. de la Rue leading the way, holding both the old women, her long arms outstretched over their bare shoulders, perhaps Mamma and Uncle William thought that everything frightening was ahead of us.

And I couldn't help thinking, exultation singing in my heart, that there was no possible way that Uncle William could see any harm in Mme. de la Rue now.

It now seemed, even, that once believing that she was the Blessed Virgin Mary wasn't so far off the mark, that this beautiful woman with hair like spun silver was about as close to the Blessed Virgin Mary as one could get on earth.

And looking at Mamma in front of me, at her lovely dark gold hair in the chignon coming loose, with the soft strands curling around her neck, and her creamy white skin, she seemed, in that moment, like an angel.

It was as if I had been staring so hard at a holy picture, at the swirls of white and gold and silver there, that I had fallen forward through the sparkly paper, and found myself gazing at heaven all around me.

I glanced at Randolph, whose face was lit up, as if he, too, saw what I did.

Leaning close to him, I whispered, "It's as if Mme. de la Rue is from heaven – like the Blessed Virgin Mary, isn't she?"

Lloyd heard me also. He and Randolph looked at me, a little startled, but then they both shook their heads, and Randolph, his eyes bright, said, "No, Lorley, I think she's the most powerful white witch in all of Guernsey."

Then, I thought, heaven must be full of white witches.

I didn't say anything to Randolph, but I kept staring straight ahead, unable to take my eyes off Mme. de la Rue.

The dark woods no longer frightened me. Even though the path had become very narrow, the black trunks, with their heavy branches, no longer seemed to have shiny, leathery leaves swaying like draperies that shut out the sky; the woods no longer felt as if awful beasts lurked there, watching us with malicious blood red eyes and sharp snouts.

Not with Mme. de la Rue leading the way.

The trees now welcomed us, their leaves breathing warmly, a forest of quiet velvet, a forest that was very still, as though everything in it was spellbound as Mme. de la Rue passed through.

We were all as silent as the woods, but when I managed to tear my eyes away from the silvery woman for a moment and look at my brothers, I saw that their eyes were alive with adventure, as if we were about to step into a cave even greater than the Creux Mahie.

As I watched them, I thought that I could hear the sea now. And I wondered if they heard it, too. But I didn't want to ask them, and break the spellbound silence.

So I shifted my gaze away from them, and looked straight ahead at the trees, listening to what surely must be the sea swirling beyond the stillness of the woods.

And then, very quickly, too quickly almost to believe, we emerged from the trees, and in that moment, it seemed as if the forest had released its hold on us, the enormous trees bowing down as Mme. de la Rue stepped forward into the clear sunlight. It felt as if the velvet trees were a great curtain that had been suddenly pulled aside.

Before me was Mme. de la Rue's house.

High on a cliff overlooking the sea, her house seemed to grow out of the ground. Even though we were now out of the thick forest, there were still clusters of tall trees with pale grey bark and leaves as sparkling as jewels. As they rustled in the sea breeze, the sound of the leaves and the water were almost indistinguishable, as if they were one.

There was no longer a path, but soft vines growing in rich green profusion over the ground, our shoes sinking ankle-deep. I would have loved to have gone barefoot through that soft tapestry of leaves, like Mme. de la Rue.

Her house was alive with green leaves. It rose, on the edge of the high cliff, the vines covering the peaked roof, the two chimneys, and the high walls, as if it were a house built not with stone but entirely of brilliant green leaves, broad lustrous leaves, like lily pads. Only the mullioned windows peered through the bright foliage, their gables also covered, like enormous green eyebrows.

And in that moment, I heard the bluebells.

It was just a few notes, a few sweet, almost impossibly beautiful notes, and my heart leapt.

Very quickly, I looked around me. It didn't surprise me that Mme. de la Rue would have bluebells growing by her house. I doubted that she would even have to plant them – I could imagine petals fluttering through the air like sapphire butterflies, flying high all the way to the South Shore, and then taking root in Mme. de la Rue's land.

Her light would draw the petals to her like a great silver sun.

But strangely, as my gaze swept over the tall, grey trees and the thick vines that spread over the ground, and the brilliant green leaves that covered the house, I couldn't see bluebells growing anywhere. Still, I heard their song – just a few notes that would start and stop again, a joyful sound that remained in my heart even when the song ceased for those moments.

Perhaps, I thought, the bluebells were behind her house, that even though the house was built on the edge of the cliff, there was enough land there for bluebells to grow – bluebells so bright that they flowed into the sea and sky.

I wanted to ask Mme. de la Rue, but I didn't want to call out to her when she was helping the two old women climb the hill.

I would ask her later, I told myself, as my eyes swept over the emerald green leaves of her house, gleaming in the sunlight.

And in that moment, the song so beautiful in my heart became stronger, no longer stopping and starting, but a lovely stream of joyful notes.

A song, I suddenly realized, that did not come from bluebells at all, but from the brilliant leaves.

From a heaven that felt very close.

A heaven that shone sapphire blue when the bluebells sang, and emerald green when the leaves came to life with their music.

I looked at Mme. de la Rue as she stood before her grey door, a door that was the same radiant silver as her hair. No leaves grew over the moulding, but curled around it like a lace edged frame.

Even the door seemed magical, and for a moment, I wondered if it, too, would sing like a heaven that had floated down to Guernsey.

Perhaps, as thick and heavy as the door seemed, it would suddenly become a mass of ripples, a mirror, and we would shimmer through it – as we heard a song of silver.

———

Marie stood back with the children as Mme. de la Rue opened the large, grey door. It looked as though it was the entrance to a medieval castle, one thick enough to barricade against the enemy. As she pulled it open, she let go of the woman who had been screaming so terribly – now as silent as a deer in the forest – and she continued holding the other woman. Marie expected to hear the hinges screech loudly.

But the heavy door opened without a sound, and Mme. de la Rue stood with the two sick old women close beside her and, bowing slightly, gestured with a graceful sweep of her arm for Marie and William and the children to enter.

For a moment, Marie hesitated, uncertain about entering this strange house of leaves, wondering what it would actually be like inside. Perhaps, she thought, the vines would cover every inch of the interior walls as well, the floor soft and brown, like the fields at home, with tiny creatures scuttling in the earth.

She knew there would be herbs and ointments and cures; there had to be. It was now clearer than ever to Marie that Mme. de la Rue was a healer and no witch, although these naturopathic healers were often called white witches by the country people in Guernsey, and by many in St. Peter Port.

Then, taking a deep breath, Marie smelled the medicines, ripe and deeply pungent, and soothing – for blending with the scent was that of a meadow in high summer, of tall plants, dry and heavy with seedpods.

She looked at William, who was staring intently at the old women now nestled against Mme. de la Rue. She was surprised by the admiration she saw in his eyes. But then, he had often told her how hard it was to treat those afflicted with senility or any kind of lunacy. Mostly, they were locked away, left in agony and isolation until they died.

Lorley pulled at her skirt, a gentle tug. She looked down at her daughter, into her blue green eyes, that were shining as though she was about to step into heaven.

"Mamma, she's waiting for us," Lorley said, in a hushed voice, and Marie then took her daughter's hand, nodding softly at Mme. de la Rue as she and Lorley walked through the door. Glancing back, she saw William and the boys following them into the house.

What amazed Marie, as she looked at the large kitchen, was how ordinary it seemed. As in any Guernsey farmhouse, iron pots, bowls, and pewter pitchers, along with woven baskets, hung from the wooden beams in the ceiling. The long table, made of wide planks, was pushed against one wall, already arranged with three mugs, a large pitcher positioned neatly in the centre. All were the soft caramel colour of glazed clay. Underneath the pitcher, there was a narrow piece of linen that extended the entire length of the table, and Marie could see tiny designs embroidered on the cloth, quite intricate stitches in red, black, and silver threads. Across from the table and chairs, there was a wide stone mantel with a bright chintz ruffle. Marie saw that nothing at all was queer about this cloth, with its pattern of little yellow flowers. And there were wicker chairs pulled close to the granite hearth, with an empty soup pot resting cozily on the wood and peat. It was as warm and comforting as any kitchen in the Guernsey countryside.

"Please, sit down. I will make you tea just as soon as I get Cecile and Jeanne cleaned and resting," Mme. de la Rue said as she led the old women into the kitchen. Then she reached for a large basin that hung from the ceiling.

Marie looked at the old women, who now stood docilely, staying very close to Mme. de la Rue, their eyes fixed on her. It seemed incomprehensible that these were the same old women who had been running like crazed, wild beasts in the woods – she would never have believed that any medicine in the world could cause such a transformation. If she hadn't seen it with her own eyes, she would have said that it was impossible.

She glanced at William and knew that he was wrestling with the same thoughts. Staring intently at the old women, and especially at Mme. de la Rue, his gaze unwavering, he said, "Do you need any help?"

Mme. de la Rue shook her head gently, and Marie saw how her long silver hair rippled with the slightest movement. "No, but thank you. They are used to me." She quickly filled the basin with water from her pump, and walked quietly into the next room, the old women following her, instinctively it seemed, like lambs with their shepherd.

They were still standing by the door, the boys beside William, with Lorley very close to Marie, leaning against her skirt. She didn't think that she could ever remember her children being so quiet.

But it wasn't a fearful silence.

And then William ushered them forward.

Marie watched Lorley walk into the room as though she was floating in a bright, blue sky, gazing in wonder all around her.

chapter
eleven

MME. de la Rue did not take long.

Marie could hear her in the next room, speaking in low, soothing tones to the old women. She couldn't make out what she was saying; her voice was too soft, and muffled by the sound of a cloth being dipped into the basin of water. The old women still didn't say anything, not that Marie could hear, but occasionally they made faint sounds, the kind that came from inside your throat, not of pain, but gentle mews of comfort.

And then came the sound of the old women lying down, the rustle of straw mattresses and bed sheets, Mme. de la Rue, her voice a bit louder now, saying, "There, let me pull the blanket over your shoulders."

Strangely, Marie felt now as though she was in the hospital in St. Peter Port where William performed his surgeries, sitting outside one of the wards listening to a Nursing Sister minister to an ailing patient – although Marie could not remember ever hearing such tenderness in a Sister's voice.

She sat beside William on one of the wicker chairs, with Lorley sitting on her knee, poised so lightly, like a butterfly on the edge of a petal ready to flutter away. Marie held her a little more closely, but Lorley seemed not to notice at all, for she was staring with such rapt attention at the entrance to the room where Mme. de la Rue was caring for the old women. It seemed to Marie that her daughter's whole body was trembling a little – fearless quivers, amazement spread over her tiny face.

William, too, was staring at the next room, at a kind of drapery strung across the doorway made of brightly coloured beads, his eyes quiet and intense. Lloyd and Randolph, like William, were also silent, as they sat at the table. But Randolph's eyes were restless, darting around the room. She watched as his gaze fixed on the cloth running the length of the table. Suddenly, he nudged Lloyd, pointing at the cloth, and said in a low voice that Marie could just barely hear, "Look at the stars, and moons, I think."

Lloyd turned and began studying them closely. "Those are pentacles, and elven stars."

"What?" Randolph said, shifting in his seat to peer at the cloth. Marie began rising from her seat, and then Mme. de la Rue walked back into the room.

Both Lloyd and Randolph stopped examining the cloth as soon as she entered. Mme. de la Rue simply looked at the boys, though, and then at Lorley, and said, with a small, kind smile on her face, "Would you like a mug of apple cider?"

Without taking another look at the cloth, Lloyd and Randolph nodded, saying, "Thank you," and Lorley slipped off Marie's knee immediately, joining the boys. As she, also, thanked Mme. de la Rue, she looked at her with adoring eyes, and it seemed to Marie as though her little girl was kneeling before a statue of some kind. And then Lorley stared openly at the cloth, even reaching out her small hand to touch the embroidery.

She heard Randolph mutter, "Better not do that, Lorley," and Lloyd looked uneasily at her.

Mme. de la Rue's smile didn't waver for a moment, and she said to Lorley, "Do you like the cloth?"

Her eyes wide, staring at Mme. de la Rue, she said, "The stars – they're beautiful."

"Yes – they are. One of the women in the next room made that for me – before she became so ill. I treasure it greatly." As she spoke, her eyes were on Lorley, and then, with the same gentleness, fell lightly over the boys. Moving gracefully, she lifted the large jug of cider from the table and began pouring it into the mugs.

More than anything, Marie wanted to get out of her chair and look at the cloth for herself. Of course, she knew what a pentacle was, the five-pointed star that was a symbol of witchcraft, an ancient one, part of Guernsey folklore, as were the elven stars, with their seven points. She told herself that all this was nothing more than some harmless sort of decoration –

Because, at this point, she couldn't believe anything bad or harmful about Mme. de la Rue. She watched her as she poured the cider, handing a mug to each of the children, and at that moment Marie felt in her heart that even if this woman with such lovely silver hair and eyes also happened to be a witch, it didn't make any difference.

"Would you like to see my animals?" Mme. de la Rue asked the children, and Marie, even though she was a little surprised by the question, felt soothed by her low, rhythmic voice.

The children all nodded, finishing their cider and leaving the empty mugs on the table. They followed her as she walked across the large kitchen, her bare feet nearly silent on the stone floor, nothing more than a soft, whisking sound, and opened a side door. Marie hadn't noticed it when she first entered the cottage – it was a very narrow door, more like a panel in the wall, in a corner of the kitchen that was in shadows, unlike the rest of the bright room. Beside the door, there was a pile of peat, neatly contained in an open stone enclosure, making it even less visible.

As Mme. de la Rue opened the door, Marie also saw that there was some sort of design drawn there, in black ink, lines that bloomed in great curls and arcs, flourishing all over the door.

But Marie only saw this in a single flash, and then the door was opened wide, and more light poured into the room. With her long, gentle arm, Mme. de la Rue ushered the children outside with her.

Marie rose from her chair then, glancing at William, who was also staring at the open door. From the look on his face, she knew that he, too, had seen the design. He got up quickly at that point, about to follow Mme. de la Rue and the children, but she grabbed his sleeve, silently motioning towards the table.

They both stepped over to peer at the cloth and saw the pentacles embroidered in heavy, black thread, poised like still spiders on the white linen. And she saw that Lloyd had been right about the elven stars, their seven points stitched in bright silver thread, and there were moons also, half moons and crescent moons and full, ripe moons in scarlet red, all combining in a sort of cosmic dance.

She found it hard to take her eyes off it, but William, at her side, said very softly, "Come, Marie."

As she and William walked through the narrow door – and Marie resisted the urge to look more closely at what was painted on the other side – she could see her children on the ground – with a jumble of curly-haired puppies and small black and white goats.

Mme. de la Rue stood in the middle of the courtyard, reigning over the children and the animals. And then Marie thought of the elven stars on the cloth and saw, once again, how really beautiful Mme. de la Rue was, standing in the sunlight but shining like a star, an Elven Queen with bright silver hair.

The courtyard was as enchanting as the radiant woman. On one side, the wall was built of large granite blocks, smooth and gleaming – not roughhewn rocks like those on the wall where they had left the car – and it rose very high, easily being twelve feet. It would have been impossible to climb because the blocks were one solid mass, as though the wall was part of the cliff itself. Marie could hear the sea far below, the sound of the waves crashing against the rocky shore. And it seemed as if the mist from the cascading, foaming water had found its way into the courtyard, floating, translucent, as if minute crystals scintillated in the air.

The cottage itself formed two of the walls, an L-shape, where the kitchen and the room where Mme. de la Rue had the old women resting were. On the wall of that bedroom, there was one small casement window, with vines growing on the sill and all around it, looking as if it hadn't been opened in years. It was covered by a simple muslin curtain, the light cloth pulled tightly closed. Marie was relieved, somehow, to see that there weren't any bars on the window, unlike the hospital ward in St. Peter Port, where the elderly demented patients were kept.

No leaves grew on the granite wall overlooking the sea, but they grew on the cottage walls, although not in the same thick profusion as on the front of the dwelling – delicate tendrils of vines, winding over the stones, with long green ribbons of leaves. As Marie watched, one of the baby goats began chewing some of the lower vines.

The fourth side of the courtyard was formed by a kind of stable, a wooden structure, the doors opened wide, where a mother goat lay on the straw, straw which spilled lavishly onto the smooth earth floor of the courtyard. One of the baby goats was nestled against her, and Marie saw, a little surprised, that one of the puppies was resting there as well. But when the pup raised its head, she saw that it must be the mother dog. Although quite small, not much larger than a bunny, she was bigger than the puppies, which were no more than a few pounds. And her hair was longer and much thicker, her floppy ears covered in silky, wavy hair, her coat black and tan.

Marie did not know what breed she was – clearly a mix of some kind – a mother dog with her puppies that were more like illustrations in a children's book, an idealized story, where the dogs and the goats were the best of friends, and the animals had pretty faces, more like little furry people.

William was very close to her, and he said quietly, "This is about as idyllic as one could imagine."

She smiled at him in silent agreement, watching the

children cuddle the puppies and the goats, a little menagerie of such innocent bliss.

Then Mme. de la Rue walked over to them, a few of the baby goats following. "Perhaps the children will stay here while we have tea?"

Marie looked at William, who nodded at her, and at the courtyard, the bright sun sparkling in the mist from the sea, the children playing happily with the animals, and felt a rush of gratitude that, after everything that had happened that day, things had, in the end, turned out so well.

She looked at Mme. de la Rue and said, "Of course. That would be lovely." She spoke as though she was talking to one of the ladies in her church group – and not a woman with silver hair flowing past her waist, standing on the ground in her bare feet, by a gleaming green house of leaves, her face as unlined as if she were a young woman.

With shining eyes that seemed hundreds of years old.

***

The tea was surprisingly good – almost like the black tea they drank at home, but with a slight taste of oranges and spices – cloves, and perhaps ginger.

Marie looked around the kitchen, at its comforting normality. Even the door seemed to blend naturally into the room. She glanced at the narrow panel, still partially open so that they could hear the children playing, the one that had seemed so disturbing before. But now she looked at the graceful swirls of velvet black paint, looping in delicate, symmetrical designs, rhythmic, slender lines, and found it harmonious. And the cloth seemed beautiful, and artistic, as well, a night sky shining in the kitchen.

Mme. de la Rue sat at the head of the table, with Marie and William beside her, and they sipped their tea quietly for a few moments. Then she said, "I am called a witch by most people. I suppose they are right."

She spoke the words as quietly as though she was offering them a piece of fruit bread. Taking another sip of her tea, she looked at them, her eyes soft and tranquil.

There was another silence then, and Marie stared at the linen cloth on the table, at the pentacles and the moons and the elven stars. Perhaps, she thought, it should seem suddenly menacing, but strangely, it did not.

William spoke first. "I have been told that you are also known throughout the island as a healer."

She bowed her head, nodding, and said, "It is my life's work."

There was silence again, a shining silence that seemed to be the natural rhythm of Mme. de la Rue's world, as she sat there, sipping her tea, looking at them with her knowing, ancient eyes.

Marie found herself becoming part of that rhythm, but then William spoke suddenly into the bright silence, "We haven't even told you our names. I am William Moore, and –"

"I know about you, William – you are a healer – and this is your sister, Marie."

Neither asked how she knew, but then she looked towards the open door, where the children were playing, and said, "And Lloyd, Randolph, and little Lorley." When she spoke Lorley's name, she smiled and looked at Marie, and said, "The fairies dance in your Lorley's head."

Marie nodded, smiling, remembering Abram saying those very words about their little girl sometimes. Then she found the words that she had wanted to say for the past few months. "I came to thank you for helping my children in the Creux Mahie that day. I don't know what they would have done without you. I can't –"

Mme. de la Rue spread her hand over the cloth, and for the first time, Marie noticed that her nails, though short, were painted silver. "I am grateful that I was there. You are welcome. You are welcome to anything that I have to give."

She spoke so kindly, looking at her with deep, understanding eyes. And Marie felt as if this strange, beautiful witch healer saw into her heart, and knew everything about her, about Abram and the terrible longing and fear, the fear that almost never left her. She realized, suddenly, that she hadn't thought about Abram since they began their trek through the woods, but now she saw Abram's face and the sadness in his eyes when he had to leave her.

And then Mme. de la Rue leaned over, and pressed her hand lightly on Marie's arm, and said, "I cannot foretell the future. Not completely. Sometimes, not at all. On this, I wish I could know. But I urge you to never stop believing that he will return."

The door didn't sing to me when I entered Mme. de la Rue's house.

And the song of the leaves stopped also, once I was inside. It was a slow cessation though, the sparkling green stream of joyful sound separating into pools, and then droplets the size of tiny gemstones, emeralds scattered at my feet.

Then the song was gone altogether, but I knew now that the leaves, like the bluebells, could sing.

I had very much wanted to tell Mme. de la Rue about the beautiful music I had heard, but she had been too busy helping the old women, leading them gently into the next room, carrying a basin of water as gracefully as a chalice.

I was hopeful that I would be able to tell her about it all later in the day –

When I had been in her kitchen, waiting with Mamma and Uncle William and Lloyd and Randolph, I knew absolutely, that even though the singing had stopped, Mme. de la Rue's magic was everywhere.

As if the silver bright halo that flowed around her hair had spread throughout her house, like a single star so bright that it illuminated the night sky.

And now, in the courtyard, the silver light of her magic melded with the golden sunshine that scintillated all around me.

A light that felt lovely and soft on my arms as I held two of the puppies – so tiny that they could nestle against my neck at the same time.

And, as I bowed my head, gently resting my cheek on their silky heads, the sunshine spread in a sparkling dance over my hair, and I closed my eyes so that the sun could dance there, also.

I felt as if I could stay like that forever, sitting on the ground by the stone wall of the house, while my brothers, at the other end of the courtyard, played with the goats in the stable.

I cradled the puppies in my arms, their hearts beating in their tiny chests.

As the sun, caressing me with its light, made me feel as if some magical spell truly had been cast over me, like a gleaming gossamer net.

But I knew that it was not the kind of spell that took you away from yourself, that turned you into someone else, like the frightening spells in my fairy tales. It was a spell that made you feel crystalline bright and more real than ever.

Like when the bluebells – and the emerald leaves – sang to me.

Filling my heart with happiness and love that melded together like Mme. de la Rue's silver light becoming one with the sunshine.

I opened my eyes, wondering if I would hear the emerald leaves sing again.

It was only then that I heard Mme. de la Rue's voice coming from the kitchen.

I lifted my head higher and tried harder to hear, straining my ears as I let the puppies settle gently in my lap.

Then I heard Mme. de la Rue say, her voice like a rich thread sparkling in a tapestry, "I am called a witch by most people. I suppose they are right."

It seemed like the most natural thing in the world for her to say.

And, in that moment the sun seemed to shine ever brighter, its dance through the air even happier.

I hoped fervently that Mamma and Uncle William would feel the same way.

I moved a little closer to the door that Mme. de la Rue had left partially open. It took all the willpower I could muster not to peek my head around the edge to see how Mamma and Uncle William were reacting to Mme. de la Rue telling them she was a witch.

But I forced myself to remain very still and wait for someone in the kitchen to say something.

But there was only silence – one that seemed very long.

My arms began waving at my sides – little flutters that did not disturb the puppies in my lap. But flutters, I hoped with all my heart, that would stream some of the sunlight from the courtyard into the kitchen, where it would dance happily around Mamma and Uncle William, just as it did around me, and make them believe that Mme. de la Rue being a witch was a very good thing.

Finally, Uncle William spoke, and his voice sounded full of golden sunlight as he said to Mme. de la Rue that she was also a healer.

His voice was very calm, as though he was sitting on our back porch with Papa, gazing at the vineyard.

And not sitting, as Lloyd and Randolph claimed, with the greatest witch in Guernsey.

My heart leapt, thankful that Uncle William could so clearly see Mme. de la Rue's goodness.

Perhaps the sunlight that surely had danced into the kitchen had helped open his eyes to the truth about Mme. de la Rue.

Uncle William continued, telling her his name, but Mme. de la Rue stopped him in her gentle voice, and named each one of us. I waited for Mamma or Uncle William to question her about that, to ask her how she could possibly know our names. But, much to my relief, neither of them did. I figured that they realized, like me, that powerful witches simply knew things like that.

I was a little taken aback, though, when, in the silence that followed, Mme. de la Rue said, "The fairies dance in your Lorley's head."

I wasn't exactly sure what she meant by that. The thought of it made me feel a little dizzy. In my storybooks, fairies had lovely, sweet faces, and wore silky dresses that flowed like rose petals all around them. With their long, graceful gowns, I knew that they would be awfully crowded in my head. And even if they could fit, I didn't know what they would do inside me – they needed to be free to flutter in the flowers and the ferns, and shimmer and sparkle over the sea.

When I heard Mme. de la Rue say, in a voice as kind as if the fairies were singing a hymn, "Never stop believing that he will return," I realized that I had been thinking so much about how the fairies could not possibly be dancing in my head, that I had missed what they had been talking about the last little while –

I did not know who HE was, but strangely, it sounded like something Rev. Pelletier would say when he talked about Jesus coming back to the world. The Reverend always made it sound, somehow, as if Jesus would be coming to Guernsey any day now.

But I couldn't understand why Mme. de la Rue would be talking about it – especially when I heard her say, after a long pause – "Thank you for coming to my home. Not many people on the island, even the many country people who come for my cures, would ever sit at the table of a white witch and a pagan."

There was a very long pause then.

At first, I thought I heard someone swallow their tea loudly, but I doubted if it was really coming from one of them – they were too far away, on the other side of the kitchen, for me to hear such a gurgle. I saw one of the small billy goats, though, chewing with great gusto, making an awful lot of noise, and figured that I had most likely heard a big bunch of leaves going down his throat.

Mamma broke the silence. In a calm voice, she asked, "What do you mean by pagan?"

Uncle William's voice cut in quickly, saying, "Marie, I don't think there's any need –"

"I don't mind questions – as long as you don't mind the answers," she said, and I somehow knew that her kind smile was on her face again. And this time, when she stopped talking, despite the noisy little goat chewing so closely to my ears, munching as though he was devouring the finest fruit bread in Guernsey, I knew that I heard Mamma murmur softly for her to go on.

I hadn't actually thought about Mme. de la Rue being a pagan, especially since often she seemed like the Blessed Virgin Mary. Nor had I really been very sure about her being a witch, exactly, but now that I heard her say she was, I had to readjust my thinking a bit. I couldn't help feeling, though, deep in my heart, that she must be a kind of heavenly witch, and a heavenly pagan. Rev. Pelletier would say that was impossible, but then, he had never seen Mme. de la Rue, a night star shining in the morning sunlight.

"I worship nature, the silver spirit in the earth, the sea, and the sky. And all the animals, the plants, and the trees." Mme. de la Rue was silent for a few moments. I couldn't hear any sound coming from Mamma or Uncle William. Nothing at all. If they had been sitting in our kitchen in St. Saviour's, I would have heard the clock ticking, the little golden hands lightly touching the air, but I doubted that there was a clock in Mme. de la Rue's kitchen. She really wouldn't need one, of course, because the sun would be her timepiece.

The silence continued, and I wondered if perhaps Mme. de la Rue had accidentally poured some of the potion that she used to calm the old women into the tea for Mamma and Uncle William – but I knew that was nonsense.

Mistakes like that didn't happen in Mme. de la Rue's world. There was no question in my mind now, and I didn't think there really ever had been, that she could cast a spell on people, using her magical medicines. But I also believed, deep in my heart, that she only used her powers to heal people.

She began speaking again. "I need to engage in devotional practice, finding the glory in the natural world, to do my healing."

"I can understand that," Mamma said softly.

I didn't understand it, for trying to comprehend everything that Mme. de la Rue was saying felt like climbing a shining cliff, in sunlight so bright that I could barely see.

I understood enough, though, to know that what she did as a pagan was what Rev. Pelletier said was a sin. To be a good Christian, you had to go to church and worship inside those stone walls and wear your best clothes and keep your eyes staring straight ahead at the pulpit. Even a glance at the trees softly waving their lovely, lacy branches outside the narrow church windows was sinful – even though the flash of tender green leaves seemed more like heaven to me than the plaster walls and hard brown pews of the church. I could easily imagine God floating for eternity in such a luminous green world, a green world that sang to him forever and ever. It was much harder to think of him staying very long in the cold white walls and bare wood of St. Saviour's Church.

I couldn't help but think how nice it might be to be a pagan. Your prayers would come out of your mouth without having to think about them. I imagined in her pagan prayers that all the flowers sang to her, not just the bluebells and the emerald leaves, but the lilies and the daisies and the roses. The trees surely made music to her, also, the willows soft and whispery – even I could sometimes sense them murmuring, but she would be able to hear the notes. And the oaks and the sycamores would have lovely, deep voices, like Papa and Uncle William, and would share the secrets of the earth with her. The sea, too, would welcome her prayers, the waves bowing down and then carrying her offerings as far as the horizon. At night, the stars would sing in the dark sky as she prayed to them, in her own shining song, reflecting the starlight above.

I could so easily imagine being a pagan.

It seemed to make so much sense. Even the Blessed Virgin Mary, who kept floating into my prayers, seemed to belong more in the pagan world than the church world. When I thought of her with her long yellow curls and flowing blue veil and silky gown, I knew that she belonged outside, in the flowers, or by the sea, or softly glowing with the stars – not hovering over a cold wooden church pew.

As I sat there, huddled by Mme. de la Rue's kitchen door, no longer listening to what they were talking about, hearing only a steady hum as they all spoke in quiet voices, I felt as if I could stay there forever in that sun-filled spot.

"Lorley, what's wrong?" It was Lloyd, leaning over me, with Randolph at his side.

I looked at them, feeling as if I had been in a kind of sleep, the way I had felt when I was in Bluebell Woods, and in the Creux Mahie when Mme. de la Rue came to help us. Being in her presence seemed to do that to me. But all I said was, "Nothing at all is wrong. I've just been listening to Mamma and Uncle William talk to Mme. de la Rue."

Randolph looked at me, his eyes shining, and said, "What are they talking about?"

But Lloyd, glancing at the open door, shook his head and very quietly said, "Let's first go over by the stable."

Randolph took my hand, and together we followed Lloyd. I put the puppies gently down on the ground so they could toddle back to the others. The mother goat looked at us, motionless, her small yellow eyes as quiet and peaceful as pebbles on the beach. I saw that a manger was not far from her side, filled with sweet grass and clover. Along the back, there was a trough with fresh water, still and dark in the stable, the thick wooden beams sheltering it from the bright sun. Then the mother dog, her short legs moving quickly, her long, curly ears flapping a little, made her way to the water for a drink.

I loved the smell of the straw, and the rich scent of the old wood. Sitting down by the stable, my back felt cool, and my face was pleasantly warm in the soft afternoon sun. Then, as the mother dog finished her drink and came over to me, climbing gently into my lap, I closed my eyes.

After what seemed like a long while, though I knew it

really wasn't, I heard Randolph say, his voice sounding very far away, "What did you hear them talking about, Lorley?" I shook myself a little to pay more attention. It seemed that I drifted off into daydreams, small ones, wisps of white daydreams, more than ever at Mme. de la Rue's cottage so high on the cliffs – getting myself lost in little pools of sunlight that made me forget everything else that was happening around me. I opened my eyes wide and saw Lloyd and Randolph sitting cross-legged on the ground, looking at me with bright, questioning eyes.

"So what were they talking about?" Randolph repeated.

Before I had a chance to say anything, Lloyd, his brown eyes light in the sun, said, "Are you feeling all right, Lorley?"

I nodded my head, saying, "Yes – I just feel so happy here, I can hardly believe that it's all happening."

"Lorley, did Mme. de la Rue say anything about the cloth on the table?"

"Or about the door?" Lloyd asked, and his voice now sounded as urgent as Randolph's.

"No," I said, looking down at the mother dog in my lap, gently curling my fingers in the baby soft fur. I closed my eyes, telling myself to think very hard about what exactly I heard. "No – I didn't hear them say anything about the cloth or the door. They were drinking tea, and when Uncle William introduced himself, she already knew his name." I looked at my brothers then and said, "She knew all of our names." I didn't tell them about what Mme. de la Rue said about the fairies dancing in my head. I was still a little uneasy about that.

"She knew all of our names?"

"Yes."

"But she didn't explain the cloth?"

"No – she didn't really have to – not after she told them that she was a witch."

My brothers looked quickly at each other for a moment, and then Lloyd said, "She just came out and said it?"

I nodded my head hard. "As plain as day. She said that she was a healer, too, and it sounded as if –"

"What did Mamma and Uncle William say?" Randolph said.

I stopped for a moment, my fingers slowly moving over the delicate, silky ears of the mother dog. "They just kept drinking their tea." I paused, trying to recall everything that I heard, but it was hard, because it all seemed so dreamlike, sitting there by Mme. de la Rue's kitchen door with the sunlight swirling around me, dazzling light that made me feel as if my skin and my hair and my eyes were sparkling. Maybe that was what Mme. de la Rue meant when she said the fairies danced in my head – although it didn't feel as if they were inside me, but outside, twinkling and shimmering in the bright sun shining all over me.

Suddenly, the strange words came back to me. I looked at my brothers, staring at me, waiting for me to continue, and I said slowly, "Right after I heard her tell them she was a witch, I think she started talking about Jesus –"

"Jesus! That doesn't make any sense," Randolph burst out, looking at Lloyd, shaking his head.

"And right after that, she told them that she was a pagan," I said, and even though they didn't look upset about that, I rushed on. "But the way she described it sounded awfully nice. And Mamma and Uncle William just kept drinking their tea."

"The witches in Guernsey have pretty much always been pagans from what I've been told," Lloyd said. "I guess some witches claimed they weren't, but I think they had to be."

"You're sure Mamma wasn't upset? She and Uncle William never believed any of this witch stuff before we came here."

I shook my head, knowing Randolph was right but also knowing that Mamma hadn't sounded unhappy. Her voice, when I thought about it, sounded the way it did when she was describing something that she thought was really beautiful – like one of the stained-glass windows at St. Saviour's, or a song that someone sang with a pure voice.

Too soon, Uncle William came to the door and said, "It's time to go. We need to get home before suppertime."

Standing there, his fair hair shining in the sunlight that was so strong in the courtyard, he looked very different than he had that morning. His blond hair and fair skin seemed much lighter somehow, as if everything that had happened that day made the sun shine more intensely on him. He had been so heavy and dark when he first came to drive us to the South Shore, but now he looked happy, his broad smile with his dimples and white teeth, his eyes crinkling in the corners, his long, handsome face as comforting as it had always been.

My brothers followed him slowly. I heard Randolph say to Lloyd that they must thank Mme. de la Rue for all her help in the cave that day, and as Lloyd quickly nodded his head, they walked into the cottage with Uncle William. I could tell they were as reluctant as I was to leave this place.

I got to my feet, resting the mother dog gently on the ground, taking one last look at the courtyard, at the puppies and the goats, the sun-drenched straw, and the bright green vines. The foliage in the afternoon light was especially beautiful, jewel bright, so lovely in that light that it was hard to take my eyes off it.

And I listened for their song. I thought I heard a few notes – not singing yet, more like a few glimmers of music about to begin. I turned to where the leaves were particularly bright, on the wall where the window was, where a rich tapestry of leaves grew around the wooden frame.

I heard a few notes, I was sure, as I gazed at the beautiful emerald greenness, and my heart lifted.

But then my eyes fixed on the window, on the muslin curtain tightly closed.

And everything then became silent.

As if that curtain had been pulled shut over the whole courtyard.

I told myself that it was time to leave. I was about to turn away, to slowly walk back into the cottage, when I saw the cloth quiver, ever so slightly.

At first I thought it must be the bright sun dancing on the window that made the curtain seem to move.

But then I saw a face peering through the open folds of the cloth.

I stood very still, looking at the old woman in the window.

Her gaze seemed very far away, her eyes lifted, looking past the high wall behind me, into the brilliant sky.

I hoped that she wouldn't start screaming again. That was not how I wanted the day to end. But then, as I stared at her face, I knew she wasn't going to do that.

Her face was serene now. With her blue eyes uplifted, looking intently into the sky, her mouth gentle, her grey hair a smooth veil, she seemed infused with an inner light.

Framed in the window, there was something ethereal about her.

I felt as if I were looking at a holy picture, the coloured paper slowly coming to life.

I thought of her in the woods. I didn't know which old woman was in the window now, but it didn't matter – whoever it was had undergone a transformation.

From crawling in the woods like an animal to gazing into the sky like a saint.

Because of Mme. de la Rue.

I couldn't take my eyes off her. I knew that they would soon start calling me, but I couldn't leave.

Then I felt a light touch on my shoulder. I turned and found myself looking into the face of Mme. de la Rue.

Her crystalline eyes were shining down on me, her whole face glowing with the same ethereal light as the woman in the window.

I looked quickly to see if the old woman was still there, and she hadn't moved, although she was no longer staring into the sky, but gazing at Mme. de la Rue. Her eyes were full of love – the same love that was so radiant in the eyes of Mme. de la Rue.

It was as if the old woman in the window was a mirror image of Mme. de la Rue, a smaller mirror, though, not large enough to capture all the beauty of the silver woman who now stood so close to me.

"Lorley – it's time to go." Her voice was very soothing. In a strange way, it suddenly made me think of my Papa, which didn't really make any sense because he spoke in such a deep, softly rumbling voice, and Mme. de la Rue's voice sounded as light and silvery as stars shining.

Like Papa, though, she made me feel safe, and, like him, she seemed to see inside me and know what was in my heart.

She stood very close to me, and I breathed in her scent – now it was a light blend of lemons and white sugar that spread into the soft sunshine all around us. The smell of spices was gone, and so was the vanilla – and I wondered if it was because of the bright sun, that its brilliant light lifted those away and left only sun bright yellow and white scents on Mme. de la Rue's skin.

I almost asked her, but I told myself there was so little time left before we had to leave.

And, more than anything, I wanted to tell her about the green leaves singing, that they had voices like the bluebells.

So as Mme. de la Rue looked into my eyes and placed her hands very gently on either side of my face, I said in a voice as quiet as the sunlight dancing around us, "The leaves sing, too, like the bluebells, Mme. de la Rue."

She nodded her head, and her hair shone ever so brightly as she said, "They truly do, Lorley."

"Like the bluebells."

"Yes – different but the same, like the beauties of emeralds and sapphires."

I looked deeply into her eyes then, and I found myself saying, "I was certain that it wasn't just my imagination, though sometimes, it runs away from me, Mme. de la Rue, and I make my family worry."

She smiled, a lovely light in her face, as she said, "Lorley, your imagination does not run. It flies. And know that it will never get away from you. You will grow wings and soar with it. As you set it free."

I was thrilled by what she said because deep in my heart, I had always believed that, truly, imaginations did fly.

And then I asked, in a hushed voice, "Are there other songs to hear?"

Her silver halo shone brighter, so much that it melded with the golden sunlight and seemed to spread over the entire courtyard.

And she said, her crystalline grey eyes moving away from my face for a moment as she looked around her, "The world is full of song, little one. Keep listening, always keep listening, with your ears, and your eyes, and your heart. And you will hear."

I nodded my head.

And I felt as if I knew what she meant, though I doubted that I could explain those words to anyone – but I understood them in my heart.

Still, though, I had to say, "But I can only hear the singing when I'm with you, Mme. de la Rue."

"That is because I'm helping you now." She paused, and looked into the sky for a long moment.

I waited.

And then I wondered if the sky was singing to her. What a grand chorus of song that would be, a hymn of heaven.

I listened, and I thought perhaps I heard a few notes, almost impossibly beautiful notes, as if the bluebells had found their way into the sky.

But just a few, and then the silver and gold silence of the courtyard returned.

And Mme. de la Rue turned her gaze away from the sky and looked into my eyes again.

"Remember, Lorley, I'm helping you now. But keep listening always for new songs, while you keep the memories of what you have heard strong and full in your heart."

Then she removed her hands from my face, hands that had been resting there as gently as white wings.

Turning to the window, she bowed her head at the old woman, who stood there, as still and lovely as a flower in the garden. She bowed in return and left the window, moving away peacefully to rest.

As I watched the old woman, I couldn't help thinking that she was softly glowing in Mme. de la Rue's halo, that the magical woman's silver light spread so far.

I looked up then, into Mme. de la Rue's face. She was smiling serenely at me, and I felt as if she could hear my thoughts as clearly as I could, that she knew exactly what thoughts were sparkling inside me.

And then, holding my shoulders, she looked into my eyes. Her gaze was gentle, as always, but her voice was louder than before as she said, "You must always be brave for your family."

I looked at her, puzzled.

"One day, you will understand. Just remember, dear Lorley, be brave. I believe there will come a time when you may have to save loved ones from a different Creux Mahie."

I did not understand how that could ever be. How could someone as small and weak as me save anyone? I would do anything I could for my family, but I could not comprehend for a single moment how they would ever need me to rescue them.

It seemed so impossible –

But I remained silent. I did not have to say this to the heavenly silver witch.

She knew.

She simply smiled and said, "I know, dear Lorley, how hard it is for you to understand some of the things that I have told you today. Do not let your mind be troubled by any of this – do not think about this now. Let my words – about your loved ones and the new songs – rest silently within you, and let them surface when you need to hear them again."

I did not know how I could make that happen.

But I nodded, saying nothing at first, as I basked in the light of her magic spreading all around us in deep waves of gleaming silver.

Then I said, "The memories of the flowers and the leaves singing, though – they will not be silent within me?"

Mme. de la Rue shook her head ever so slightly and said, "Their songs will grow stronger and stronger over time."

Then we walked into the sunlit kitchen, where everyone was waiting for us.

No one said a word as we entered the tranquil room.

But there was so much love there – and for a moment, I felt as if Mme. de la Rue and I were in Bluebell Woods once more – with Mamma and Uncle William and Lloyd and Randolph with us also.

And the bluebells sang so joyously that I let myself imagine that we all could hear them.

Everyone was very quiet in the car on the way home, and Marie was grateful for that.

She needed time to think. She knew that she had done the right thing by going to see Mme. de la Rue – she was convinced of that – but she had not been prepared for what had happened there.

Nor did she understand it all.

The witchcraft part no longer bothered her. The woman who shimmered like beautiful, aged silver was a gifted healer. She knew that as surely as she had a heart beating in her chest – and if worshipping the moon and the stars and the woods and the sea helped Mme. de la Rue do that, then so be it.

How Mme. Laporte would be mortified. She would never understand for a moment why Marie would venture through those woods that were like the haunted trees in Grimm's Fairy Tales, or dare to go into that cottage in the first place, that great mound of leaves that seemed to grow out of the ground in a mysterious burst of magic. And then calmly drink a witch's tea, with pentacles dancing on the tablecloth and pagan symbols spiralling all over the door.

Mme. Laporte would tell her that she had lost her mind.

But she knew that thanking Mme. de la Rue for saving her children had been the right thing to do. And that living a moral life could help keep her husband safe. It wasn't as if she still believed that God was this harsh taskmaster in the sky who doled out favours to those who did exactly what they guessed he wanted. She simply believed that trying to be good created more goodness in one's life.

But if she had ever attempted to explain that to Mme. Laporte and, for that matter, the ladies at the church, she could easily imagine their appalled reactions. Drinking tea with a known witch and a pagan would hardly be perceived as doing what was morally right.

Marie would not let her mind dwell on what they would think. Instead, she let her heart fill with the love and kindness and beauty she felt in the presence of Mme. de la Rue. The white witch's care of those women, demented and so pitiful, was an act of pure compassion.

And Mme. de la Rue's devotion to healing had impressed even William. While the children were in the courtyard with the little menagerie of animals, Mme. de la Rue showed them the large room where she kept her potions and ointments and elixirs. Marie hadn't realized how big the cottage actually was, appearing from the outside to be much smaller, covered in such thick foliage, blending into the woods the way the sea and the sky melded together on Rocquaine Bay.

Her Healing Room, as Mme. de la Rue called it, seemed to grow out of the ground also. Walking into the room, Marie felt as if she had stepped inside the trunk of a great tree. The floor and the walls and the high ceiling were all a deep, mellow brown, coursed through with thick black veins. At first, she thought that the same pagan symbols that were painted on the door in the kitchen were also doing their shadow dance on these walls, but when she looked more closely, she saw that the room was made entirely from highly polished wood, the dark grain running through it in exotic spirals. Where such unusual wood came from, Marie couldn't imagine. It felt so like the interior of a tree that, initially, she thought the room was circular, but then she realized that there were actually five walls, five points like the pentacles on the cloth, and she saw how artfully the room had been created. They stared in silence as Mme. de la Rue led them past the floor-to-ceiling shelves, filled with bottles and jars of various sizes and shapes – tall bottles that contained long, frothy stalks and murky, viscous liquids – others wide and shallow that held ointments and pastes – in containers that were made out of either clear or amber brown glass, shining like dark jewels against the walls. She could see one jar, on a shelf close beside her, where a kind of fungus bubbled slowly, as it undulated against the sides of the jar, a grotesque growth. Shuddering, she had to look away.

William had asked a lot of questions then, noting the labels that were affixed in a precise spot on each bottle and jar – even on the tiniest bottles, some no larger than thimbles, with ornate glass stoppers like little diamonds in the narrow apertures. Each label was written in a very small, meticulous script. Hundreds and hundreds of receptacles lined the shelves, and Marie now wondered how Mme. de la Rue could have created such an apothecary.

By herself – living alone all through the years. Her only companions, and, from what she understood, relatively recent companions, were the very ill, old women she cared for so lovingly.

How, she marvelled, could Mme. de la Rue be so strong?

Doing such good work, in isolation, knowing that many on the island, in their ignorance and fear, shunned and mocked her.

A truly gifted woman. A magical woman.

Now, as Marie sat in the quiet car, the rumbling of the engine the only sound as they made their way home through the forest, she looked at her brother, his eyes intense on the rough, narrow road winding through the thick woods. She felt deeply grateful that he was with her. And then she glanced back at her children. All three seemed lost in their own thoughts. In the eyes of both Lloyd and Randolph, the sparks of their great adventure were still bright, and in Lorley's eyes, she saw a look of wonder, as if she had just gazed through the gates of heaven.

Marie knew that the look in Lorley's eyes, the wonder from what they had experienced that day, was in her own eyes as well.

She was so very thankful for their time with Mme. de la Rue.

For her magical strength.

For helping her keep hope alive.

And even though Mme. de la Rue claimed that she could not predict the future, that she could not tell her absolutely that Abram would survive the War, still Marie felt renewed hope. Closing her eyes, she remembered Mme. de la Rue's words, "Never stop believing that he will return," and she let the words flow through her – in a stream of lovely silver light, shining from the goodness in Mme. de la Rue's heart.

And she would remember that light when the dark fears about Abram returned, as she knew they would. The light that would drive away the darkness.

chapter
twelve

WILLIAM WAS GROWING anxious about going to the War.

He was afraid that they were never going to send him. Two months had passed since he had been told that he was needed at the Front, and still he remained in Guernsey. Soon, it would be Christmas.

His only consolation was that at least he could be with Marie and the children and fulfil his promise to Abram to watch over them. Lately, though, Marie had seemed much stronger. Seeing her like that helped him not worry about her as much, and it eased his mind greatly. Ever since they had been to see Mme. de la Rue – the day he had received word about going to France – Marie had been so much better.

The bewitching Mme. de la Rue had a very powerful effect on them both. But he shook his head as the word 'bewitching' came so readily to his lips because he did not believe for a moment that the woman could cast spells or any such nonsense as that. After that strange, and he had to admit, strangely sublime day, he believed absolutely that Mme. de la

Rue was a gifted healer. And a bewitching one, in the sense that she had a captivating, enchanting presence, so strong that he understood how Marie could see a kind of glimmering halo around her, as she claimed.

And when he thought about little Lorley, the poet William Blake's words came to mind, for she surely saw "heaven in a wildflower" as she gazed at Mme. de la Rue.

He was thankful now that he had taken them to that cottage on the South Shore, even though he had had such grave misgivings. Truth be told, he had not believed in any of the remedies that many of the superstitious farmers and many others, even from St. Peter Port, obtained from the old women on the South Shore, claiming that they were cured by the strange concoctions.

He and his colleagues had always scoffed at this so-called folk medicine, dismissing it as delusion and ignorance, nothing more than compelling evidence of the placebo effect.

He did not scoff at it anymore. Not that he would share any of what he had seen at Mme. de la Rue's cottage with his colleagues. They would not understand.

They wouldn't want to believe him. To think for one second that some old woman could devise a remedy that was more effective than what modern science had produced would be impossible for them to accept. As they frequently stated, they were men of science, of rational thought; their knowledge elevated them far above the plebeian folk medicine practitioners. At worst, they mocked the old women as the crazy coven, though not believing that any actual witchcraft occurred. But his colleagues believed that the women could do real harm and were all headed towards the fate of that Dugas.

They rather conveniently ignored the fact, though – and this had always bothered William – that many of their own presumed scientific cures were quite crude. Most of them were still providing morphine syrups to teething babies, even dusting their gums with powders containing mercury, a substance that was too toxic for babies, William was convinced. Too many were recommending to patients suffering from chronic migraine headaches that they sit in a warm tub with a low voltage current passing through the water. William had argued forcibly against it, citing the risks associated with such a procedure, but some of them continued the practice.

Truly, what he had seen at Mme. de la Rue's cottage had opened his mind to things he had not thought possible. He had never heard of most of the plants that she used for her healing potions, and he had been utterly shocked by the quantity and variety, as he stared at the shelves that rose so high, the bottles on the very top touching the ceiling.

And in one corner of her apothecary – and as he thought of the word, he knew how his colleagues would balk at calling it such, but it was an accurate descriptor – she had shown him a glass jar containing, innocuously, a few pieces of bread growing a luxuriant layer of deep green mould.

He had shaken his head, saying, "I don't understand."

"I use the mould to cure skin infections. It is amazingly effective. Would you like to take a vial with you? I'm sure you have patients in need," she had said.

And so he had taken a vial containing a concentrate of the mould, for the treatments he was presently prescribing for such infections were largely ineffective.

Now he sat in his office in St. Peter Port, at the oak desk that had been his father's, a desk made from the same gleaming wood that had been used to build the magnificent ships of his father's company. Leaning his head against the high back of his leather chair, he stared at the vial from Mme. de la Rue that he had placed on the polished surface of his desk.

Unfortunately, he had come to the conclusion that he couldn't offer it to any of his patients as a cure. As much as he believed in the strength and, undeniably, the intelligence of Mme. de la Rue, he couldn't in good conscience prescribe anything he knew so little about. The idea was absurd, really, that a mould grown on those ridiculous pieces of bread could produce anything of therapeutic value, and yet, compared to some of the cures that he and his colleagues relied upon, it wasn't so beyond the pale.

Even so, being back in his office, far away from that strange, enchanted cottage on the South Shore, he realized that, as tempting as it would be to try it, he couldn't, not without proof of its safety and efficacy.

But he remained conflicted because he had seen such compelling evidence of Mme. de la Rue's ability. She calmed those ailing, old women, using a compound that seemed vastly superior to the chloral hydrate or the somniferous drugs that he and his colleagues used. These drugs – quite new to medicine – worked more like an anaesthetic, often leaving the patient in a state characterized by lassitude and extreme fatigue, with greatly compromised mental acuity.

Whatever concoction Mme. de la Rue used, and now he wished that he had brought a sample of that medication back with him, had had remarkable results, something that his arsenal of drugs never produced.

Mme. de la Rue had impressed him with her healing abilities in a way that he had not thought possible. And the kindness she demonstrated towards those demented women had affected him profoundly. When he questioned her about it, asking her how long she had been caring for them, she said that it had been a couple of years, not long after Mme. Dugas had died so tragically.

"You know about that?" he had said quickly, but as soon as the words were out of his mouth, he realized how ridiculous his question was because, of course, she would have known.

"A failure on my part," she had replied. "I tried to help her, but she would not let me. Her remedies were very different from mine, quite dangerous in my view. Her decline was rapid and I knew, too late, that I should have more forcefully intervened. After that, I vowed that I would be more vigilant caring for the aging women on the South Shore."

He could see her standing there as if it were yesterday, showing him her medicines, humble yet so powerful.

Now, he picked up the vial, holding it carefully in the palm of his hand, and he knew in his heart that it would work. And he deeply regretted that he couldn't use it.

But he would keep it, as a reminder of her.

***

He was still staring at the vial when Reginald walked into his office. For a moment, he thought it was Abram.

The boy had always looked much like his father, but during the six months that Abram had been gone, he had grown surprisingly tall, his arms and chest more muscular, his face lean, like his father, with the same dark shadow of beard.

No one would have thought that the boy was not yet fifteen years old. He actually looked older than many of the boys who had been sent to the Front. William thanked God that they were in Guernsey, where everyone knew Reginald Vidamour and how young he actually was. In many parts of England, boys the age of Reginald, with scarcely a trace of beard on their faces, looking not a day over fourteen, were lying about their ages and managing to enlist. William knew his nephew would have done the same.

"Reginald! Good to see you. Sit down, please," he said.

"I figured you wouldn't have any patients now, Uncle William."

He nodded his head. "Right. I still try not to see anyone on Wednesday afternoon. I have quite a lot of paperwork to complete, although I'm afraid I haven't accomplished much." He motioned to the stack of papers, documents, files, and bills that were placed on his side table, a neat stack that his secretary had organized for him before she left for the afternoon.

Reginald was staring at the vial. "That's an unusual bottle. What kind of medicine is it?"

William looked at his nephew and knew that he couldn't tell him that it was a remedy from Mme. de la Rue. He didn't want the boy's thoughts to return to that day, and the awful days that followed.

That day spent at the South Shore had been very hard on Reginald. When they returned, long past suppertime, the boy had been wild with worry. In retrospect, William knew that they should have brought him with them and let Reginald act as the protector of the family, as he had promised his Papa.

And then the very next morning, they received the awful news about Passchendaele. William still found it surreal somehow that that day at Mme. de la Rue's happened while the battle of Passchendaele was being fought in Belgium. The thought of them in that cottage that sprouted out of the ground like some enchanted thing, sitting with a woman who seemed so surreal herself, while Abram was in that battle was still hard for William to make sense of in his mind – from heaven in a wildflower to hell in the mud of Passchendaele, it seemed. All in one day.

It had been a very long, torturous week, waiting for more news about the battle, waiting for the list of men who had died, and several more days passed before they knew with certainty that Abram had survived.

It had been such a struggle for Reginald, so firm in his delusions that he should be a soldier fighting the War with the Guernseymen, and fearing that his Papa was dead, believing that he should have been with him in the trenches.

No, he did not want the boy to start thinking about that difficult time, so William slipped the vial into the pocket of his suit jacket. "It is used for infections, actually," he said, and then leaned back in his chair, looking at the boy. He smiled kindly and said, "How are you doing, Reginald?"

"Everything is fine on the farm." Then Reginald paused, staring at his hands, as large as a man's now, hands rough and calloused from the heavy work in the grapes. "It's just the same as always, Uncle William, the same thing day after day."

"You're doing good work, Reginald. Your Papa will be very grateful when he returns."

The boy looked at him, his face lighting up for a moment. "That's what keeps me going," he said. "But I find it harder and harder to do, Uncle William, knowing the War is being fought in France and I'm stuck in the fields," he said.

William got out of his chair and walked over to him, putting his arm around his nephew's shoulders. "Believe me, I understand, Reginald. But your Mamma needs you more than ever." He paused and then said quietly, "And you know that I will be leaving soon."

Reginald nodded, looking slowly around the office. The tall shelves were filled with medical texts and journals, from the gleaming floor to the high ceiling. Sitting snugly between the bookcases was a table laden with a heavy black typewriter, and in the far corner of the room was the examination table, covered with a white cloth, shining brightly in the rich oak of the room. Reginald had always felt comforted by his uncle's office, he reflected, as his eyes came to rest on the rug, a dark crimson colour, with deep gold and sapphire swirls emblazoned around the edges, blending warmly with the glow of the wood. Finally, he said, "I can't believe that they are really going to send you. You're needed here, Uncle."

William moved away from Reginald then and walked over to the window of his second floor office, a very wide window that took up most of the wall. A tall chair, like the one at his desk, was placed in front of it, turned so that he could look at High Street, lined with the shops on St. Peter Port's bustling main road. And beyond that, he could look at the sea. On that bright December day, the water was deeply blue and stretched endlessly under the clear sky, water, it seemed, that would never meet land.

As William stared at the water, still silent, not yet responding to Reginald, lost for a moment in his contemplation of the sea, it suddenly seemed to him that they were never going to send him to France, that the boy was right, that this limbo of waiting would never end, just as the water before him seemed without end.

Finally, he turned away from the window and answered his nephew. "Honestly, I just don't know, Reginald. There is plenty of work to do here in Guernsey, but the need is so much greater in France. I haven't heard anything about the Regiment for some time." He paused, walking over to his desk, flipping through the pages of his calendar. "Here it is December 3rd, and there really hasn't been any news since the middle of November."

"That's why Mamma sent me to town today, actually, to see if you had heard anything."

He shook his head. "Nothing at all, but tell your Mamma not to worry. The last information I received was that after Passchendaele, the Regiment was no longer in the trenches but in training somewhere in the north of France, away from the Front Lines."

"That can't last long," Reginald said.

He couldn't lie to the boy. Reginald wouldn't believe him. "Yes, they will be in battle soon enough. You're right."

Reginald stood up then, smoothing down his rough trousers. "I best get back to the farm. I still have a lot of work to do."

William walked over and put his arm around the boy's shoulders again. "Just tell your Mamma that there isn't any news –"

Reginald nodded. "I know, Uncle, and I will tell her that the Regiment must still be in training."

William watched him leave, squaring his shoulders as he walked out of the room.

Like a soldier going to fight in the trenches. On his own.

Reginald knew that he should return to the farm as soon as he could. Walking down the stairs from his uncle's office, he told himself that it wasn't fair to leave Herbert to prune the grapevines without him. For a strong harvest next year, the work was crucial, and Reginald knew that he was more skilful than his brother; he had learned from Papa how to sculpt the dark grey bark so that the grape vines would be heavy and rich each year. It wasn't that Herbert couldn't do the pruning well, but Papa had always said that Reginald had a gift for it. And when he was working with Papa in the vines, before the War, before everything in his life changed, it had all mattered to him.

But now, each day as he worked in the fields, it seemed as if the hours grew longer and longer, that the day would never end. And it was becoming more and more difficult to conceal how he felt. Herbert, still working with a zeal that Reginald could no longer muster, as hard as he tried, sensed the change in him; he knew, though, not to try to talk to him about it. But the endless rows of vines, barren now, their grey branches extended wide, looked more and more to Reginald like rough crosses, but crosses without any Saviours hanging there, no symbols of salvation, but of never-ending servitude.

He didn't know how much longer he could stand it, he thought, as he stood on the High Street, not seeing the people that bustled past him, some close to him on the sidewalk, others on the cobblestone street. Nor did he see the brightly coloured storefronts, their iron filigree doors open wide for the Market Day crowds on Wednesday afternoon.

Reginald looked past all that and gazed at the wide expanse of sea. It was such a dark blue that day, not like the turquoise waters on Rocquaine Bay, where the bright waves filled the whole sky with light. Those days of running along the sandy beach, exploring the caves like daring young privateers, now seemed as if they were behind him forever.

There was only the farm, and the longing to go to the War, a longing that was always there, looming in front of him, always beyond his reach.

A ship was coming slowly into the harbour. At first, he thought it was a battleship, and his heart leapt inside him, but as it came closer, slowly, ceremoniously, he could see that it was a freighter, its tall stacks billowing smoke into the wide sky. It was an impressive ship, and Reginald could not take his eyes off it.

He let himself imagine that the ship really was part of the great fleet of the British Navy, perhaps even the H.M.S. Dreadnought. He had a picture of it in his room at home, a drawing that he had looked at so many times that he had every line and curve of the ship, every smokestack and gun turret, memorized, etched in his brain as if it had been drawn there as well.

And he allowed himself to dream not only that it was the

H.M.S. Dreadnought but that he was on that warship, and that it was not coming into the harbour, but sailing far out to sea, taking him to the War in France.

On a ship that ruled the seas like a great grey Poseidon, its high mast reaching into the sky like a mighty spear.

Taking him to Papa's Regiment.

chapter
thirteen

THE BATTLE of Passchendaele was over, though Abram knew Passchendaele would never really be over.

They had been in the trenches for less than a week before the battle began.

Before the attack, Abram had thought that it could not get much worse. Crouched in the trench – filthy, amidst the rats and the fleas and the smell of the crude latrine – waiting always waiting for the sniper's bullet, knowing that the enemy was doing exactly the same thing, with only that narrow strip of No Man's Land between them.

And always there was the smell of death.

From the shallow graves, from the decomposing corpses that they couldn't possibly retrieve from No Man's Land, from the boys that he had watched die.

When the rain came, the water pooled in the trenches, the sides becoming slick with mud, and their clothes and their boots were drenched as the earth began moving, becoming a slow black sea that wanted to pull them under, down into the depths of the earth.

No crevice in the Creux Mahie was as awful as that dark sea of mud that spread through No Man's Land.

And soon, too soon, men were drowning in the mud.

Filled with the bodies of the dead and dying.

Strangely, when the battle at Passchendaele began, Abram welcomed it, as he had been grateful for the first rain on his face.

Anything to get out of the trench.

Anything to heave himself out of that hole in the ground, to strike blindly at an enemy, an enemy that was no more human to him now than the putrefying corpses in the trenches.

And in the writhing fury of the battle, Abram no longer felt human either. He was a creature risen out of the stench and the sludge of the trench, fighting for his life, and thought of nothing else, his eyes as empty as the dead all around him.

They had gained ground, gained some of the precious land that was nothing more than an expanse of thick, black mud.

And then in that space of six days – six days that sometimes felt like six years and sometimes felt like six seconds – time somehow so distorted in the trenches, the clock with the golden hands in his home in Guernsey had no power here – the Germans gained it back, after all the death in the cruel mud.

Still, the rain continued.

And now the next battle was about to begin. They were in the north of France, near a town called Cambrai.

They had received the orders from General Haig himself, from an unreal world, it seemed to Abram, where orders were still printed on clean white paper.

Once again, he crouched in the mud.

Waiting for the next order, to charge out of the trench with bayonet raised.

It was then that the terrible fear came, that he would never see his family again. And he saw Marie, with her blue green eyes as bright and shining as the sea, and her long golden hair as soft as the flowers that grew everywhere in Guernsey. And he saw his children, all five of his precious children, each one of their faces filling his heart.

This had not happened at Passchendaele. And the black despair rose within him, darker than the dead world that now fixed its grim, skeletal arms around him, pulling him down into the abyss like the men who drowned in the mud.

He shut his eyes, willing their faces away, forcing away the despair, for he knew that to survive, he must.

When he opened his eyes, he saw the hand on his arm.

It was so white that for one awful moment, Abram thought that it was the hand of a dead man. But when he turned, he saw that it was Billy Larocque, one of their youngest soldiers.

He didn't know how the boy could be so white. He was crouched over in the trench, leaning into the side, his boots nearly submerged in the water. Like all of them, his uniform was filthy from the splatters of the mud and the dark blood, a horrible kind of camouflage that made the men who still survived blend with the dying and the dead.

Abram knew how dirty his own face was. His was the same as the other Guernseymen who were now back in the trenches, wild animals who lived in a hole in the ground, fighting for their lives.

Somehow Billy, with his fair skin, very fair for a boy who came from Guernsey – his mother was Irish or Scots, he couldn't remember anymore – had a clean face and hands.

Perhaps he had washed in the water pooling in the trench. Abram hoped not. He could understand why the boy would want to try to clean himself. No farm animal in Guernsey would ever be kept as filthy as were the soldiers of the Royal Guernsey Light Infantry. So, as he stared at that white hand, and into a face as clean as if the boy's mother had just scrubbed it with her washrag, he thought that he must warn Billy about the trench water. He would get very sick if he swallowed any of it. Billy leaned over then, and said in a voice quiet enough so that only Abram could hear, "I'm afraid that I'll never see home again."

Abram looked at the boy, at his pale eyes that were almost as colourless as his skin, at the dusting of freckles on his face, and thought how much younger he looked than Reginald.

Of course, that was not true. He knew that Billy had just turned eighteen when he enlisted last spring. It was the boy's colouring that made him seem much younger. And his fear.

Even in the despair that Abram carried like a dead man on his back, he could see how much the boy was suffering, how frightened he was.

Abram could still see that. He hadn't lost that yet.

And so he looked into the boy's timid, yearning eyes and said what he knew he had to say to the boy, "You will, Billy. Everything's going to turn out all right. You'll get home to your mother."

He spoke the words in a soft voice, and as he did so, he prayed even more softly that he was telling the truth.

chapter
fourteen

I ALWAYS WENT to the mailbox at the end of our lane with Mamma, holding her hand.

Like her, I was anxious to see if there was a letter from Papa.

And always now, I would be looking for Mme. de la Rue.

I couldn't seem to stop myself, even though as I stared hard at the grapevines on either side of the long lane from our house to the road, I knew that she would never be walking on those narrow paths. There was nothing for her there. Plants that she needed for her medicines grew in the woods and by the sea; here, there were only the barren vines.

But I still looked for her in the grey branches spreading out from the naked stalks. If I looked long enough, the vines became the arms of old women, reaching out for someone to help them, long, crooked arms praying for someone to ease their pain. And then it was easy to imagine Mme. de la Rue suddenly appearing there, her long hair a shining silver, making the vines come to life, no longer dull grey but radiant as they caught her light. Sometimes, I could even see their aged faces in the gnarled bark, becoming softly loving, their rough, ravaged fear leaving them – as Mme. de la Rue passed by, her presence a caress.

Imagining her there made me feel closer to her, made me remember that day on the South Shore, that day that still filled me with wonder. I had not seen her since, even though two months had passed. I went to Bluebell Woods as often as I could with my brothers, hoping to see her in the meadow, her graceful body moving like one of the flowers freed from its roots, petals swaying in a slow dance.

I worried that I hadn't seen her again, but just the past day, when I had asked Mamma, she reminded me that Mme. de la Rue had the old women to care for – and many others who came to her for her medicines. Mamma told me that I must be patient, and know that I would see her again.

"Just like we will soon get a letter from Papa," I said to her then. And after I spoke the words, I said a silent prayer, the same prayer I said in my heart many times each day, the words "Please keep Papa safe" spilling out quickly, with a longing inside me that was so enormous it hurt.

And when I said the prayer, I couldn't help but send it not only to God and Jesus, but also to the Blessed Virgin Mary and Mme. de la Rue.

I believed that they were working together to keep my Papa from harm.

God, though, was more like the grandfather of the world, with his wise beard, taking care of us from his throne in heaven; I never thought of him moving around too much. It seemed to me that he needed Jesus and the Blessed Virgin Mary and Mme. de la Rue to spread his love and kindness to everyone. Jesus, I imagined to be in France most of the time. It just seemed that someone who had died on the cross would be the best one to be close to the soldiers in the trenches. And the Blessed Virgin Mary, I thought, moved from our little island to the War in France like the bright blue sky shining over us all, her love spreading wide like her blue veil, her white hands reaching out in the soft clouds.

But it was Mme. de la Rue who was especially close, and I believed that she was somehow melding her powers with everyone from heaven to keep Papa from getting hurt.

I knew that I couldn't tell anyone in my family that, even though I wanted to – but there were times in the past week, as everyone grew more and more worried when still no letter from Papa came, that I wanted to tell them everything. Tell them about Jesus in the trenches and Mary in the sky and Mme. de la Rue so close to us in Guernsey – using her magic with all the holiness in heaven to help not just Papa but all the soldiers.

But I could never say any such thing. Only once, not long after going to the South Shore, I had tried saying a little about it, sharing with Mamma and my brothers at the dinner table how much Mme. de la Rue seemed like the saints in heaven. Before Mamma had a chance to speak, Reginald said, "She's a pagan, Lorley. She doesn't even go to church."

He tried to say more, but Mamma shook her head at him, saying softly, "We'll stop talking about this now."

After that, I kept very quiet about it all, but I knew that even though they said Mme. de la Rue didn't go to church, her eyes had seen heaven. Many times.

And I believed that she was doing everything she could to keep Papa safe.

We were almost at the end of our lane. Before Mamma opened the mailbox, she looked at me and said, "Say a prayer that there is a letter from Papa."

I nodded and closed my eyes. They were all there, Jesus and the Blessed Virgin Mary back from France, with God floating a little above them, his great grey beard swirling in a soft mist around them. And right in front was Mme. de la Rue, shining more brightly than ever.

When I opened my eyes, Mamma still seemed to be praying, standing with one hand on the mailbox, her eyes shut tightly.

I stared at her hand, pale and small against the black mailbox that sat squarely on top of the fence post. The door opened wide, like our oven, made out of the same heavy cast iron, though it never frightened me the way the stove did – there were no bright flames licking inside it like the long tongues of devils. It was more like a turtle, really, with a thick black shell, a friendly head and little flippers ready to peek out at any moment. And sometimes, when Mamma opened the mailbox, I liked to think that a tiny bobbing head would suddenly appear, small pebble eyes squinting.

But that day, all I longed to see was a smooth white envelope containing a letter from Papa.

I pulled lightly on Mamma's skirt because she seemed to be getting a little lost in her long prayer, and I knew what that was like, when a prayer wrapped around you like a dream, holding you so deeply that it becomes very hard to open your eyes. But I was anxious to look in the mailbox, and I didn't think I could wait much longer.

Mamma immediately opened her eyes, shaking her head a little. "I'm sorry, Lorley. I'm taking too long."

I nodded, not saying anything. Perhaps, I thought, she had as many holy faces in her prayers as I did.

Mamma let go of my hand then and opened the mailbox. I stretched my neck up as high as possible and could just see a single letter, lying there, small and ghost white. Mamma plucked it out quickly, staring hard at the writing on the face of the envelope. She suddenly looked as though she was crying, but there were no tears on her cheeks or any sounds coming from her throat.

"What is it, Mamma?" I asked. I could not believe that it was one of the letters that everyone feared – the letters that began coming to Guernsey after Passchendaele.

After that battle, when I first heard everyone saying the word Passchendaele, right after we went to Mme. de la Rue's cottage on the South Shore, I thought they must be talking about a meadow, a place where there were lacy pink flowers growing in pale green grass, filled with so much sunlight that the sky was nearly white.

Because it was such a beautiful word, Passchendaele.

But then I was told that it was the scene of a great battle, where some of the soldiers in Papa's Regiment were killed. And I couldn't understand it. How, I thought, could anyone fight in a meadow – a meadow filled with flowers that must surely sing in the sunlight?

I couldn't stand to think of the blood spilling over the pale petals and the sweet clover, of it all being trampled with heavy boots, of the soft young grass becoming a grave.

Very quickly, though, I learned that Passchendaele was no meadow, but a place more desolate than the worst cave in Guernsey, a place where, they said, men died choking in the mud.

When I heard that, I wanted to run away to the cliffs as fast as I could, to look at the bright sea and let the wind wash the terrible words out of my mind.

But I didn't, because I had never seen Mamma so worried in all my life. I had to stay close to her.

And I tried my best not to hear the name of that place or think of that sea of mud, a devil's sea, where long, twisted claws pulled the soldiers under.

I couldn't believe that Papa could be anywhere so horrible. I couldn't stand to think about it. There had to be some mistake.

But then the letters began arriving, and everyone was saying the word over and over. The letter that told you that your Papa, or your husband, or your son, or your brother, had died at Passchendaele. The letters all said the same thing – only the names and the dates were different, I heard Mamma saying at the time to Uncle William. She had started crying when she told him that.

So many of the sad letters were sent to families in Guernsey. I imagined those sad letters being carried there by small white birds somehow making their way over the wide sea to our island – birds, I thought, without eyes, so that they couldn't see all the sadness they held.

That morning, standing beside Mamma at our mailbox, I could not believe that one of those letters had flown to us.

"Mamma, what is it?" I repeated. I wanted her to say something, to wake up into the Mamma I was used to.

And I was desperate to know what letter had arrived.

Although I already knew that it had to be some terrible mistake.

If one of the sad letters had found its way to our mailbox, then I knew that it had been dropped there by one of those poor sightless birds that had woefully lost its way.

Mamma finally looked at me, and I saw the tears welling in her eyes now. She tried to speak, but she was having a hard time making her mouth move, as if all the stillness and sorrow had turned her face into a mask.

I shook my head then and said, "I know it's a mistake. That can't be about Papa." My voice sounded too loud; the barren branches of the grapevines now seemed to be quivering a little, their silence in the sunlight disturbed, their arms reaching out even more plaintively.

Mamma knelt down, putting her arm around me, and then showed me the envelope that she held in her hand.

I stared hard at the writing. I did not understand.

It was the letter that we had written to Papa several weeks ago, after we received the news that he had survived Passchendaele. Mamma's careful script, with its curls and soft strokes, words like little flowers spread over the page, was on the face of the envelope, addressed to Papa in his Regiment. I couldn't read handwriting yet, but I could recognize Papa's name and the letters R.G.L.I.

Scrawled in the top corner of the envelope was a word in black ink, the letters not like Mamma's lacy, gentle script at all, but a scribble – spidery letters that looked as if they would soon start scurrying over the thin white paper.

"What does it say, Mamma?"

"It says that Papa is missing, Lorley."

She held me even closer then, buried her face in my hair, her arms around me as if she never wanted to let me go.

Almost, it seemed, that she was afraid of losing me, too – that I would run off to the cliffs and vanish into the deep granite rock or wander into the dark heart of the woods and never find my way home.

Then all that would be left of me would be the word MISSING in spidery black letters.

I hugged my Mamma with all my heart, saying, "Please don't worry, Mamma." I wanted her to know that she would never lose me, that I would never become a missing person.

And I longed to find the right words to make my Mamma believe that Papa would not be missing for very long, that soon a white bird with sweet, kind eyes that could see far into the horizon would carry an envelope across the ocean from France with the words SOLDIER FOUND in joyful green letters that flowed all over the white paper.

I could not do that, though, because knowing that my Papa was missing filled me with too much fear and sorrow.

And even though I could hear his voice now, telling me before he left for the War, "Don't be afraid, Honey. And don't be sad," that was all I could feel now, ropes of sadness and fear twisting inside me, writhing like snakes.

I started to tremble as those ropes tightened, even though I tried with all my might to make my body calm and smooth again. I closed my eyes, and I tried to imagine the bluebells singing.

But I could not hear them. And the trembling would not go away.

Mamma held me even closer to her chest as she said, her lips still pressed lightly on my hair, "Let's go back to the house. We must try to get through this, Lorley."

Together, we slowly rose from our knees and began walking down the long laneway to our farmhouse. As we neared our back porch, I could hear the voices of my brothers in the kitchen. The screen door was open, and I could see them all sitting around our large oak table. Reginald, Herbert, Lloyd, and Randolph were eating slices of the fruit bread Mamma had baked that morning, and each had a large mug of apple cider beside him.

Mamma stopped for a moment. Randolph was telling a story, but I couldn't quite catch his words, nor, I was sure, could Mamma. But as he finished speaking, all of my brothers burst into laughter, and I knew that Randolph had shared with them one of his funny tales that we all so loved to hear, stories and laughter that we had rarely heard in these past months of the War.

Mamma and I looked at the painfully bright white envelope in her hand, and it seemed as if the devilish black letters were hissing at us.

I knew that she did not want to walk into the kitchen, nor did I.

Now, I longed for one of the blind white birds to swoop down and drop the letter on our long oak table. So that we would not have to.

But my Mamma raised her eyes to the sky and then so did I. I prayed to Mme. de la Rue, and I believed that she did also, a silver bright prayer that would keep the darkness from spreading over everything in our world.

It was Lloyd who first saw us as Mamma and I walked silently into the kitchen.

Randolph was taking a big drink of his cider, his hazel eyes warm as the laughter filled the kitchen, the room as merry as if we had all just joined together in a Christmas song.

Herbert was still laughing hard as he reached for another piece of fruit bread, and even Reginald, for the first time in what seemed like forever, looked relaxed, the creases on his young face no longer there.

Lloyd had been laughing, also, as we entered the room, gazing in his gentle way at Randolph, his eyes soft and admiring.

But he turned his head a few moments after we entered the room, and his laughter stopped abruptly, for as soon as he glanced at our faces, he knew that something was terribly wrong.

"What is it, Mamma?" Lloyd said.

Even though his voice was quieter than usual, as he spoke, all of the laughter in the room suddenly stopped.

In the silence, I stared at the gleaming golden oak table, now as dull as a dying log in the forest, at the fire in the hearth, no longer warming the room, at the flames that now seemed threatening, as if they were about to leap from the grate.

Worse was the black stove, for as my eyes fixed on it, thinking about my Papa missing, never had it been so full of the devil. I feared that if I lifted the lid off the burner and stared into the depths of the stove, I would see sinister red eyes glinting at me from the embers.

Lloyd's gaze remained on Mamma's face, but Randolph saw the envelope clutched in her hand. "Is that from Papa?" he asked very quietly, all the cheer that had been in his voice gone so quickly that it was hard to believe it had ever been there.

It was the same for the entire kitchen, which, just a few short moments ago, had been so full of merriment, and was now as silent and somber as an ink black tunnel in the Creux Mahie.

Before Mamma could answer, Reginald's chair scraped over the slate floor and, in a few strides, he was at her side. Herbert's chair scraped even more loudly in his haste to follow him.

"What does the letter say? Please let me see it, Mamma," Reginald said, his voice much stronger than Lloyd's and Randolph's, sounding very much like my Papa.

Mamma kept the envelope held at her side, her eyes loving as she looked at each one of us, slowly, her eyes so clearly asking us to try to be brave, as she said, "Your Papa is missing." Then she raised her hand, showing us the awful spidery letters that suddenly seemed alive, crawling over the dead white face of the envelope.

Silence once more fell like a grey shadow over the room, and after what seemed like a very long time, Mamma said, "We must pray for the best. Papa may already have been found by now. We can't give up hope."

As she spoke, Reginald's eyes hardened. He stared at the fields through the kitchen window as he said, "I'm going to do more than pray, Mamma. I'm going to find him. I want to enlist," and his voice trailed off for a moment. Then he turned and looked at Mamma, saying, "Once I get to France, I won't stop looking until I find Papa."

Very quickly, Mamma began shaking her head. "Reginald, you can't do that. You are not old enough. They won't take you."

She looked at each of my brothers, and I felt that, at that moment, she wanted arms long enough to reach around all of them in one great embrace and hold them against her heart and never let them go.

My brothers, though, had their eyes fixed on Reginald. "I know I can't enlist here," he said, "even though I'm bigger and stronger than many of the Guernsey lads who are eighteen. But they know how old everybody is in Guernsey, with the recruitment in the parishes. But they won't know me in England. And besides, I heard that they don't care if you lie about your age. As long as you stand at least five feet three inches and have a thirty-four-inch chest, they'll let you join. The recruitment officer gets two shillings sixpence for each new soldier." Reginald finished, looking at Mamma, his eyes no longer hard but shining with each word he spoke. Eyes as bright, I suddenly thought, as the bayonet I had seen my Papa carrying when he marched in St. Peter Port before leaving for the War.

"You must not do that, please, Reginald. I know it wouldn't be too hard for you to board a ship for England and do what you're saying, but don't, please. Your Papa would never want you to put yourself in such great danger. Not at your age. Please, my son," Mamma said, and her eyes, now, were shining too, but it was a fearful light, like a candle flickering to stay alive in a black cave.

Then she looked at Herbert, Lloyd, and Randolph. I followed her gaze.

Suddenly, they all seemed to be exceptionally tall, growing before my very eyes, as if I were Jack in the fairy tale, watching the magic beans become an almost impossibly high beanstalk, the green leaves shooting through the clouds.

But I knew they weren't really any taller. It was my fear playing tricks on me – because when Reginald said that boys only had to be five feet three inches tall to become soldiers, it frightened me to my deepest bones. All that I had to do was look at my Mamma, who I knew was five feet two inches on her tiptoes, as my Papa always said, and see how much Reginald and Herbert towered over her. And then I looked at Lloyd and Randolph, who weren't taller than my Mamma, but Lloyd was getting close, and Randolph, not all that far behind.

In my fear, they seemed to be growing like magical beanstalks.

Beanstalks that wouldn't rise into the clouds but would twist and creep their way over the ocean to the War.

My Mamma didn't see beanstalks when she looked at my brothers, but I could tell from the fear growing stronger in her eyes that she saw how dangerously tall Lloyd and Randolph were also.

Reginald broke the silence that had descended onto the kitchen. "I'll go alone. Herbert, Lloyd, and Randolph will be needed here more than ever in the vines."

"No, Reginald, do not leave Guernsey," Mamma said.

Herbert looked ready to argue with Reginald and say that he was going to enlist, also. His eyes seemed desperate. Even Lloyd and Randolph looked as if they were trying to will themselves into growing taller.

Suddenly, I could no longer bear seeing their faces longing for the trenches, in their great longing to find our dear Papa.

So, telling myself to move as softly as though I was a petal being touched by a breath of wind, I slipped out of the kitchen. Luckily, the screen door was still open. I could never have managed to leave as silently as I did if Mamma had closed it when she walked into the kitchen to tell my brothers the terrible news about Papa.

I tiptoed down the stairs of our porch, and over our gravel yard, now trying to imagine being invisible because I knew it helped me move as if I were a misty ghost.

As soon as my feet touched the grass, though, I began running as fast as I could, long, swift deer legs springing out of my body.

I was not even sure where I was going.

But I knew that I had to get far, far away from Mamma's eyes full of fear, from my brothers' eyes, too bright, too burning, too ready to flee to France to search for Papa.

I found myself heading towards the cliffs.

I wanted to gaze at the turquoise sea that spread like a halo around our island – see the white mist shimmering as if angels had just floated over the water, leaving sparkles glimmering in their wake.

I even wanted to gaze upon the deep lair where the sea monster lurked beneath the rocks – because it always made me feel safe, knowing that the angels would never let the monster hurt us – because in Guernsey, the radiant white angels were never far away.

And I remembered how I always believed that even when the sun did not shine, did not gleam with the white rays of angels, and the long grey clouds came – God was still there, leaning over our island with his great grey beard, keeping our island free from harm, keeping our island magical.

I needed to see it all –

But just as I neared the cliffs, I saw a silver mist shimmering near the steep precipice. The sun, though, was so bright that I could not see clearly, but the gleam of silver felt so beautiful that I had no fear as it moved towards me.

Then she said, "I am glad that you came, Lorley," and the mist cleared as I found myself gazing upon Mme. de la Rue.

Gently she took my hand in hers and led me away from the cliffs. Down the narrow path we walked together in silence. I didn't need to tell her that my heart was singing to see her. She already knew.

How she knew I didn't think I would ever truly understand. But now she could feel my thankfulness for seeing her at this moment, and, also, my painful fear that my Papa was missing, and my just as terrible fear that my brothers were going to leave to find him.

It didn't take us very long to reach Bluebell Woods. If I hadn't felt so wide awake, I would have thought that Mme. de la Rue had cast a gentle spell over me, lifting me into the air and letting me fly with her to the woods.

For, ever since Mme. de la Rue had taken my hand, time had stopped.

As it had on that day so many months ago, when I first gazed upon her silver hair that fell shimmering past her waist and looked into her eyes as clear and beautiful as gemstones, the colour of the sea when the sun shines so brightly the water appears crystalline.

"Can you hear the bluebells singing, Lorley?"

I looked at the silver trees, their slender arms reaching into the sky, their leaves a pale gold spread over the earth.

The bluebells now lay beneath that earth, and I could imagine a lovely blue sea of petals where they lay rippling underground, waiting to rise in the spring.

I shook my head. How, I wondered, could I hear them when I could no longer see them?

"Listen, dear Lorley. Open your heart to them. You don't have to see them to hear them sing."

I tried very hard, but as I did all the fear about my Papa began twisting inside me again.

Mme. de la Rue let go of my hand and gently held my shoulders. She tipped my head so that she could look into my eyes.

"Never stop believing your Papa will return. Listen for his voice. He is telling you to be strong and brave."

"But how can I hear my Papa when he is so far away, and no one even knows where he is?" I said, and in that moment, I longed for my Papa more than I thought possible, my heart aching to be with him, wherever he was, lost in the War.

Mme. de la Rue's eyes were jewel bright, eyes that shone with my great yearning. "You must try, Lorley. If you let yourself hear his voice, then you will find hope as silver bright as a sky filled with stars."

"But it is not just me who needs to hear my Papa. So does my Mamma, and my brothers," I said, my heart aching even more as I thought about them.

"You will share your silver bright hope as the stars share their light in the sky," Mme. de la Rue said, gazing upwards. She raised her arms then, and I knew she was praying. After a long silence she said, "And then your brothers will choose the right path."

"But which path, Mme. de la Rue? I do not want them to go to the War."

"I cannot know which path, but, through you, they will choose the right path."

"But can you know for sure about my Papa and my brothers?" I asked, trying my hardest to understand all that she was saying.

"I cannot foretell the future, never in its completeness, though I have visions. But you know that dear Lorley. And I know that, in this moment, you must listen for your Papa's voice," she said very gently.

And now her words fell over me in a silver spray of magic.

And I heard, at first very low and soft and then rising, my Papa's voice.

His words floating in the clear silver light.

Telling me not to be afraid.

And my fear became less.

As hope rose inside me like silvery blue flowers slowly growing out of the earth.

And even though I could not see the bluebells, I began to hear their song.

It was not the same as the first time they sang to me.

But still a deep blue heavenly song.

One that was somehow both sad and beautiful.

the story continues
in 'the heavenly
silver witch'
the sequel to Island
of Silver

excerpt from 'the heavenly silver witch.'

I STOOD on the high cliffs, gazing at the turquoise waters that sparkled as if the stars had gently fallen from the sky to shine in the sea.

And then, as if I were one of the stars, I fell slowly from the cliffs into the warm waters. There was barely a splash, and I found myself floating in the sea of stars.

Yet the sky above was bright with sunlight, as golden and white as the angels that I could see flying high above me.

A magical day where the sun and the stars shone together, sharing the sky.

A day so magical that on the shore I suddenly saw my Papa standing there, his dark eyes filled with the golden and silver light of the sky and the sea.

I began swimming through the glistening waters towards my Papa, as fast as I possibly could, wishing, more than I ever had in my life, that I truly were a mermaid with a sparkling emerald tail.

My Papa began walking into the water to meet me, his

arms outstretched, his eyes smiling with love, ready to take me into his arms.

But I could not reach him.

No matter how hard I swam, there was always more water between us.

When I awakened, my heart ached, for all I wanted to do was fall back into my dream, with my Papa gazing at me, his heart full of love, a love brighter than the stars that danced in the sun's light.

Something must have startled me from my sleep, but I could not imagine what it was. I always fell so deeply into my dreams, the silky cocoon of sleep wrapping all around me, that I almost never awakened until the morning spread its bright wings in my room.

I only stayed in my bed for a few moments before I got up and walked to the window. The moonlight was luminous through the glass, a spray of silver light so bright in my room, that for a moment I thought that Mme. de la Rue was standing outside my window, her heavenly light shining with the silver moon.

And then I saw my Papa.

Papa had come home, my heart exulted.

He was standing in front of our house, his head raised, staring at the windows on the second floor. After being gone for six months, and missing for fourteen long days, he had returned from the War.

It was midnight, and too dark to see his face in the deep shadows cast by our tall granite farmhouse.

But I knew it was him.

My heart was so glad that it filled my chest, so light with joy, as though I was on the cliff in my dream again, about to float in the sea of stars.

I was about to call 'Papa', when I heard our front door slowly open.

Another figure moved in the deep shadows and stood beside my Papa.

And then, without saying a word, Reginald and Herbert walked out of the darkness cast by our house and into the bright moonlight.

I uttered a cry.

For it was not my Papa. It had been Reginald standing in the darkness.

And now I felt, once more, as though I was falling – not gently into a sea of stars, but crashing onto the jagged rocks below.

At first, I couldn't move as I watched Reginald and Herbert race across our wide yard, heading to the trees at the far side of our property. Before very long, they would vanish into the woods.

And I knew they were running away to the War to find our Papa.

I remembered what Reginald had told Mamma, the day two long weeks ago when the terrible letter arrived telling us that Papa was missing. Reginald had wanted to leave then, board a ship for England where he would enlist in the army. Once he was in the trenches, he would search for Papa. And now he was doing that, and taking Herbert with him.

I stood there, as all that flashed through me, my eyes fixed on my brothers. And each moment that passed, they were becoming less like my brothers, running as if demons were chasing them, and more like shadows flitting over our yard in the night, flickering silhouettes in the silver moonlight.

I knew it wouldn't be long before they reached the woods, their shadows melding into the black towers of trees that stood like dark sentinels.

Always, I had believed those trees watched over our house, protecting the vines, protecting my family, like a warm velvet cloak. But now they seemed like guards who were about to enfold Reginald and Herbert into their dark branches and take them away from us.

As I stared at their fleeting shadows that would soon vanish from sight, I knew I had to do something. They had to be stopped.

I turned away from my window and began walking very softly to my Mamma's room. I slowly opened the door and slipped silently into her room.

I knew she was exhausted. She had spent all morning and afternoon with poor Mme. Sarre, who had received three letters that day, not the MISSING letters but the far more dreaded letters, letters that told Mme. Sarre that three of her sons had died. All three in the same battle. She had been told that two of her three sons, the twins, were buried side by side, and she was grateful, heartbreakingly grateful for that. Mamma cried when she heard that, and had spent the day doing everything she could to help Mme. Sarre, and others, who were suffering so badly.

Now, though, as I tiptoed very closely to her bed, she did not look the way she had when she kissed me good night.

The light grey powder of fatigue was gone from her face.

In her deep sleep, she was as beautiful as she was in her

wedding photograph. Her silky golden hair flowed to her waist, like her wedding veil, in long, delicate waves. And her nightgown seemed to be the same creamy lace as her bridal dress, flowing in soft ripples over her shoulders and down her arms. She was a lovely young bride again.

But thinking of her wedding picture made me think of my Papa, standing beside her, so handsome with his sleek black hair and dark flashing eyes and his tender smile as he gazed into my Mamma's eyes.

Now, though, Mamma was alone, my Papa so far away. I did not want to see her as a bride without her dashing groom by her side.

That was too sad. And then I thought of the fairy tales my Papa had always read to me. I let those enchanted stories shine within me, as I gazed upon my Mamma.

Her golden hair began shimmering, and very quickly, as if Mme. de la Rue had sprinkled her magic over us, my Mamma became a lovely Sleeping Beauty – deep in her blissful dream, waiting for her prince to return, who would bring her back to life with a kiss.

I wanted her to remain Sleeping Beauty for as long as possible.

So, I tiptoed slowly out of the room.

I could not take her away from her dream of her prince, my Papa.

Moving very quietly, I walked across the hall to the bedroom Lloyd and Randolph shared. I felt as if I were a luminous ghost once more, as invisible as I had been the night I stood outside Reginald and Herbert's room, the night that now seemed so long ago.

The door to their bedroom was open. I could hear Lloyd

and Randolph sleeping deeply, their breathing long and even. They were exhausted after working hard in the vines that day.

I took a few silent steps into their room and saw them lying in their bed beneath their wide window. The draperies were pulled open and the moonlight spread its light like a great silver halo over the room, as if Mme. de la Rue's beautiful light was shining over them also.

I was about to wake them.

I knew that I could brave those black woods – where the long dark branches waved their gloom into the night, where the woods breathed with creatures lurking there – if Lloyd and Randolph were by my side.

Secretly, I always thought of them as my knights in shining armour, for their brave lion hearts gleamed the brightest gold.

But just as I was about to awaken them, it came to me, in a flash, that they would never let me go with them. They would fear that I would hurt myself. They would say that I must stay with Mamma.

I gazed once more at the moonlight spreading its silver stars over my brothers as they slept.

As beautiful, I thought once more, as the light that shimmered all around Mme. de la Rue.

And I remembered what she had told me in Bluebell Woods, on the day when I was so terrified, the day I learned that my Papa was missing.

She told me that, through me, my brothers would choose the right path – which surely meant I had to be the one to find my eldest brothers and bring them home.

Alone. I had to do it alone.

I could feel Mme. de la Rue's silver light glowing, now, all around me. And then I knew that I would not really be alone. The heavenly silver witch would be with me – her halo of starlight shining over me.

So, I left Lloyd and Randolph in their room.

And walked silently out of the house, into the darkness and the starlight.

afterword

Island of Silver is a work of historical fiction – but it is based on the lives of people whose home was Guernsey more than one hundred years ago. Abram and Marie were my grandparents; Reginald, Herbert, and Lloyd were my uncles. And Randolph was my beloved father.

Because of my father with his great lion heart, I wrote this novel.

Lorley is my own creation, but she is named after my maternal grandmother, who was a magical storyteller with long, silver hair.

acknowledgments

I am deeply thankful to Frank Eastland, who chose to publish my novel. His kind and thoughtful mentorship, his endearing sense of humour, and his heartfelt encouragement will not be forgotten.

I also wish to thank Janet Silburn, my Editor, and the Creative Team for their expertise and tireless support.

Throughout the writing of this novel, I so often thought of the wonderful students I had the privilege of teaching. Those English classes, with those remarkable students, continue to inspire me each day I sit down to write. To all of you, thank you.

A constant source of inspiration, as well, through all my years of writing has come from my sons. Thank you, Jeff and Marc; your loving support means everything to me. Also, thank you, Cassandra, my daughter-in-law, and Karen, my sister, for your wholehearted encouragement.

Above all else, thank you to my husband, Joe. Without him, I would never have embarked on this writing journey that began so long ago. So thank you, Joe. You are the love of my life.

about the author

Island of Silver is Bonnie Henderson's debut novel. She received her degree in English Literature at Western University. After graduation she worked at various jobs, from bookselling to fashion buying. She found her true profession, though, when she became a high school English teacher. Through her teaching, Bonnie discovered that her love of her students was as powerful as her love of literature; these combined loves strengthened her passion to write. Now retired, she devotes her time to writing, reading, running and hiking. She lives with her husband, Joseph, in St. Catharines, Ontario.

thank you for reading

If you enjoyed *Island of Silver*, we invite you to leave a review and share your thoughts and reactions online and with friends and family.

Publish Authority

www.ingramcontent.com/pod-product-compliance
Lightning Source LLC
Chambersburg PA
CBHW051506050726
47594CB00010B/3992